STOLEN
Honours

DIANE LEWIS

Copyright © 2020 Diane Lewis
All rights reserved
First Edition

PAGE PUBLISHING, INC.
Conneaut Lake, PA

First originally published by Page Publishing 2020

ISBN 978-1-6624-0895-3 (pbk)
ISBN 978-1-6624-0897-7 (hc)
ISBN 978-1-6624-0896-0 (digital)

Printed in the United States of America

Prologue

"You broke it!" Mary's shrill screech pierced the peaceful hallways of the large house. The home was never considered opulent for the day. But it was certainly not squalid. It was a moment's ride on the rail to the city spiral. Mary's voice reminded Bethy of one of those screeching alarms. "You little twit, you broke Dad's favorite album! Do you know how hard it is to find a long play record? They haven't made LP records in over four hundred years!"

"I'm sorry!" Tears streamed down Bethy's face. "I just wanted to…" She sobbed "Hear the music again. I just…" She gasped air. "Wanted to…" Her words were broken by heavy sobs.

"Well, neither of us will hear that record again." Mary stormed from the room. Her voice rounded the corner and continued to echo from down the hallway. "Can't trust you with anything!" Mary's shriek of anger turned to murmuring, then it came louder again. "What do you think Dad is going to say when he gets home? Why can't I just lock my room?" Her voice came from downstairs now.

"I'm…I'm…sorry," Bethy cried. Her voice was barely audible and drowning in the sobs. She slunk to the closet. She thought, *Maybe if I hide, they won't be able to find me.* Closing her eyes in the darkness, she crouched down to rest her head on her knees. What would she tell Mom and…Dad? It was an accident. She was just trying to record Janis's songs on her new D-corder. Her mind raced with the horror of punishment. Would Mom and Dad just sell her for slave labor on the outer moons of Jupiter, sent to the ice mines of Uranus to pay the cost of the broken album, or worse, ground her?

The terror of confronting her mom and dad flashed through her mind with horrible images of punishment and finally rested on the most heart-wrenching of all: "I am so disappointed." Her father's voice echoed in her mind. Their trust in her would be destroyed. She knew she was not supposed to be in her dad's study with the antiques, but they were so neat. The voice on the record, the soulful emotion caught on the vinyl disk. Bethy wished for a moment she could go there, maybe to hear Janis in person and replace the record. The image of the hot and dry summers with the dark smoky room and Janis Joplin with her guitar made Bethy stop sobbing and catch her breath.

The ice mines would almost be good right now, as warmth surrounded her and a bead of sweat gathered on her brow. She wondered if the air-conditioning had stopped working in the house. Something didn't seem right if she closed the door. And then why was this much bright yellow light in the closet, and when did it start blowing bits of…? She sneezed and then slowly lifted her head off her knees. The world came into focus as the tears dried from her eyes, evaporating into the sunny summer day.

Suddenly she was scooped up and shoved aside as a horn blared beside her. She nearly tripped as her foot caught on the crack in the…pavement. She froze as the realization set in that cement had not been used for decades. Suddenly, the world crashed in around her, a world she had only seen in pictures.

"What were you doing in the street?" the tall man yelled over the noise of the busy street, out of breath, as he knelt down beside Bethy and looked at her eye to eye. "Are you hurt, kid?"

Bethy's hopes that the strong arms scooping her up were her dad's had dissipated as she stood, taking it all in. Her eyes fixed on the long slender metal things moving past them, rounded at one end with pointy bits at the boot. *Cars.* She remembered the description of rubber wheels, actual rubber. Short buildings surrounded them, only five or six stories high. A few buildings in the distance were only a little taller and made from the cement stuff with strips of glass up the sides. "I don't know." Her quivering voice timidly squeaked as she continued looking around.

"Where are you from? Where are your parents?"

Bethy noticed the woman standing behind him, looking bewildered. She bent over to whisper to the man, "It is almost like she just appeared in the middle of the road."

"I know. I saw," he replied.

Bethy looked around, fear in hear eyes. "I don't…know?" She started to weep. "I don't…know…where I am." Her shoulders shook as she buried her face in her hands.

A small crowd started to gather around them.

"You should take her to the hospital. They can sort her out." An elderly woman bent over her cane hobbled up, clicking her cane on the cement, emphasizing each syllable.

The man stood up. His colorful floral button-up shirt remained wrinkled even after he stood. He placed his hand on Bethy's shoulder and looked over to his friend.

"Really? You would have her turned over to the establishment?" the short black-haired woman ranted at the old lady. "We care more for her than *they* ever will, and *we* just met her. No!" She took a deep breath to calm herself and then turned from the old biddy to her friend. "We'll take her to the club. We have a little time before it opens. She doesn't look injured." The black-haired lady looked back sternly at the old woman and then to the rest of the crowd. "The only thing they would do is send her home. Or if they can't find her parents, she will fall into the system where she will be lost. They won't care! Besides, what if she doesn't want to go home? You know *that* is exactly where they will send her. She should decide for herself." The black-haired lady stood tall as a mother lion defended her own child.

The crowds started to shrink away, intimidated by look of a small motherly lioness and the flower-shirted man in charge who did not like being second-guessed once he made up his mind on something.

A shadow of doubt crossed the man's mind. "What if she was kidnapped?" He spoke softly to his friend, "If she doesn't know where she is, it makes sense someone brought her here. Maybe against her will." He looked away as she puffed a little more. Stepping back, he shook his head.

"Yeah, you're right."

The man knelt back down and held out his hand. "Hi, I'm Rick, and this is Bridget. You want ta' come with us? We can at least get you through the day and then figure out tomorrow when it gets here."

"I'm Bethy." She wiped the drying tears from her eyes and took his hand. She wiped her eyes again with her sleeve, taking a deep breath. Rick stood back up. A smile crept on Bethy's cheeks as she found herself grateful of her growth spurt months ago. Now she looked at the bottom part of his untucked colorful floral shirt instead of the hairy legs below the ragged jean shorts. Each step clopped as his sandals slapped the bottom of his feet. She looked up with her new height, and she almost reached the bottom of his gathered hair.

"How old do you think she is? And what is she wearing?" Bridget whispered, looking at the cartoon drawing on her shirt that shimmered into a scene with the character running through the landscape and then stopped. She looked up at Rick. A slightly amused and shocked look crossed her face as her mind wandered to futuristic technology before her mind came back and smiled. "I haven't seen those before. They look"—she smiled—"comfortable?"

"A stand against the social norms or maybe vacation to Tomorrowland," Rick defiantly announced, and then he smiled back, oblivious to Bridget's concerns. "I think she'll fit right in."

"I'm six years and two months old," Bethy said proudly, and then started looking around as she walked along the street. These buildings don't obscure the blue skies. A couple of small cloud wisps passed over head as she paused a moment to feel the sunlight fall warmly on her skin. Her cities were vast and tall; she could still see the buildings reaching for miles, piercing through the little white feathery clouds even on the other side of the mountain range where she lived. Looking to the left, her eyes fell upon the focal point of the city, the light-reddish domed official looking building with columns surrounding the base of the dome, reaching well above any other building within the city.

They walked to a street with various sized buildings. They continued through a couple streets with one- and two-story buildings, each unique. The different buildings were shoved together like in a vertical nightclub sandwich. The clubs along the street held enticement that might lure a teenage boy at night, but during the day, they merely beckoned with intrigue. Bethy followed them into the dark club. She stood still for a long minute as her eyes adjusted to the dim light. The aroma of greasy food, stale beer, and cigarettes greeted them at the door. At that moment, she realized her stomach had been ignored far too long. The inviting club lay ahead of her. Two booths lay nestled next to the wall in the corner to her right, and directly ahead of her lay the bar with glass bottles of different liquids on top of a rise in the floor, providing a good view of the stage in the left back corner of the club. The main floor between the bar and the stage was dotted with tables.

"Are you hungry?" Bridget asked. "Can we get you something to eat?"

Bethy looked around at the place, remembering her manners. "Yes, please, what do you have? What…" She hesitated, not wanting to irritate the only friends she had found in this time. "I…what would you recommend?"

Bridget smiled, amused by Little Miss Manners.

"The cook makes a great cheeseburger, and that always makes me feel better when I'm scared." Bridget knelt down to hug Bethy. "You're going to be okay." She smiled.

"Cheeseburger." Bethy felt her mouth start watering at the thought. "I have not had beef since our last family trip. It is so rare at home." Bethy hopped onto the stool, bouncing a bit happily, looking forward to what the cook created for her. Hamburger. Wouldn't her sister be so jealous.

"We always have local talent coming in. You will have fun here. You are welcome to stay down here to listen. I'll set up a place upstairs for you to stay with me as long as you need." Bridget winked and then turned to leave the room.

Agent Hajjar stood on the catwalk overlooking the movement below in the Cannery Wharf Jaunt Port. He leaned forward, resting his arms on the thick steel railing. His hair was still long from the last assignment, flicking annoyingly on his closed eyelids. He stood still, listening to the sounds around him. There was a constant stream of people flowing in from the sky rails and elevated walkways into the port; they moved through the open arched entrance under the giant clock, through the tall sequoias, like wooden columns on either side of the pad. Looking up through the canopy of leaves hundreds of feet above, he was reminded how tall the city was with the skyscrapers reaching miles above the tops the trees that surrounded him. With the artificial light provided by the partial-transparent-solar-luminescent dome, this gift from the Americas to Queen Elizabeth IV would have died, drowned by the shadow of the buildings above.

The constant hum of excitement from the people moving through the port, like the hum of data through a transceiver sending information to the outer planets, always calmed Hajjar when his nerves were on edge. He opened his eyes, exhaling to watch the movement of people like the water of a brook weaving around the trees and pillars in the port. His dark brown eyes scanned the crowds below, coming and going from their destinations.

People in sets of two and three maneuvered through the crowds like fish swimming upstream. His eyes fell on a family: mother, father, and two children. They were carrying their luggage through the large archway made from marble, depicting the noble achievements of lasting peace in United Euro States after the war. Historians said the design was reminiscent of the Arc de Triomphe in Paris.

Hajjar smiled at this thought. The Arc de Triomphe was destroyed over a hundred years ago in the Great Global War, and very few pictures remained in general population.

In truth, the entrance did not look much like the Arc de Triomphe. This archway, though roughly the same height and width, was not as grandiose and took only three long strides to pass underneath, entering the Jaunt Port. The back side of the arch was littered with digital displays broadcasting departure and arrival times or a large luminescent clock in the center. The round crystal surface displayed an ancient clock, the kind with hands, taking up the entire area of the screen, but it has the digital display smaller in the center for those who no longer knew how to read the hands for the time.

Hajjar again returned his thoughts to the crowds below weaving through the trees. The twelve trees stood like ancient Greek columns along the center of the port. He wondered where their roots found nutrients; the port was built fifty stories above what they used to called street level. He wondered if they filled in the few stories under the port with soil and how much trouble the city may have had to clear the under-dwellers out of the lower wards of the city to fill in their refuge with soil.

The family Hajjar spotted earlier had made their way to the jaunt pad between the wooden columns of sequoia; he watched them huddled tightly. The older girl jumped up and down, clapping excitedly. Her younger brother shook his head with dread and apprehension, probably inexperienced in jaunting, having recently completing his class learning the technique. The boy had to be about eleven, minimum age for jaunt class. Hajjar watched as the boy's dad knelt on one knee, grasping his shoulders then wrapping his arms around him in a tight hug. A long moment passed as they closed their eyes, calming themselves while holding each other's hands, and then vanished.

Most people nowadays travel from one place to the next by jaunting. The power of the mind is used to instantly transport people across earth, even across worlds, and even the outer planets and settlements in the outer asteroid fields. Jaunting is the quickest way to travel for those capable of learning the technique.

Hajjar closed his eyes and remembered his first jaunt. He stood up, keeping his hands on the railing a moment, lost in memory before turning around and leaning back on the rail. His memories wandered back, eighteen…no, nineteen years ago, back to when he was barely six, to *his* first jaunt. It would be another four years until he became the youngest kid to jaunt through time.

Hajjar remembered sitting on the bed, looking out through his bedroom window as his friends as they waved back at him on their way to the Kid Space. Sure, he didn't really see them heading there, but he *knew* they were going. He could hear his mother on the link to Pepper's mother.

"I wish my Ryan could go to the park too," Hajjar's mom, Nasheen, elaborated. "He has pox. It is contagious."

"How long?" Pepper's mom reminded him of a songbird with her chirpy voice. A miniature image of her stood on the dining room table with her jogging pants and hair pulled into a tail.

"The doctor said it will be two weeks." Nasheen looked back at her son, Ryan, peeking out from his bedroom.

"Twoooo weeeeeks!" The sassy whine of Pepper came clearly into the room as a smaller figure joined her mother's on the table. "The Knight Brigade won't hold the red fort without him!"

Ryan ran over and quickly joined his mom at the link, looking at his cohorts. "You, Brice, and James will have to hold your own." He remembered stating bravely but desperately wanting to join them in their conquest.

"But James just got back from vacation, and we will be outnumbered. *And* he has *cool* stuff from the trip to show us." Brice ran in to join the projection of Pepper and her mom. Ryan wondered if he remembered to breathe. "How will we get the blue base? You are a part of the offensive plan we practiced…"

"No!" Ryan's mom, Christi, stood stern. She looked at Ryan more than at the gang of kids in the link.

"But, Mooooooooom?" he remembered pleading, begging.

"No!" The image of Pepper's mom turned to the group, placing her hands on her hips. "You do not want pox!"

"We will keep in touch." The discussion was over, and Ryan would be quarantined in his bedroom indefinitely. He ran back to the window touching the screen, removed the dark filter, peering outside.

Mom always said we were privileged to have our place. The loft was high enough in the scraper that bits of sun actually filtered through the buildings, sending colored shards of light like a kaleidoscope reflecting from building to building dancing into the room where he stood. She said some people living closer to the ground levels may never see daylight. Ryan realized now that the ground level was about where he stood now, fifty to a hundred stories above the ground, and the levels underground were dark and scary and reached almost half a mile below the surface of the planet.

Ryan looked down to the enclosed walkway connecting the two scrapers and then to the darkness of the chasm with no bottom. He imagined what the ground might look like. He saw his friends then bouncing and running around Pepper's mom.

He pressed his head to the glass, straining to see them as they disappeared into the next building.

He closed his eyes, imagining them getting to the Kid Space. The corridors opened into a giant room filled with lots of different structures to play on and in.

They would be running to their favorite—the maze of colored tubes leading out from a central base. The tunnels looped around, up and down, changing color as they neared the next base. The colors radiating out from the base could be changed from the home screen in the base.

Pepper would no doubt be guarding their base from her position within the top entrance while James and Brice started to infiltrate the blue tunnels. James would be crawling through the south corridor to the blue base; at the same time, Brice would be making his move, crawling in from the east for a two-sided attack on the blue base. Ryan was supposed to be the third advancement of the attack they planned for today. The two would distract Nigel, Anthony, Nancy, and Hillary, drawing them from their base, and then he could sneak in, touching the screen, changing the color to red, his team's color. They would play this version of base tag for hours until their parents made them come home and clean up.

Ryan could remember closing his eyes, wishing so hard to be there that he could feel the tubes around him, smell the plastic and rubber of the blue base, and hear Brice's and James's voices. Then he opened his eyes to find the blue screen in front of him and Brice's wide-eyed shock crawling in from the side entrance.

"You came!" Brice started vibrating with excitement. "How did you get here? How did you get past your mom? It was almost like you appeared there, and are those red bumps itchy?"

Ryan looked around the tunnels, the screen, and the giggling Brice. None of this was his bedroom.

Excited, they returned to the red base to celebrate their victory.

Hajjar smiled, remembering the short-lived victory as Pepper's mom found him with the group.

"Nasheen! Do you know where your son is?"

The small image of Ryan's mom sprang up from the small disk Pepper's mom held out in front of her. "He should be in his bedroom. That is where I left him just a moment ago."

"Well, he is here."

"I didn't hear the door open. And he couldn't have gotten there so quickly…unless he…but he is too young to jaunt."

"Apparently not!"

Hajjar chuckled with the amusing memory of the two weeks following that jaunt. He spent the time with his best friends out of school, quarantined together. They used hydro-tazers to blast each other with water each time they started scratching at the irritating little red spots.

***

"I thought I'd find you up here." Agent Johnston's voice broke through the white noise of the crowd, jerking Hajjar back from his memories.

He turned to look at his partner. She looked as she did every day, pantsuit with heels that clicked on the floor, announcing her entrance to a room. It might strike fear into the minds of those who had a guilty conscience and knew her reputation. Her deep red hair streaked with white was the only indication that she was older than she looked. It was pulled up into a bun atop her head with pencils holding it in place but allowing wisps to escape captivity, falling about her face and shoulders. Why did she have to intrude on his sanctuary outside the Bureau? Her piercing green eyes almost seemed to read his thought, and moments after the thought passed through his head, he regretted thinking it. He was honored to have been selected by the top agent to be her apprentice when entering the force.

She was the youngest to graduate from the academy and become an agent, or that was until *he* graduated six months younger than she was. She had the best record in the Bureau for the last fifteen years, even working solo as a Senior Time Detective Investigator for four and a half years until she requested to be his mentor. But that was over three years ago. He should still be honored, or that's what he kept telling himself to replace his growing frustration. He was made a full partner a year ago but she still…he took a deep breath. Sometimes he just wanted to be treated like the equal partner that he was.

He shook his head. Maybe that was the frustration of the assignment they had just closed.

"I didn't think you ever left the grounds. Too much danger." Hajjar's sarcasm cut close to truth.

Johnston shook her head, slightly rolling her eyes as a dedicated parent accused of not having a life. "The chief wants to see you." Agent Johnston said once that each case gave her white hairs; she must have had thousands of cases to explain the overpopulation of white hairs starting to be more noticeable than the dark red ones.

"Why didn't he tag me?"

"He did." She tossed him the earbud. "I'm not your secretary," she added. "You know that you should never leave the safety of the Px Shield without this." And then she handed him his red leather-bound Field Notebook. "It is too dangerous." Her voice picked up a motherly tone to it as she turned to look over the crowds below.

Hajjar paused to slide his earbud into place. "Why can't we just get an implant like everyone else?" Hajjar muttered, looking longingly at the cybernetic on the people below.

A stereo response came with Chief Stewart in his left ear and Johnston standing on his right side. "You know why." Johnston shook her head, slowly muttering something about petulant youth. Chief Stewart's voice came with a steely resolve into Hajjar's ear.

"Yeah...yeah." Hajjar rolled his eyes and sighed, repeating mantra from a handbook. "As part of the Time Bureau of Investigation, we must be able to blend into any culture anytime, anywhere. I know, I know," Hajjar stated with frustration. Agents are called on to travel to any place or any period, investigating distortions in the timeline to correct and reset history from unique individuals who may also hold the ability to time jaunt. If an agent fell or died while performing their sworn duties, any cybernetic enhancements might alter the timeline and require putting a second agent at task to fix an already corrected timeline.

Chief Stewart's deep voice reverberated through the earpiece, chuckling softly. "I need to see you in my office, Agent Hajjar."

"Be there in a few minutes." Agent Hajjar sighed. He looked over to see Johnston already walking away from him, headed toward the lift down to the floor. *Always playing catchup*, he thought as he briskly jogged to her side.

They rode the lift down to the entrance level and out through the archway under the clock to the elevated walkways outside. The gentle warm glow of the sunlight transitioned as they passed under the archway into harsh glaring boards advertising anything and everything. The light refracted from each reflective surface on the surrounding buildings. The two walked in silence. It's not the kind or silence that comes to a couple after years or decades together, running out of things to say. No, this was the silence of two people who had never confronted issues that constantly loomed upon them.

They left the port and entered into the inner city sublevels where the buildings butt up next to each other so tight that some cities resembled a blanket of quills on a porcupine, piercing through the clouds into the outer atmosphere. The gleaming pointed tips of the scrapers jetted out, daring anyone from the planets and solar system above to come and get skewered on them. He looked down into the darkness of the buildings' sublevels. In this city, like a porcupine, you can always find parasites next to the skin, feeding on the host. Hajjar shivered thinking of the city underbelly, glad to be living far away from the campus.

They walked through the glittering shards of sunlight and into the side of the next building, through two more buildings to the elevated light rail which carried commuters through the smaller buildings into the next city, and then on toward the glistening dome of the Time Bureau campus.

Getting off at the Greenwich Station, they walked the remaining distance to the campus entrance. The tall red stone walls surrounding the campus made Hajjar feel like he was walking up to a fortress. The walls stretched in a circle with a mile radius, surrounding the center of the campus, the center of the Px-Dome. The entrance arch ahead was closed to unauthorized personnel, closed off by two heavy steel doors.

Hajjar and Johnston instinctively pulled out their identification badges within the issue field notebook to present to the guards. Two guards dressed in black uniforms lowered their weapons to their side, stepping forward to take Hajjar's ID. Three more stood behind, eyes alert to all movements outside the gate. Hajjar proceeded into the alcove where the guard slid the ID into the reader as a life-sized image of Agent Hajjar appeared next to him, along with his full biometrics and DNA signature. He placed his feet in the designated area, standing relaxed with his hands lowered to his sides. The image slid over to rest in the same spot he stood. The images lit up, identifying his field notebook, high-intensity beam weapon and of course his Walther Pk380, old but reliable. Once confirmation of the identity was verified and all potential weapons were confirmed, the guard handed the badge to him, and they proceeded through the heavy steel doors into the first room. He stepped through the opaque field then paused for the ambient light to change green before proceeding to the final checkpoint with the two guards, each stood behind, to the right and left behind him.

A young woman with amber eyes stepped up to him face-to-face, looking him in the eyes. Her calm demeanor, along with the eerie shade of her eyes, always made Hajjar feel uneasy.

He wished he was a full category 3C psychic. Back a couple hundred years ago, the world organization started recognizing psychic abilities and categorizing them for use and danger. The ability to read thoughts was given a rating from 1 to 5, with mere impressions as 5, the ability to read full thoughts and see impressions of images as 3, and being able to remotely access another person's brain to be a passenger along for the ride, seeing, hearing, and witnessing the thoughts of the person as category 1. The ability to project thoughts into a person's mind was ranked from D to A, with being able to project impressions to sway feelings only as a category D, being able to project images and complete thoughts as category C, and most impressive was being able to control a person's actions and thought like a puppet as category A. He met a C3 physic once, outside of the agency. They talked all night. Though she was connected to everyone around her, she felt alone. There was no one categorized higher than that still living now. One time there was a person categorized as B2. They were mad and had to be locked away to protect the public from deadly nightmares and unconsciously attacking each other as his mind became overwhelmed with the horrors of the inner thoughts from people near him.

The D2 psychic standing in front of him focused on him, narrowing her eyes as to look through him. His vision blurred for a moment, then came back into focus. He always felt slightly violated by the mind probe.

"He is clear." Her voice echoed in the chamber. "Welcome back to the campus, Agent Hajjar." She smiled and then walked back to her desk to wait for Johnston. Metal doors opened in front of him, revealing the luscious green campus.

Hajjar stood a few minutes, waiting for the metal doors to open a second time for Johnston to step out and join him.

Johnston walked from the last security check, turning toward the archives.

"Aren't we going to the chief's office?"

She paused, turning back to him. "We?" Johnston looked to him with amusement. "TDCI Stewart wants to see *you*. This assignment is all you."

Johnston paused in the campus mall to admire the mosaic patterns of colors in the flower gardens. Purple, pink, and white flowers were arranged like Celtic knots through the rectangular campus center, stretching from the three-story brick administration building all the way to the center of the dome, where the 144-story archive stood tall with the clock tower displaying the time on all four sides, using actual clockwork mechanisms, a technology long since abandoned for tiny silicone circuit boards.

She looked at the single spire like a giant javelin thrown into the center of the campus reaching a kilometer taller than the archive. It projected the domed shield from the top like a shimmering bubble. The blue sky above the dome glittered in small spots where birds or insects passed through the field. She marveled a moment at the thin barrier protecting them all from the potentially harmful fluctuations in the timeline by the few able to not only jaunt over distances but through time. The paradox shield, called the Px-Dome by the faculty and students, enclosed the entire campus. Outside the glistening Px-Dome, the metal city buildings loomed on all sides, closing in on the placid green campus, sometimes casting their ominous shadows on the residents.

The sunlight warmed the air. Johnston passed the brick academy buildings lining either side of the mall filled with grass and trees. Young recruits were on the other side of the windows, sitting at the desks and learning the rules to follow for people who have the ability to disrupt time outside the Px-Dome so that they can return home without accidentally rewriting history. Other students who wanted to remain with the Bureau were sparring, learning weapon techniques for all periods, learning investigation techniques, and learning the challenges and demands of TDI like her.

She walked straight to the archives at the far end of the garden. All the best agents were historians at heart. They had a love of sifting thought dusty volumes, which felt of parchment; looking for historical evidence that just didn't make sense; and those events that just didn't add up in history and led to the thrill of the journey to the time and place to investigate.

She continued into the archives, closing her eyes to breathe in the aroma of accumulated knowledge and history in the form of dust that gave the oldest and most intriguing of the historic volumes a rich scent. She imagined the knowledge oozing into her brain by diffusion, making her feel wiser just by standing there.

She opened her eyes and looked up through the lobby with the glass veranda open to the first ten floors where the most recent volumes were kept. These archives held all known literature, from ancient stone tablets, papyrus scrolls, to the recent digital streams and theoretical articles released moments ago. Even the Dead Sea Scrolls were held within these walls, recovered from libraries of Jerusalem during the Great Global War.

The important work of the Bureau was done here. Historians investigated the literature for anomalies, items, or events out of place with the reality within the dome protected by the paradox dome. They looked for items that suddenly appear, advancing the technology of civilization decades ahead of the schedule and the inventor who had no background prior to becoming rich from the invention. Most of a good investigator's time was spent sifting through historical documents, looking for anomalies worthy of investigation.

Johnston walked up to the research hub, a digital monitor containing the location of all literature within the archives.

"Hey, Liz." Jen's voice echoed through the room, followed by a few of scowls from archivists with their fingers over their lips, and the others actually broke the silence themselves with shushes.

Jenn casually glided over to Liz, ignoring the wave of glares that followed her.

The two hugged.

"How was your trip to Poland? The start of WWII must have been fascinating." Jen greeted her friend and continued excitedly, "I know you can't tell me all the classified stuff, but at least tell me when and where along with a few juicy bits. I like to live vicariously through our friendship and your time jaunting." She stepped back from the hug.

"Wait, what?" Johnston asked in an excited whisper.

"I thought you'd tell me about all your trips." Jen paused. "Well, not *everything*." She leaned in to emphasize, "Not the classified *would tell ya, but I'd have to kill ya* stuff, but everything else." Her eyes met Johnston's.

"What are you talking about?" Johnston looked to the scowls brought on by interrupting the silent sanctuary of the archive. "Would you like some coffee?" Not that Jen needed any more.

"You *weren't* there." Jen frowned.

"What made you think I was?"

"I have the photo from the archive. I can't tell your age in the picture, but you are saying you haven't been there…"

"Well, not yet. Do you have the photo?"

"Of course." Jenn looked around cautiously. "Caffeine?"

"Or maybe some vintage wine from one of my trips." Johnston paused. "Then again, maybe not. I may need to keep my wits about me for this photo."

"I'll grab the photo and meet you at the cafe on the edge of the campus." She started to her desk then turned back. "But I'll take a rain check on the wine." She tried to hide the smile but winked. Johnston smiled and then lowered her head, shaking it with amusement.

***

The view from the coffee shop gave a great vantage point to watch the people as they came and went from the buildings, mostly students attending the academy with their books, learning history and precision with their jaunting. A few professors strolled through the grounds, watching the young teenagers with a parental gaze. Occasionally, she spotted an agent constantly darting their eyes, alert to every movement and not lowering their guard, keeping alert and guarded even in the sanctuary of the campus.

From the window, she watched a group of students sitting under a tree, chatting with books open around them. Suddenly, the girl with long brown hair blanched as she looked up at the clock tower. Frantically, she gathered her books, sprinting to the brick building across the garden, leaving her friends laughing. Johnston smiled and remembered how the punishment for running into a classroom a few minutes late was far less than time jaunting backward a few minutes to walk into class on time.

Jen sat at the table, looking out the window and taking the seat with her back to the door. Sometimes she would sit in the seat facing the door to watch Liz fidget uncomfortably, trying to keep an eye on the door directly behind her with the wariness of a feral field agent. Johnston walked over from the counter holding two mugs. She leaned over to set the mug with white froth and chocolate dust in front of Jen, who smiled, leaning forward and wrapping her hands around the mug. Johnston set her own mug with the chain dangling over the side in front of her seat and then sat down. She slowly pulled out the metal basket filled with an assortment of tea leaves from her mug, setting it aside on the small plate. And then she lifted the saucer and poured a dribble of cream into her tea and swirled it lightly with the spoon before placing the spoon next to the basket on the small plate.

Jen lifted one hand from the mug to slide the envelope over to Agent Johnston. And then she returned her hand to the mug, interlocking her fingers around it.

Johnston took a sip of her tea and then opened the envelope to study the picture. The image was old, predating crystal screens. It was rare for Johnston to hold a glossy black-and-white photo. In the background was a white cathedral with a tall archway over the entrance. Two bell towers on either side of the marble entrance gave a peaceful enduring symbol of stability. In front of the cathedral stood a statue of a warrior, sword held high, calling the charge into battle. In the foreground were piles of rifles and ammunition with a group of three solders wading through the sea of weapons. The solders wore distinct round helmets that flared out at the bottom, and the long thigh-length coats gathered in the back. She could only imagine the long black boots hidden by the piles of weapons and the SS insignia on the collar too small in the picture to see.

"Look there. That is you." Jen pointed to the left-hand side of the picture, almost. "Isn't it?"

Jen's finger pointed to the woman on the left-hand side heading out of the picture, behind the piles of ammunition. Her features were crisp, though the movement of her hair suggested she was moving briskly. Her face turned, looking over her shoulder with a focused gaze at the soldiers. It was like looking into a mirror about ten to fifteen years ago. She had the light-colored eyes, defined cheekbones, and the dark hair pulled back with wisps falling out.

Johnston self-consciously ran her fingers over her own hair, pulled back, and then started twiddling the wisps of hair with her fingers. "It looks like me, but it can't be." Johnston pulled out her compact magnifying glass to look closer. "I can't quite tell the age of her." Johnston looked for white running through her hair or wrinkles, and then determined the image was far too small for the details to be apparent. "Traveling into a war is strictly prohibited unless on a mission. The probability is too high that any action might influence history." She looked hard at the person in the photo. She lifted her head, shaking it slowly. "The first thing I need to do is get a plan. Figure out when and where this might have been taken."

"I know the when, where, and the background information about this picture." Jen lifted her chin with a smirk. "I work the archives. That is what I do, and damn well. You don't think they keep me in the archives for my outgoing personality and witty sense of humor?"

Johnston's gaze lifted from the picture to Jen's grin. *Witty sense of humor indeed*, Johnston thought, raising one eyebrow and smiling.

"Looking at the context of the picture." Jen slid the image to the center of the table within her reach, facing Johnston, pointing with her finger as she continued, "That monument of the man lifting his sword to charge is most likely Jan Kiliński, because that statue was in front of the Field Cathedral of the Polish army. Mr. Jan was a shoemaker who helped lead the Warsaw Uprising against the Russians in 1794." She looked up from the picture, eyes gleaming. Her smile sagged seeing Johnston's raised eyebrows. "You may not be as interested in that." She looked back at the picture. "That cathedral was in Warsaw, Poland. The interesting thing is that it was originally built in a baroque style, as seen in this image. But around 1834-ish, the

Russians converted it into an Orthodox church with the Russian dome style that is seen in Moscow, and it stayed that way until World War I. After World War I, between the years of 1923 to 1927, the church was converted back to its original baroque style. Then it was partially demolished in the Warsaw Uprising of 1944. The cathedral is in Krasiński Square, Warsaw. And in the beginning of World War II, the statue was located there. After the German invasion of 1939, the weapons from the Polish army were piled around the base of the statue."

Johnston leaned forward, resting her chin on her hand, her eyes wide. "Wow, you got all that from this picture?"

Jen looked up, her cheeks lifted by the corners of her grin. "Well, yes, and I analyzed the picture a few days ago. With the help of the archive, it has the highest probability of being taken on October 16, 1939."

Johnston's gaping jaw curled up into a smile. "All that by yourself? No help?"

"Yes, by myself." She took a deep breath. "Aaand the research books. I had time to look all this up. If you weren't going to tell me about your trip, then I would look it up in the archives. It's not top secret if it's in the history books."

"You never cease to amaze me. It is no wonder you are the top investigator identifying anomalies."

"Yeah, but you get the fun of traveling there. I have never time jaunted. I got here on my grades and determination. I am stuck in 2593, living vicariously through reading historic records and through your stories." Jen faintly smiled. "What I wouldn't give to go with you to the past."

"You know I can't." Johnston smiled. "I would love to have you join me on a jaunt, but I can't. Taking someone on a joined time jaunt has never been achieved before. Even in theory, it would take a psychic rated at a minimum of 2B to be able to project the destination so clearly that you would be able to feel it, smell it." She closed her eyes. "Be there." She opened her eyes again. "And still a 2 to be able to read the traveler well enough to make course corrections in their thoughts mid-journey. And when I was tested, I only ranked in reading thoughts. I couldn't influence others."

"Yeah, I know." Jen smiled. "But it is fun to wish you could take me to Paris in the late nineteenth century for some wine and great emerging painters."

"My first solo assignment." The words felt good to Hajjar. TDCI Stewart never really said why he was being called into his office, and Johnston gave no indication as usual. It had to be his first lone assignment, and it was about time. Seven years with Johnston and now a chance to prove himself. He was always top of his class, accomplishing things faster and younger than anyone else.

Hajjar paused to enter the lift to the ninth floor. The doors slid open as he stepped inside.

He paused, closing his eyes and steadying his nerves the way Johnston had taught him. The cocky grin lifted one cheek. No apprehension, not even a hint. He thought, *I am ready for this. I have been ready for years.*

He would be again the youngest to meet this milestone achievement. He was skilled and knowledgeable enough for a mission without a senior officer at such a young age, and why shouldn't he be there? He was the best in all his classes and wouldn't compromise, especially when he knew he was right.

He excelled in history, always getting perfect scores. Once, after getting his test back on the Great Global War, he would have gotten yet another perfect score but for one question. He remembered rereading the question to see why it was graded as wrong, and to his annoyance, he was correct. He was sure of it and set out to prove it after all.

The fourth-grade teacher sat loftily at his desk, smug in his supposed knowledge of historic events. Ryan Hajjar took his test up to Mr. Wells, along with the recent publication proving his correct answer. Ryan placed the test down on the desk, requesting Mr. Wells to reconsider the answer based on the evidence presented in a recent publication on the Treaty of Constantinople.

The delegates representing the countries at the signing of the treaty were all present with each of their flags waving. According to the history book, one country chose to protest the last-minute additions to the treaty by not signing. Though hotly debated, recently flight records and accommodations for the president of Kurdistan indicated that she was present at the signing but chose not to sign the treaty until the changes were once again removed.

Mr. Wells refused to consider the evidence sitting right in front of him, stating that photographs taken at the treaty did not show her being present. The debate got louder and louder. Ryan stood facing the desk, both hands holding the edge with his thumbs on top of the desk and his fingernails digging into the desk underneath; he continued taking deep breaths through his clenched teeth. He closed his eyes.

"Why can't you accept the idea that I am right?" Ryan demanded. He had done the research. He even he felt like he was there in the warm dry summer, the sound of the flags waving in the breeze. He breathed out, clenching his teeth, and then he opened his eyes to be surrounded by a combination of Turkish and Eastern Orthodox architecture. He looked ahead of him to the group of men and women wearing ceremonial outfits, generals with full bars, stars and cords draped from their shoulders alongside leaders in brilliant suits, all signing a parchment. He was among a group of people holding cameras, notepads, and tablets.

Looking over the group, he saw the Australian prime minister shaking hands with Kurdistan's president off to the side, away from the signing of the treaty. The two were discussing and smiling in agreement. Australia played down their role brokering the treaty after the president of Kurdistan refused to sign, but after this day, they worked on a peace treaty that would meet all country's requirements to ensure a lasting peace. But the most important thing was that she was there. The Kurdish president was there.

"I was right. Take that, Mr. Wells!" He jumped up, pumping his fist into the air.

Moments later, the unexpected ten-year-old was whisked away for questioning. Who was he, and how had he managed to infiltrate through the nine layers of security to get within mere yards of the signing? What was his intention?

They pulled him out of sight of the delegation and stashed him into a secure location. There he sat in a solid gray room with no windows and only one door, with two very scary men in black suits leaning in, yelling questions at him in a language he could not understand. The fear started to well up inside him as he looked back and forth from one man to the other. One would start yelling as the other man stopped to take a breath, until both were interrupted by a knocking on the door. Both men looked at each other with confusion, then the one that resembled a tree trunk stepped outside the door for a moment. Ryan heard fragments of a conversation as the man was clearly yelling, but the response came calm and precise.

The new man in a dark suit stepped in, stating something to the two men in the same language, and handed them a set of papers. He followed up with a statement and a look, making the tree trunk man stalk over, unlocking the chains from Ryan's ankles and wrists.

The tall clean dressed man in a gray suit with a short haircut walked over to Hajjar, kneeling down and looking him in the eye. The gray eyes of the man in the suit relaxed. "I need you to put this on and come with me."

Ryan placed the metal ringlet over his head; the man adjusted it so that it sat snug on Ryan's head. He then stood a moment longer, feeling disoriented. Hand in hand, the two walked calmly out of the facility.

Now that they were alone, the man with gray eyes knelt down in front of Hajjar. "I'm Mr. Hennessy. You are not from around… now, are you?"

"Now?" Hajjar asked.

Mr. Hennessy sighed. "Let me adjust this." He pressed a few buttons on the head jaunt dampener around Ryan's head to set a destination. "Here we go." And then he pressed a final button.

Within minutes, Ryan started to fall into dreams.

Ryan Hajjar was taken immediately to the academy to learn how to control time jaunting so that he wouldn't randomly find himself in a different time and place. He stayed there, unable to go home until he showed proficiency, still the youngest human to jaunt through time. And he continued to set the standard in his classes.

The lift doors slid open, and Hajjar stepped out through rows of wooden desks to the glass office at the end. He stopped at the door, rapping on the frosted glass quickly then stepping back, placing his hands to his sides.

The milky frosted window in the door changed to a clear glass, revealing the chief behind his oak desk. He raised his hand, summoning Hajjar to come in, and the door slid open. As Hajjar turned to close the door out of reflex, the door was already closed, and the window returned to a milky frosted color.

"Have a seat, TDI Hajjar." Chief Stewart placed a folder in front of him. "I have an assignment for you."

Hajjar flicked a smile, trying to hide it behind professionalism. *Can't look too eager to beat another record.*

The chief handed the folder to Hajjar. "We need you to investigate an anomaly."

Hajjar forced back a smile, hiding his emotion as he opened the folder to see the information upload into his Field Book screen. "This is a recording device…" He paused to change the screens and read further into the report. "After sitting in storage for twenty-eight years, the device was discovered in an inventory audit in 2405. The device was first made and sold in 2402…191 years ago." His voice trailed off. "Is this right?" He looked up from the report. "So it was sold to the pawnshop in 2377? This would be 216 years ago." His disappointment was dripping from his words.

"Don't look so sad, Hajjar." Chief Stewart smiled slyly.

"If tech before its documented time of introduction with intent to gain money or gain a tech copyright first, it would not be sold to a pawnshop. Especially if we have the potential to retrieve it without the pawnshop knowing the tech that they hold. Clearly the owner didn't know what he had until fifty year later."

Chief Stewart rose from his desk, annoyed. He turned and looked out his window, taking a deep breath. "The tech is not the only issue." He breathed out slowly. "This is why I said an anomaly and not an investigation of *some* tech." He turned to the window. Hajjar could barely make out the chief muttering something about not being ready for this assignment.

Hajjar flipped the page, annoyed at the accusation that he was not ready. He pausing to read further into the report. "Is this correct? This can't be a first generation recording?" His eyes widened.

"We haven't retrieved the tech yet to confirm the authenticity and quality." The chief turned to face Hajjar. "We have to treat it as first gen recording until we recover the device and verify the recording."

Hajjar rose to look at Chief Stewart. "First I need to recover the device and interview the attendant in the shop and find out who sold the device to them." He looked back at the pad. "We will see where the investigation goes from here."

"Good plan. Don't let me hold you up." The chief held out his hand. Hajjar shook it then turned to head out of the office.

Johnston sat looking at the picture with amazement and then looked up over the picture into Chief Stewart's office. She *had* to investigate this, but how much information should she tell him? She breathed deeply, willing her feet to move. After a long moment, she stepped forward, taking another breath. She closed her eyes and knocked on milky frosted glass window. The glass cleared a moment as Johnston opened her eyes to see the chief beckoning her in. She exhaled and opened the door.

"What brings you in to see me?" The chief leaned forward, touching his fingertips together and resting his elbows on the table.

"An anomaly I need to check out." She looked down at the picture then set it in front of Chief Stewart.

"It looks like World War II. I'd guess Poland, maybe Warsaw. Why is this picture worth risking your life?"

Johnston twitched a slight smile. The chief knew his history. Warsaw 1939, and he knew how dangerous it would be. "The back part of the picture, behind the statue, the profile." She pointed. "I need to"—she paused to emphasize—"to check this out." She looked him in the eyes.

"This is you?" Chief Stewart paused. "I don't like the idea of a good agent risking their life on a personal investigation. There is a reason World Wars are off-limits. Too much could be compromised, even for a paradoxical photo."

"I'll be careful. Any danger and I'll jaunt back." She bent over, placing her hands on the chief's desk.

"Your life is not just what I'm talking about. What if you get captured carrying tech? They are in the first years of World War II. Imagine how the war, even history, would change if the Polish resistance—or worse, the Germans—got their hands on our tech." He placed his chin on his thumbs with his index fingers touching his nose. "I can't let you risk it."

"I'm going. I have the time to take off." Johnston stood back up. "I need to take care of this myself."

"Very well." The chief leaned back in his chair. "I will remind you the Paradox Shield protects agents from the effects of rewritten history from an incident." The chief leaned forward, folding his hands in his lap. "Since you are too stubborn, listen. If your actions result in a breach of normal timeline development, we will not hesitate to send an agent in to take you out to recover you and your tech before your inevitable actions occur."

"Acknowledged." Johnston stiffened then turned to leave the room.

The chief's voice followed her out of the room. "Good luck."

***

Johnston returned to the research department in the depths of the library. *How do I safely get to the center of Warsaw in 1939?* Her thoughts rushed through her head. The place just fell to the German invasion. Most records and photos of the time were lost in the destruction. Those saved in the original invasion were surely destroyed in the uprising years later.

Hours passed as she combed through document, photos, and images, looking for a place to jaunt in. If the population even saw a person jaunt, a person just phasing into existence in front of them, who knows how they would react. Johnston's worry started to distract her. She breathed, regaining focus. *I'd either be shot the moment I arrived, or just being witness to something like that would change history as we know it. Then I'd be* taken care of. She closed her eyes, thinking of ideas. *Given my research, there is no way I can pop into Warsaw at that time and not be seen or guarantee not being seen.* She walked through the labyrinth of books and records, pulling more files and documents.

Hours passed more quickly as a plan started to unfold. The engrossing research kept her occupied as time slipped away from her.

History became even more captivating when her life depended on it. She rested her head on the back of her hand. All the lights in the building were turned off. A figure emerged from the shadows.

"You should go home and rest." Jen squatted down at the table, placing a hand on Johnston's shoulder. "The books will still be here tomorrow."

Johnston rubbed her eyes with the back of her hand. "You just don't want me drooling on your beloved books."

Jen closed her eyes and sighed, smiling. "You got me. It is all about the parchment."

"Yeah, I knew it." Johnston looked at Jen, straining to keep her eyes open.

"Come on, Liz. Let me get you home." Jen led the sleep-deprived Johnston from the small desk in the center of the room with rows of matching desks surrounded on all sides by books.

***

Johnston slowly lifted her foot out of the water to turn off the hot water reheating the bathtub. She sank deeper into the water. The heat of the water permeated her muscles, soothing the tightness in her back and shoulders. The collected tension behind her eyes started to defuse into the water, throbbing less intensely with each moment sitting in the tub.

She opened her eyes to see the steam curling off the surface of the water, then off her arm as she lifted her hand out of the water to wrap her fingers around the wine glass and raise it from the stand next to the case file she needed to review, but not this moment.

She scooted up in the cast iron tub, bringing her shoulders out of the water to take a sip. Setting the glass back down, she started an inner dialogue, first in Polish and then repeating the same dialogue in German, focusing on the dialect and accents specific to the time.

The sanctuary of the bath was merely the calm before the storm. She couldn't let her guard down until she was completely confident or until she was back home safe.

Rolling her shoulders, she tried to will the muscle tension and lactic acid buildup from hours of hand-to-hand combat training to loosen. What she wouldn't give for a back massage.

I have the self-defense practice ready, she thought in Polish, and then repeated the same phrase in both high and low German. *I can disarm a person once close enough to grab their hand.*

She flipped open the folder. "The forest southwest of Warsaw looks like the most likely place to meet up with Pilecki and the resistance." This time she focused on the specific enunciation and pronunciation her speech coach grilled her on and repeated a second time in German.

She briefly reviewed the images she was able to dig up, though extensive review might result in jaunting there prematurely.

She set the folder aside. Closing her eyes again, she slid down further into the water. Her inner dialogue continued first in Polish. *What should I wear?* She opened her eyes a moment and smiled, continuing her inner dialogue, practicing Polish. *I'll take a dark button-up shirt like those of the factory workers with pants and boots. This will allow good versatility and ability to hide my H-EMP guns and movement to attempt to disarm before pulling tech. It will be both practical and appropriate for the time. Farm women were starting to wear these clothes to work the fields with the men. It would not be common for another two to five years, but it would be passable. Though a tight French braid would be better tactically for potential combat, a tight bun atop my head would be more appropriate for the time.*

Now that the location, dress, and language were planned, she stretched. Her muscles weren't protesting any more.

She rose out of the tub, placing one foot on the floor, and grabbed a towel to wrap around her, tucking the corner in beside her. She wandered into the living area with smooth movements, trying not to slip on the tile or spill her glass.

Sitting on the love seat, she looked around the room, her sanctuary, where she felt relaxed surrounded by her memories. She looked at her small laser gun from Lenard. She got it during her first case where she saved Mr. Tesla from a man traveling back to get revenge on the man who created the weapon that had killed his child. The best thing was that he never knew the danger he was in. He never even knew she was there.

She looked over to the books from Louis and Charles and then reached over to turn on the lamp. She loved the lion's head in the slender pentagonal base and the flower stem that looped into a golden glow that illuminates the side of the love seat with warm reading light. The light made other memorable items emerge from the darkness. She looked over to her favorite, a sketch by her favorite artist, Leonardo. There were so many questions that she wanted to ask him but couldn't in fear of inspiring him in directions that he would not otherwise pursue.

She lifted the glass to her lips to take a sip. Her eyes lifted to a painting over the electric fireplace of pastel lilies painted largely with wide brush strokes. Yawning, she picked up the little pill bottle, tapping the side with her finger until two white tablets fell neatly into her hand. Setting the bottle back down beside the lamp, she dropped them in her mouth and washed them down with the rest of the wine.

She took the medication only when she was deep in a case preparation. Once the case language and location started intruding on her dreams, she wanted to stop dreaming. She didn't want to wake up in the forests outside of Warsaw, surrounded by the resistance or worse, German soldiers, while wearing her cute blue pajamas with her favorite cow cartoon character.

Johnston slowly inhaled with her eyes closed. She exhaled, feeling the boots on her feet, the weight of the thick soles grounding her. Inhale. The loose dark pants allowed her movement, including a kick if needed. Exhale. She stretched her arms out and lowered them to her sides, feeling the light green cuffs on her wrists and the jacket heavy on her shoulders. Inhale. She pulled hair tight into a bun on her head, holding in the emotions the way good women were tough, then. Finally, the stun gun, small and slender to resemble a Polish Radom VZ-35, a military pistol from the time attached to her holster in the small of her back and a small single-shot Derringer-style stun gun stuffed in her boot.

Now placing herself there, her eyes closed as she continued. Another breath in and she slowly exhaled. She pulled the image of the woods outside of Warsaw. Inhale. Right now, Kampinos Forest (Kampinos NP) securely formed into her mind. Exhale. She could smell the woods and the chill of the frost at night. Inhale. The rustling of the leaves in the trees and the sounds of fighting in the background echoed in her ears. She felt the image of the first part of October 1939 firmly in her mind, along with the crisp fall air on her skin, biting her nose. Exhale. She felt her breath in a cloud escaping her lungs into the frosty night air. She breathed in the chilled air as it frosted her throat. She opened her eyes to see her breath leaving her mouth as a fog. Into the chilly dark Polish night.

Dropping to a crouch, she listened to the sounds around her, the rustling of leaves as the breeze slowly weaved its way through the limbs above. The darkness surrounded her, along with the silence of night while the birds slept in the trees. She slowly exhaled with relief that her arrival did not disturb any animals that would flee and give away her location. With stillness around her, she sat still, allowing her eyes to adapt to the darkness. Sounds of the gunfire and bombs echoed in the distance behind her toward Warsaw. Something caught her attention as an outline of the woods slowly came into focus, illuminated by the moon through the forest canopy.

Silently, she pulled the compass out of her pocket. The letters *N*, *S*, *E*, and *W* faintly glowed red in the darkness with an arrow hovering between north and east.

She turned the compass so the arrow aligned with north and then turned her body to align with the arrow. The river should be north of her position if she had jaunted to the right place. Closing the compass, she slipped it into her back pocket.

This would be so much easier with GPS, but the first satellites wouldn't be launched for another twenty years. And even then it was just for show. No, this would have to be done low-tech. She looked up into the darkness with trees and branches silhouetted in the ambient light of the stars and silver of the moon.

Slowly, one step at a time, she placed her foot down, listening intensely both to her movement and any other noises from the forest around her. Her movement though the underbrush of the forest was painfully slow, and she barely made a sound.

The trees rustled overhead as the cold breath of autumn permeated the canopy to bite her nose and cheeks. The breeze picked up, creating a crescendo of leaves murmuring. Her steps quickened in those moments as her movement were muffled by the sounds of nature. She wanted to find the resistance before they found her, or worse, she was found by a German soldier.

A flicker of yellowish-orange light in the woods ahead caught her attention. Crouching down, she slowly moved in. As the firelight got closer, she could see it start to cast, dancing shadows on the bushes ahead. With each step closer, she could begin to hear voices. The deeper voices of men mixed with a few voices that sounded crackly of boys. *Though in light of the invasion, their childhood would have been long gone*, she thought.

She slunk up to a shrub on the edge of the penetrating firelight. Crouching in the darkness, she waited to listen. Blocking out the sound of the forest, she could faintly hear talking over the sound of the crackling fire. She rocked forward, placing one hand with fingers spread on the ground, and she focused on the speech. German or Polish? Potential friend or foe? She closed her eyes.

Crack.

The sound of a broken stick splintered the near silence, bringing her back to the immediate surroundings. She heard the second heavy step close behind her. The sound was quickly followed by the unmistakable sound of a bullet loading into a chamber. "Hands up!"

There was a slight relief as she recognized Polish. Johnston slowly raised her hands and stood up. She heard sounds of other men running through the brush, loading their pistols in mid-sprint.

"Who is it?" One voice cracked with fear.

"What are they doing here?" Another deep voice tried to remain hushed, though the excitement was loud and clear.

Two more silhouettes moved through the darkness more slowly than the others, cautious in their approach. Both men had their hands confidently placed at their side, probably resting on a side arm, but not convinced it needed to be pulled.

"Who are you and what are you doing here?" the deep voice from one of the silhouettes asked.

Johnston paused to incorporate bits of their accent into her reply. "I'm trying to get to the river, to my sister in Warsaw. I need to find her." She adjusted her Polish, attempting to mimic their dialect. "I need to find her."

The silhouette lowered his hand from his belt. At the same time, the three standing with their guns pointed at her lowered the muzzles a few degrees. The youngest of the men with the cracking voice stopped rattling his gun.

Johnston kept her hands raised but allowed a small sigh of relief.

The deep voice came from the darkness behind her, directly behind her. "Bring her to the camp." He walked by, looking her in the eye. "We can find out more there."

The procession of young men wandered in toward the camp with Johnston in the middle. She remained holding her hands up above her head. She stepped awkwardly, handling herself to keep the illusion of a civilian. Three more men walked calmly behind her, one still with a gun aimed at her.

Single file line weaved its way through the shrubs into the firelight. Johnston's gaze scanned the nine faces around the firelight, pausing a moment on the young man with a cleft chin, low serious brows, light piercing eyes, and a bump halfway down his nose. Pilecki.

Johnston sat on a log near the fire.

Pilecki crouched, looking Johnston in the eyes. "Where is your sister?"

Johnston widened her eyes and focused on tears, looking at the ground between her feet. "Warsaw. That is the last I heard from her, three streets over from the monument to Jan Kiliński and the cathedral." Her eyes glistened moist with tears as she looked up into Pilecki's eyes. She watched him get up to converse with his men as she lowered her head. She watched them intently with her head lowered. All three men looked back at her. Pilecki rubbed his eyebrows and then moved his hand to his side, walking back to the fire.

He squatted in front of her again, placing his hands on her knees. "Who are you?" His eyes met her tears.

"I should ask the same of you. And what are your intentions with me?" She forced sobs between each word.

"We only want to help you," he said reassuringly.

"But who are you?" She wiped a tear with her sleeve.

He sighed. "Peter." His finger slipped to his eyebrow then brushed aside his hair. "That is all I will tell you of us. The less you know, the safer we will be."

Johnston pursed her lips and then looked up at him with her hands clasped in front of her chin. "Can you help me?"

"We thought that area was shops only. No people live near there." His hand slipped to his eyebrow, looking her in the eye. "Where are you from?"

Johnston fought back a smile to keep the innocence in her eyes. "No, the shops are a few streets over, and they all have apartments above them, where my sister lives." She sobbed a bit more. "If you won't help me, I'll go alone."

Pilecki sighed. "No, I think we can help you. We are heading to the city soon."

Johnston smiled, forcing her eyes to water a bit more. "Thank you." She leaned forward, grabbing his hands. She heard at least three weapons being cocked and pointed at her. "Oh, sorry." She backed off with her hands up. "Sorry, sorry!" She retreated to the ground she was sitting on and slowly lowered her arms.

"Sir…sir." A young man tapped Pilecki's shoulder. "We have some consensus," the young man tried to whisper in Pilecki's ear.

Pilecki looked down long and hard at Johnston before moving to join the men.

Johnston sat with her legs crossed in front of her on the log, each elbow resting on her knees. She connected her pointer fingers and rested her chin on her thumbs. Closing her eyes to filter out the background noise, she focused on the murmurs, making out bits and pieces.

"…don't trust…spy."

Pilecki's voice was recognizable. "We take her with us."

She heard murmurs of protest from the group.

His voice interrupted murmurs. "If…spy, we shouldn't let out…sight. She knows…and camp location. I truthfully…we… about her accidentally…captured. Then she wouldn't last torture and interrogation."

An agreement settled through the group. Nods of unity in the decision passed from each man to the next one at a time. Once all agreed, they returned to the firelight.

"We'll take you." Pilecki walked up, casting a shadow over her.

She looked up at him. "I don't want to be a burden. I can just follow the river in and find my way into the city."

Her statement was met with an annoyed and frustrated look from Pilecki, who did not like her questioning his authority.

"Yes, sir, thank you." She swallowed her satisfaction but still exhaled a sigh of relief. "When do we head out?"

"Tomorrow night we will head out right after dusk. The moon won't rise until early morning. We will have enough time to take the river. As long as we miss the patrols, we will make it into the city."

Pilecki leaned over to look harshly at Johnston. "Don't do anything to bring attention to yourself. You are already a liability we don't need."

"I understand," Johnston whispered.

"Good. Now rest." Pilecki stood back up. "We all need to be alert and ready for anything tomorrow night."

Johnston could hardly sleep. The excitement of being in the presence of the founders of the Polish Secret Army made her mind race. The questions she would love to ask him, just pick his brain about tactics and plans to fight the Germans without potentially altering history. Johnston breathed a sigh of disappointment knowing the reality and turned over, faced the fire, and focused her thoughts.

"You still awake?" Pilecki's deep voice startled her.

Slowly she removed her hand from the pistol under her backpack-makeshift pillow, moving it to the ground and pushing herself to a sitting position.

Pilecki smiled and then continued scanning the edges of the darkness for movement.

"For the record, I did not want you to join us on the trip," he whispered as he continued to scan the trees for movement and sound of more unwanted visitors. In a low whisper, he continued, "I think you will compromise our group and get us captured or killed."

"I know. That is why I was awake." She turned to sit slightly ahead and to the side of him, not blocking his view while she scanned the darkness behind him and then continued, "I can handle myself."

He glanced at her then chuckled. "You may come from a farm, but a farm girl won't handle a pistol with the accuracy and precision you will need if you face a German. I doubt that you have ever killed before. Could you take a life?"

Johnston hesitated to answer, knowing the truth but not speaking it.

"In that moment of hesitation, they would have killed you," he stated.

So many things she wanted to say, but she could only ask, "Then why are you letting me come with you?"

"Because you are greater liability to us on your own. You have seen us and where we are camped. This could get us captured. At this point, your capture and torture might put an end to the rebellion before it begins."

"Then why haven't you killed me?"

The look of hurt answered the question. Then he put it into words. "We may be desperate to survive, but we are better than them. If we stoop to their levels, killing anyone that is merely an obstacle or challenge to the master plan, then we are no better than they are. We must keep our humanity. Otherwise, we become no better than those SS wolves."

Johnston smiled, relieved and happy to hear that a person in history that she respected just reinforced that respect. "You can leave me in the sewers and move your camp after you drop me off."

"We plan to." He looked at her. "Why is it so important to get into Warsaw?"

"I told you." Johnston looked at Pilecki then up at the sky. "I'm looking for my sister. When last I saw her, we parted on tenuous terms. I promised our parents…" Her voice trailed off. "I just need to know she is all right."

Pilecki nodded then went back to scanning the darkness. "Get some rest. You'll need it tomorrow."

Johnston lay down under her blanket, placing her head back on the pack, her hand slid under and on the gun underneath.

The night passed slowly, filled with subtle noises, stirring Johnston out of her light sleep. Each time another member took watch, Johnston instinctively tightened her grasp on the gun beneath her pack, trying not to alert anyone to the fact that she was awake.

After hours that seemed like decades, the skies lightened to a purplish blue with streaks of pink and red that feathered across the sky. The birds woke, starting their morning routine as the sunlight slowly reached the top of the tree canopy, turning the dark silhouette of leaves into green foliage.

Johnston savored every moment of true nature, not the small patches confined to the middle of her sterile glass and metal urban sprawl. She laid motionless for a moment before she subtlety moved the gun back into its holster at the small of her back.

The group was lively for the lack of sound. The majority of supplies were packed and stashed, covered by foliage and tall brush. Within an hour, the remnants of the camp were stowed. Johnston looked around with amazement, taking notes for future infiltration. The small clearing appeared vacant. Patches of shrubs near the tree line dense with ferns hid small bundles of supplies, all covered in green to blend in. The place where a small fire once danced was now covered by a long tree trunk, moved from where the men sat the night before. The tufts of grass and pine needles were carefully returned to almost their natural state. She had to look hard to see evidence that they had even been there.

She knew now there would be a long time to dusk. The group set, tension building, wanting for the darkness to be on them while Mother Nature continued at her normal slow speed. After the hues of reds and pinks on the horizon, night swallowed the entire sky. Johnston paused to marvel at the billions of stars stretching across the sky. Back home, the pollution and light from the city blocked all the stars, even miles outside the iron and glass sprawl.

"Let's go." Pilecki jolted her back to the task at hand. They loaded two small boats with the minimal supplies to remain light and agile in the water to avoid any German patrol lights.

Silently, the boats slid into the water. Johnston sat in the middle where she could be harmless. The men slid the paddles out from the side of the boat then silently placed them into the water ahead of them. With one hand down, pulled back on the paddle, and their other hands on the end of the paddle pushed forward, the boat cut through the water. Each man slowly pulled the paddles out the water and then placed them again into the water ahead of them.

Both boats slid through the water, one slightly ahead and to the right of the other. They hugged close to the shoreline to be covered by the tree limbs reaching out over the water. The men sitting along with her sat straight, listening and alert, scanning the shoreline wary of movement. The man in the back of the boat paddled in sync with the men in the front by dipping his paddle on the opposite sides of the boat.

The silent tension built with each stroke of the paddles as they slid through the darkness closer to the city. Suddenly, a hand grabbed her shoulder as Mark, the young jittery man, pointed to the left along the shoreline. Johnston's eyes darted to see the movement and flashlight he was pointing at. Everyone froze to watch as the beam of light scanned the tree line ahead of them and then moved to the opposite side of the river. The soldier in a domed helmet passed along the opposite shore, paused, then turned to walk back into the tree cover on the opposite shore. Johnston looked behind her to see Pilecki wave his hand in a forward motion. Paddles were dipped into the water to continue forward as the men continued scanning the shoreline for more encounters.

The hours passed at a snail's crawl. As they reached the edge of the city, the half-moon started cresting over the horizon. It was now two-ish in the morning. The seven hours spent rowing into the city felt like seventy.

The boat glided up to a round grate covering a dark hole leading into a brick wall. The man in the front steered the boat up to the man-made cave as the side of the boat came alongside the opening. Mark's nerves jostled the boat a little as he rose to grab the clasp on the grate, stepping out of the boat. He unhinged the clasp and swung the grate open. Pilecki briskly got out of the back of the boat and into the round cavernous opening. Mr. Glittery continued to scan the shoreline as Pilecki pulled the boat alongside the opening so Johnston could get out. Johnston and Pilecki pulled the boat into the opening past the grate. The three in the second boat followed suit, and soon both boats were pulled into the opening of the grate then closed and locked.

Pilecki pulled out a map, lighting the area with the flame from his lighter. Looking first down to study the map then back up to the tunnel, then to the map again, he finally made eye contact with Johnston.

"These sewers will take you where you want to go. Take these tunnels past the next three junctions. At the fourth junction you turn left then continue past one more junction. There you will find a ladder that will take you to the street. That will be the neighborhood your sister lives in. We are also heading to the fourth junction, where you are turning at, but we will leave you there."

"Thank you." Johnston secured her backpack.

They sloshed through the muck past the three intersections and stopped at the fourth. Johnston reached out her hand. "Here is where we part ways. Thank you. It has been an honor to meet you."

He shook her hand and nodded. Johnston could see something in his eye, worry of doing the right thing, but at what cost? She knew that she would not compromise his mission, but there was no way he would know that.

Johnston shook the hands of the five other men and wished them a safe journey. And then she turned down the tunnel to the left. She climbed the ladder to the top, slowly lifting the sewer cover to look around. The light from the partial moon gave an eerie glow to the buildings. The colors drained by the low light almost painted the cityscape into a black-and-white picture. The three-story buildings looked light gray with the ornate designs around the windows, doors, and up along the top of the building dramatically with the stark contrast of the moonlight and the black shadows. The silence of the vacant streets gave Johnston an uneasy feeling. She slowly and consciously climbed out. Carefully, she returned the cover to its place.

Quickly, she glanced around again, noting the deep shadows that looked like pools of oil that could swallow a person and hide those prying eyes. She darted to the safety of one of the shadows in the alley.

She found a corner to hide until dawn when the warm light would fight back against the darkness and reveal her hiding spot. She took a moment to rest. She would need to stay alert in the morning. Light sleep interrupted by sounds as subtle as rustling paper kept her on edge, but it was better than nothing. The morning came slowly, turning the black-and-white city into a colorful image with each brushstroke of sunlight that broke through the shadows.

Johnston continued down the alley to peer out the opening. The alley opened onto the city square. A cathedral stood tall at one side of the square, a testament to the consistent influence of the church through the history. A tear came to Johnston's eye, knowing that within the next five years, that cathedral would be used as a hospital for wounded soldiers. It would draw attention, becoming a target in the bombing raids, nearly demolishing the cathedral as the Germans tried to destroy the catacombs deep under that became a sanctuary for the wounded. Johnston took a moment to admire the chapel, reflecting on its longevity before its utter destruction, then rebirth thirty years later after the war.

In the center of the square stood a familiar silhouette of a man holding a sword skyward in defiance. Her scan of the square revealed seven soldiers around the pile of ammunition and weapons.

As the early morning passed, she hovered at the corner of a building, overlooking the square, scanning the soldiers and people coming and going through the area. By midmorning, a person carrying a camera passed through as two solders stalled, looking down between the photographer and the statue. Johnston quickly scanned the side of the pile nearest her to see a familiar figure. The figure looked just like her, but fifteen years younger. Johnston looked over her shoulder at the soldiers and then continued walking down an adjoining street.

Johnston scanned the soldiers to see them distracted by the piles of ammunition and the photographer, and she slid from the shadows to pursue this person. Johnston carefully slipped behind the photographer, avoiding his attention. The figure darted down an adjoining alley off the road. Johnston came to the entrance to the alley and placed her back to the corner of the three-story baroque building. She quickly turned her head to glance down the alley to see the mysterious woman looking nervously back and forth. She stood fiddling with both hands, working the lock above the door handle. Her head swung toward the end of the alley where Johnston quickly ducked behind the corner of the building.

Johnston rested the back of her head against the building, glancing up and down the street for anyone who may have noticed her. She slowly exhaled and looked again. The woman was gone from the alley.

Johnston rounded the corner then slowly continued down the alley toward the door.

Suddenly, a German voice announced his presence behind her.

Careless, Johnston, careless. She chastised herself then raised her hands and turned to face him.

"Who are you, and what are you doing?" The German cut through the ambient noise.

"I was checking things out." Johnston was not happy with her German dialect. It sounded a century off.

"You need to come with me." His rough voice was followed by a rattling of his gun when he used it to point the direction he was herding her to.

She glanced behind her then stepped closer. The soldier grinned deviously.

Johnston grabbed his gun with her right hand, pushing it up and to the side. She twisted, turning her back to him, holding his right hand over her shoulder in front of him and using her left hand and body momentum to reach his hand.

In the fast moment, she squeezed her finger. The shot rang in her right ear as she wrenched his hand further and the gun fell from his hand. She grabbed his hand with both of her hands. She stepped back, bent forward, and threw him over her shoulder.

Hearing steps behind her entering the alley, she spun, placing her left knee hard on the breastbone of the solder, pulling the gun from the small of her back with her right hand, aiming it at the chest of the soldier. In the next moment, she pulled her gun from her left boot with the other hand, aiming it down the alley to where she heard the footsteps.

The German soldier twitched as a quiet thuff as the energy charge from her gun knocked him unconscious. Johnston slowly returned her gun to the small of her back and rose to her feet. She looked around and decided to drag the body behind the corner and cover it with the loose trash.

She held her breath, inching down the alley away from the unconscious body. The footsteps continued past the alley opening, and she exhaled in relief.

Slowly, she holstered her gun, listening down the alley for any footsteps to return. Satisfied that she was out of danger, she continued.

She glanced up and down the next alley and then tried the door. *Was the door unlocked? No the door handle did not move. Locked,* Johnston thought as she pulled her tools. She closed her eyes, inserted the tool, and maneuvered through the tumblers, then she twisted, opening the door.

Slowly she pulled the door open, returning her tools to the backpack. The door creaked as she slunk in. She closed the door behind and locked it.

She came in from back-alley door. It opened onto the stairs, leading to the second-story kitchen. She silently moved though the kitchen to the servants' quarters. A creak in the floor on the first floor caught her attention as she moved to the stairs. She searched each of the remaining rooms on the first floor.

Carefully moving from room to room, she determined two things missing from the home. One, the person. The woman she was most likely following now was long gone, and also missing from the house were two objects from the mantle, a book from the shelf, and seven paintings from the walls.

She slipped the gun out briefly before she placed it back into the holster and continued to investigate further. The items from the mantle left footprints in the dust. The first item was a hexagon shape, short on the back with a wide area in the front. The second item had a round base like a goblet or a vase. The final missing item looked like a book from the shelf and paintings from the hallways; the dust imprint left several clear rectangles in the hallway main entrance.

Johnston carefully retraced the path of the intruder, looking for items out of place. At the entrance, she found a smudged footprint with bits of slightly moist mud dried on the edges. Johnston cringed, knowing she might have just gotten an intact image of her own footprints. If only she had been more careful entering, but it was too late now. The morning and previous day were dry with no rain. The dried mud was probably not from here. Carefully, she took some samples and noticed a long black hair matted in the mud. She collected it for future analysis. She moved into the kitchen where she found another long black hair on the floor and collected it too.

After a final search of the house that didn't turn up any additional information or evidence, Johnston packed up her items and calmed herself for the return trip to the campus.

Breathe in, the calm campus like the calm island in the turbulent sea of time fluctuation. Tout, the agency, a stone, brick and mortar structure standing against the encroachment of new technology on old values. Breathe in, feel the trees and the campus mall with students studying. Out, the solitary sanctuary of the basement library within the paradox shield. In, Johnston, Agent 11878 entrance to the shield.

Hajjar stepped out of Chief Stewart's office and closed the door behind him. He stood with his chin a bit higher as agents at nearby desks started to look over at him. He strutted to his desk with the portfolio tucked under his arm. Touching the folder open, the images appeared above the paper-thin surface. He studied the contents, and with a glance, he transferred the data onto his field notebook. His field notebook was the first thing issued to him when he graduated from the academy and became an agent. The sleek black leather portfolio was about nine inches by six inches, and half an inch thick. It was roughly the size a hardback novelette from the nineteenth century. To the untrained eye, it looked like a black leather travel journal filled with pages of heavy paper with a thick sturdy front and back cover. And to any person other than Hajjar or anyone without clearance, it would always resemble a travel journal, opening like a book with fifty pages and a pen tucked into the binding. When Hajjar picked up the Field Notebook, a fingerprint DNA scan would be taken from anywhere he might touch on the outer surface, and no unauthorized bio-signatures within a five foot radius. With the successful login, the wealth of knowledge would open.

He sat studying the data on the device sold to a pawnshop in the year 2377. His finger flicked across the page of the field notebook, tracking his focus as his eyes paused on specific words. They opened into further description of places and people.

The device was sold to RedWing Pawn. The address in Detroit, Michigan, popped up underneath. Hajjar gestured, and the crystal display in the notebook erupted as images of the pawnshop rose from the screen to stand above his open notebook in 3D. The address, date, and time remained on the flat crystal top paper-like pages, with the shop standing in front of him centimeters above the desk. July 27, 2377, the sale was completed. No time stamp. He could go back to the date and do one of those classic stakeouts where you sit and watch the place until the perpetrator showed. But who was the perpetrator? What does he or she look like? He leaned back in his chair, rubbing his temples with his fingers.

Wardrobe…an outfit to blend into the year 2377 would be necessary. The trip to wardrobe stirred images of 1950s Hollywood costume sets. Racks of vintage outfits hung, meticulously maintained, ready to wear. None of the outfits were digitally printed as most cloths or costumes were created nowadays. These were made using the techniques of the time they were made for. Eleven, thirteen, eighteen, twenty-one, twenty-three centuries, each long rack represented different millennia that stretched from one end of the thirty-meter long room to another. Each rack was divided into decades with different outfits for regions of the world. Each outfit was designed to blend in, making each agent trusted but not unique and memorable.

Hajjar stood in front of the section for 2370s. A young sassy woman peeked around the end of the rack of clothing. Her rose red lips matched her hair. She stepped up to stand next to him with a small crystal tablet scanning the fashion of the times.

"Sarah." Hajjar grinned, still working up the courage to ask her out for a drink or to hang out after work. He couldn't tell if she was flirting with him or if she was this cheery to everyone. But one thing was for sure. He liked her smile that warmed the room.

She took him to an elliptical table, setting her crystal tablet down. The surface of the table lit up, extending the information from her tablet onto the crystal surface of the table, pulling up an image of Hajjar projected at one-fifth scale above the table. "You are going in as agent investigating *questionable merchandise*." She spoke down to the table. Her right hand lifted into the air to flex her index and middle fingers in air quotes to emphasize *questionable* and *merchandise*. "Or are you planning to be a tourist interested in purchasing something *unique*?" Again her fingers flexed.

Hajjar looked over to his image hovering above the crystal table. At a sweep of Sarah's fingers, the image transferred to full size, hovering over the floor with the clothes from the rack—a Hawaiian shirt unbuttoned with a bright blue shirt underneath, baseball cap, cheap gold-rimmed sunglasses, and a large camera around the neck.

Hajjar grimaced at the image. "I don't have an exact time on the transaction." He exhaled. "Maybe I'll be an agent of the time period, like FBI, CIA, or something. So if I miss the transaction, I can project the authority to question the clerk." He looked over, catching a smile as Sarah picked up her small tablet again, flicking her fingers on the surface, and the full-sized image changed, replacing with a sleek black suit with dark sunglasses. "That is better." Hajjar grinned. "Do you have a badge?"

"Of course, we do." Sarah flicked her hand toward the rows of drawers at the end of the room.

"I think that is the best." Hajjar's voice trailed off as he walked around the image, studying it, himself, from all sides. *Now the next part of the investigation would play out*, he thought.

Sarah left and returned with the black suit from the rack and a light blue button-down shirt. Holding it in front of him, she nodded. The classics never really get old; they just get more ingrained in the minds of the public. Hajjar stepped into the rectangular change room to slip into his new identity. The blue shirt slipped on, fitted with the sleeves down past his wrists. The shirt was a nonintrusive, passive color with hints of white stripes. He threaded the belt through the loops and tightened the solid silver buckle. He pulled the collar up to place the dark blue tie around the back of his neck, around the front twice, behind, up through the back, and down through the front, and finally tightened with minor adjustments. Finally, he bent down to slip on the boots. He straightened his tie one last time and then slipped on the suit, crisp lines of no nonsense getting to the bottom of the investigation. *Adding a little bit of intimidation never hurt*, Hajjar thought to himself.

The FBI would still be a prominent force at this time, he knew. "Agent Hajjar, FBI," he said, looking at himself in the mirror. "My name is Agent Hajjar, FBI." He flipped the badge open and closed again in one fluid motion while holding out his right hand with a smile as to shake the hand of his projection standing in front of him.

He stepped out to be greeted with "Oooh, nice." Sarah clasped her hands together, smiling. "You look textbook FBI from the times."

The image Hajjar wanted to project was almost complete. Now for the final touches.

With the notebook flipped open, Hajjar scanned the page on the time. English with an accent, neutral brogue. More northeast American or slight British would work best for his image. No hint of his native accent. He did not want anyone to put a finger on his origin. Tensions would be escalating about that time.

Pulling up the layout of the area, his eyes scanned for a possible jaunt location. Jaunting into a populated area was too risky. The possibility of being observed was too high, unlike jaunting out. The air vacuum created a small sonic boom that could be explained as a meteor or aircraft testing.

The area map had five shops lined up with a long parking lot stretched out in front of the shops. Each store was separated from the next by a small alley about two feet wide. The coffee shop on the street corner with tables and umbrellas outside the front might give a good vantage of RedWing Pawn next door. On the other side of RedWing Pawn were three more shops—a women's apparel shop, a quilting shop, and finally a pet shop. Each store had a metal back door and a large dumpster near it. He decided to jaunt in behind the RedWing building near the dumpster where he would be hidden, and then walk to the coffee shop to watch the place before heading in.

Hajjar grinned and nodded in satisfaction of a good plan. He straightened his jacket, threw his shoulders back, lifted his chin, and walked through the halls up to the jaunt pad on the eleventh floor. The ambient lighting illuminating the walls, floor, and ceiling became a solid cocoon of gray, pliable for the imagination to project the destination.

Hajjar exhaled slowly, closing his eyes. Using the methods taught to him in academia, he filled his mind with the layout of the land behind the RedWing Pawnshop. Inhale. The gray brick building with two large windows on either side of the glass door. Exhale. The red sign in the shape of a wing glowing above the entrance planted in his mind. Inhale. Inhale. He moved his focus around to the back of the building; the metal door in front of him dead bolted, but no camera for another six months. Exhale. He reached to the big green dumpster to his right. Inhale. He focused on the sound of the traffic from the four-lane road nearby, finished six months ago. He could just feel the midafternoon sun warming his right cheek.

The smells of the dumpster suddenly invaded his nostrils, more pungent than he imagined it to be. Slowly, he opened his eyes, squinting to let his pupils adjust to the bright afternoon sunlight. The dumpster was a few feet away, though the smell seemed closer.

The dead bolt door in the back of the RedWing was painted a cherry red with a gray trim. Hajjar looked around, listening to the sounds from the flies and the wind stirring some packing paper and a plastic bag swirling them up a few feet in the air, dancing like two litter fairies. Hajjar walked through the wind swirl, breaking up the dance. He focused his thoughts; he was here on business.

Rounding the corner, Hajjar sat at the table with his field notebook and pen. The table farthest from the coffee shop entrance gave the best view of the RedWing entrance.

"Can I get you something?" The voice came from nowhere. Hajjar jumped a bit before looking up at the girl. She bounced on her short heels, and a blue ponytail gathered on top of her head with a purple and pink bow. Her white shirt was freshly pressed, and she wore black pants with a black apron. She stood holding a pen with a bobbing daisy on the end and a small notepad, ready to write. She radiated far too much excitement for this to be anything other than her first job.

Hajjar looked to her and scowled. "April." He paused. "I'd like house blend. Black." He paused, looking back up at her sudden look of intrigue. "Yes?"

Her eyes widened. "Nothing. You look very official and mysterious, like how did you know my name?"

Hajjar looked flatly at her then cocked one eyebrow in amusement. "It is on your name tag."

"Oh, yeah." She looked down a small silver bar on her chest with *APRIL* spelled out. Her face turned a slight shade of pink as she continued, "I'll have that right out for you, sir." She turned to walk away then stopped, looking at her notepad, turned, and marched back.

Hajjar looked up slowly. "Yes?"

"What size—petite, moyenne, or grande?"

"Grande." Hajjar smiled. "Please."

"Okay." Again, April turned in a bounce, leaving on her mission.

"Thank you, April." Hajjar smiled kindly at her. He wondered what would have happened if he flashed his badge. Kids could be so easily impressed and distracted. He decided she would probably forget his order.

Hajjar looked back at his notebook and then lifted his head, turning his attention back to the pawnshop.

A young man—short with shoulder-length hair, blue jeans, and a T-shirt with a yellow circle with a wedge removed from the side—was leaving the pawnshop with a paper bag in hand. He took two steps outside, pulling out an old cartridge for a game system. Briefly his attention turned to Hajjar, and then quickened his pace back to his car.

Hajjar sipped his coffee, watching the door while a young man or woman—Hajjar couldn't tell from the cap and baggy black shirt—walked into the pawnshop with their hands tucked in their front pockets, shoulders slumped. *Teenagers these days*, he thought. *No self-pride.*

Half an hour passed before an older man with streaked gray hair got out of his car, pulling out a large box with random items sticking out of the top. He carried the box up to the door, carefully balancing the box on one knee as he hopped while reaching out to pull the door open. Quickly, he stepped forward to catch the door, stopping the box with his other hand before it fell. He slid in through the door, performing this clumsy dance.

Hajjar finished his coffee, slowly evaluating the area and deciding his next move. He got up from the table, placing a bit of money down under his mug. Now was as good a time as any. Hajjar adjusted his jacket and instinctively reached to lay a hand on his belt where the badge was clipped. Walking with long brisk strides, he headed straight for the door and pulled it open, pausing to cast his long shadow into the store all the way to the counter. He scanned the store with his piercing gaze.

The teenager tipped their blue cap with Murphy Moo cartoon on the front to the young store clerk then picked up the single bill on the counter and turned to leave.

Agent Hajjar met the eyes of the store clerk with solid white hair behind the register. A quick glance at the name tag revealed "Ryan Schmittgall, Manager."

"Mr. Schmittgall." Agent Hajjar held out his right hand. "I am Agent Hajjar." He flipped open his identification with his left hand, paused for a moment, and then he flipped it closed again. "I'd like to ask you a few questions. Do you have a moment?"

"Oh, yeah, sure." The man shrugged. "You can call me Ryan."

"Well, Ryan." Hajjar smiled, recognizing an advantage "Ryan, that is my name too." He smiled like a fox. "I'm looking for a key item to my investigation." Hajjar took a step closer to the counter. "I have a lead that it might be sold here, if it hasn't already been." His eyes narrowed, looking at Ryan, dropping his smile to a flat expression.

"We will help you in any way we can. We always turn over questionable items to the authorities." Ryan took one step back, raising his palms a bit off the counter. "Just describe the item and I'll see if it is in inventory."

Hajjar relaxed, and as he did the tension in the store lifted a bit. "Thank you. It would be a small slender object about five centimeters long." He held up his index finger and thumb to the approximate length. "About one centimeter wide and three millimeters thick, about the size of a stick of gum." He continued to hold up two fingers. "With…"

"Colored circles along one side." The young girl with short black hair stepped up. "Yeah, I don't know what it is." She placed the small slender object on the counter. "I offered five bucks to that girl for it."

"What girl?" Hajjar's voice rose as he recognized the object, picking it up.

"That girl, the one you just passed when you came in. The one with the blue hat, with a *OK cow, moo?*" she said with a weird expression like a popular kid oblivious to fictional art. "She said someone will come asking about this." She handed him the device. "And wow is that freaky quick!" The clerk whose name tag read Lisa peered wide-eyed at Agent Hajjar, then to Ryan, and back to Agent Hajjar.

Before she could say another word, Hajjar turned, sprinting for the door. He could have slapped himself in the forehead; how could he be so blind? Murphy Moo was a cartoon character from his childhood, not this period.

"Hey!" Ryan's voice trailed Hajjar sprinting out the door. "Are you going to pay for that?"

Hajjar paused outside the door to look for a glimpse of a blue hat. Two buildings away, the person in the blue hat and black T-shirt turned into the alley. Hajjar sprinted past the two buildings to the alley, pulling his EMP gun from his belt. Stopping just shy of the corner, he waited, placing his back to the wall, holding his pistol with both hands close to his chest. He paused for a moment. He faintly heard murmuring down the alley.

He whipped around the corner.

Gun extended.

To find the alley empty.

He slowly lowered his pistol, peering down the alley again. Had he missed something?

He looked down to the ground, spotting fresh footprints that stopped halfway, meeting a second set of fresh footprints. He studied the tracks a moment, pulling out a digital scanner recording the 3D image of the indentation patterns. It looked like tennis shoes, but analysis of the scan back at the Bureau would give more details. He then walked over to the second set of tracks to scan them. These were larger, looking almost like tire tread. Pocketing the device, he stood up to head back to the pawnshop.

Ryan was still waiting behind the counter. "So what is that thing?" His eyes gleamed with hope of a payoff, or at least a good story.

"Top secret evidence," Agent Hajjar stated. "What can you tell me about the girl?"

Ryan walked over, pulling out his stack of papers for that day. He removed the top sheet. "She said she was Elinor Dashwood of 13 Queen Square, Bath. She didn't have an ID."

Hajjar looked over to the young clerk. "You said someone would come asking about this?" He looked to her badge. "Lisa."

"That's what she said. It was the weirdest thing." Lisa walked over to stand next to Ryan, looking up at him hesitantly.

"Go on." He nudged her shoulder with his own shoulder.

"She said to hold it. That soon someone would come looking for it and ask a bunch of questions. I didn't realize she meant within a minute or two later." Her eyes widened. "Wow, the FBI is really resourceful."

"What did she look like?" Agent Hajjar looked at Ryan, then back to Lisa.

"Tall, slender, green eyes." She squinted her eyes, thinking. "A bit younger than me. I really didn't see her hair under the rim of the hat." She held her hand to indicate a height as tall, slightly above her head, just shy of six feet.

Hajjar looked up above to the register camera. "Does that record?"

"Well, yeah." Ryan looked up at the same spot in the ceiling.

"May I see the recording?"

"Yeah, right this way." Ryan led the way into the back room. "Lisa, watch the register." Ryan opened the door to the computers.

Hajjar pulled out a small piece of metal about five centimeters by one centimeter by two millimeters with buttons along the top. He held it to the computer, pressing a series of three buttons. A red light on the top blinked twice, and then three seconds later, it blinked again.

"I have the image. Thank you for your time." Hajjar held out his hand.

Ryan was frozen with his mouth slightly gaping open. The thing Agent Hajjar held was like a slimmer sleek version of what he had just bought for five bucks, but he had never seen either of these before. And his daughter was always current on technology innovation. "Oh, um, wow…um, yes…Thank you." He grabbed Hajjar's hand, shaking it.

"If she returns for any reason or you remember any details that you feel relevant, please call." Hajjar held out a card freshly printed with a shiny badge in the left side and his contact information with a direct line to the Bureau.

"I will." Ryan smiled, looking down at the card.

Hajjar nodded and then turned to leave the store. He headed two doors down to the same secluded alley for his own jaunt back to his time, his office.

"What did you find out on your vacation?" Chief Stewart's voice was curious with a hint of concern.

Johnston paused with her hand on the back of the chair. She closed her eyes and smiled a moment before looking at him and continuing to the front of the chair to sit down. "It was… thrilling," she said dryly.

"Did you find what you were looking for?" Stewart looked up from his folder.

Johnston settled into the chair, taking a deep breath. "Yes, the lead resulted in a discovery, a known act of time travel to steal art and valuables from houses in Warsaw at the start of World War II, most likely with the knowledge that the city would be utterly destroyed, leaving no evidence after World War II."

"You are sure the person jaunted into the area?"

"Yes."

"What makes you so sure?"

"The person had intimate knowledge of the city to avoid capture. They maneuvered to specific houses with the desired artwork. They left from the third floor, not the front or back door. I am not sure what was taken, but I'm sure some quality time in the archives will reveal a lot. I brought some evidence back that is being analyzed."

TDCI Stewart made a slight growl as he settled his chin on his folded hands. He looked like he was praying but for the intense concentration in his open eyes. "The suspect enters war zones or intense battles to take rare and valuable items and artifacts." The words sounded like a statement needing reassurance.

"Yes."

"Relying on the war to hide the evidence of the theft."

"Yeesss." Johnston frowned, drawing out the word, tilting her head to the side and hoping to see where he was leading. "Why?"

TDCI Stewart growled again and then pulled up an image on the screen, scanning down the page. "Do you know what the suspect looks like?"

"Female, early twenties, dark hair, light eyes." Johnston fought back the need to fully disclose the description.

The moment of silence stagnated as the chief started looking through a folder that he pulled from the corner of his desk. Stewart looked up at Johnston again then back at the crystal.

"Why?" Johnston tilted her head a bit to the side, raising one eyebrow. "What are you contemplating? I know that look."

He looked up at her, then back at the screen, frowning. "I am not completely convinced of this, but this case may fit your profile. Opportunistic theft of valuable items during segues or battles." He took a long look at the crystal before passing it to Johnston. "Based on your description, it fits, but I know you are not telling me everything." Johnston took the folder from his hands, slowly opening it. "If it doesn't fit the profile of your current investigation, maybe you would recommend the agent I should send in to investigate it."

Johnston looked up at him over the folder, raising her eyebrows. "You want my advice on assigning an investigation?" Johnston looked back down onto the crystal to scan the information. "Ahhh…The subtle plan of attack fit the profile, as well as the strategy to hide the missing items using a war to do so." She leaned into the screen, reading intensely, suddenly looking at TDCI Stewart. "Is there a description of the suspect?"

Stewart shrugged. "We have the description of the Royal Family and some soldiers and generals, but not of the staff of the party that left the castle smuggling the Honours to safety."

The left side of Johnston's lip frowned as she looked back down at the crystal. "First, they are the Honours of Scotland, so I want to investigate this." She slowly drew the sentence out, trying to convince her head that this was not only the right idea but the smart thing.

Johnston could feel Stewart's smile before she saw the corners of his lips flick down into a somber scowl.

She continued, "It fits the profile, and if it is who I think it is, it might fit the items she would want." Johnston paused, looking back at the crystal a moment. "I need the data analysis from the trip to Warsaw while I am in Scotland, but that will give me a couple days to research. I need the most accurate information from the Warsaw analysis."

"The most accurate history outside of the Px Shield is within the file I passed you. I didn't expect that will change."

"That is handy to have. I will need the altered history and our protected history to infiltrate and correct the timeline." Johnston looked up at Stewart. "You look happy."

"Well, yes. I have my best agent on the job." He grinned.

"Somehow I think you had this whole thing planned." Johnston sighed. "Subtle." She shook her head. "Subtle, leading me to think it was my idea and not an assignment from the agency."

"I don't know what you are talking about." TDCI Stewart's eyes glinted with satisfaction behind the unsmiling face.

"Well played, sir. I'm still looking into this. If it doesn't fit my profile, I'll recommend a replacement, but from what I'm seeing…" Her voice trailed off into thought as she packed the folder under her arm and stood from the chair.

"Regardless, you are the only person skilled and qualified for this assignment."

Johnston sighed, closing her eyes a moment. She opened her eyes and reached for the door before turning to face Stewart. "I'll keep you posted."

"I expect so." Stewart's voice followed her out of the office.

***

The aroma of nostalgia greeted Johnston as she opened the door.

She walked into her flat, tossing her folder along with her field notebook on the right cushion of her love seat as she passed. Pausing a moment to look at the field notebook, she sighed, continuing to the kitchen. She reached up for a round bottomed wine glass, setting it on the counter. She looked over to the clock. Two days had passed here. Another sigh escaped her lips. A week in Poland was two days here. She grabbed the half-filled bottle in her right hand and the glass in her left. She took a hard look at the semi-plunged cork in the bottle and then at the glass held in her left hand. She slowly closed her eyes, exhaling at her lack of foresight and wanting to pour the glass. She was frustrated on why humans hadn't grown a third or fourth arm by this point to help in situations like this. She appreciated the new cuber-bionic extra appendages that accomplished exactly this. They were multiple arms like a mutated twentieth-century Spider-Man. She opened her eyes, gave up dignity, and grabbed the cork with her teeth, pulling it from the bottle. And then she poured the wine into her glass. The bottle sloshed as she kicked off her shoes and walked into the main room in her loft. She sat the bottle on the stand next to the love seat. With her head slightly tilted back, she took a sip and then sat down, grabbing the folder.

Her purple leather-covered field notebook flipped open with ease. The glass clinked as its base connected with the lamp base. The yellow glow of the lamp was not necessary for the crystal, but she liked the atmosphere it gave to the room when she started her reading. Plus it was a gift from her sister during her first years at the academy to remind her of home. It was one of the few times they got along.

These items stolen from history glared out at her and grated on her nerves with a deep burning sense of wrong. There was wrong, like lying to the agency when "not taking historic souvenirs" such as a pen, bottle of wine, or lamp. These have no historic impact or significance. Thousands were manufactured, and it held no critical role in the timeline. The Scottish Honours…this was wrong. The wrong of an abomination, something that should never happen, for history's sake.

According to the history outside of the PX shield, the Honours of Scotland were lost in the 1660s; they were lost after Cromwell's invasion and rampage through Ireland and Scotland, never recovering. This differed from the current history in the library of the TBI. According to currently accepted history, the Honours of Scotland were smuggled out of Dunnottar Castle and buried in Kinneft Parish and recovered in the 1660s.

Sometime between the Cromwellian invasion in 1651 and the discovery of the Honours in 1660, they were gone. They should have been found in the parish, but they weren't. They were stolen from history.

The worry lay heavy, dreading the possibility of failure. A lot more research was needed. She would only have one chance at finding the person and the Honours. The scenario ran through her head like a swarm of mosquitoes buzzing softly in and out, clouding the problem.

"Could the Honours have been taken in transit between the castle and the parish?" She focused her thoughts. "Unlikely. It would make sense the Honours would arrive and be hidden, then dug up from the floor. But how would they do it without the priest knowing?"

She started thinking about the profile of the thief, the person who would not want to draw attention to themselves. Killing the priest would be out of the question; even rendering him unconscious during the theft would draw enough attention from the Time Agency to investigate.

This profile was assuming this was the same thief that was in Warsaw.

Johnston lifted the glass to her lips and tapped the field notebook's display. She could feel the tension and pressure of making the wrong decision start to soften as she swallowed and set the glass back down.

What if she could drop in on the priest to ask him about the Honours, verify their presence, and determine if they even made it to the chapel? It was possible the Honours were taken in transit from the castle. Any causality would be blamed on Cromwell and overlooked by historians.

She took another sip. Something bothered her, and it took a moment to put her finger on it. What bothered her was the fact that the Honours went missing during the Cromwellian invasion and not from the catacombs of Edinburgh Castle. The Honours were stored there and lost for a hundred years. This would have posed the perfect opportunity for them to slip away into the mysterious ether of stories and never found. Who would dedicate an agent to guarding the Honours for a hundred years? That alone would become legend, drawing attention to the Honours and thus rewriting history in the process of fixing it.

"The thief must have wanted the challenge as much as the items. The challenge of planning and executing the heist is as much of a thrill as getting the prize, and then having it in the personal collection might bring back the memories." The Ruger Pistol she brought back from Warsaw brought a grin of pride and accomplishment. "This thief is not much different than me, yearning for the challenge and escape from boredom." The memories distracted her from the thoughts swarming in her mind for a moment, and then she forced herself back to the task at hand.

How could she verify the Honours didn't make it to the chapel without going there first? And if she decided to infiltrate, would she enter the English side or the Scottish side of the conflict?

The positions for infiltration played out in her head like a Shakespearean tragedy.

She could infiltrate Cromwellian troops as a servant. The English had little value for women at that time. This would give the advantage of infiltrating and moving through the ranks undetected, or more appropriately ignored as not worth the time or attention paid. *The downside*, she thought, *or sides.* Johnston sighed with her head back on the seat and her fingers spinning the base of the glass, creating a scratching sound on the table. "First problem: as a worthless woman, I wouldn't be able to get close enough to the castle to watch the comings and goings for a large package four and a half feet long, and other items. The second problem: I still have a Scottish temper and won't be able to stand by while constantly insulted, or if a soldier decided to look on me as an object to have." Her mind did not want to imagine the possibilities. "I don't think I'd be able let him rape me. I never have, and these Honours are not worth a first time for rape of any reason. I'd probably act in defense and end up in a difficult situation. I'd either be killed, change history as warrior woman, then killed by an agent before history was irreversibly altered, or mysteriously disappear from incarceration, blowing cover and unable to try again." Johnston sighed again, thinking the play out. The twiddling of the glass stopped a moment as she opened her eyes, looking at the shadows on the ceiling like Rorschach blots.

She wondered a moment about her own sanity. The shadows started looking like warring factions of primitive humans with spears and clubs, approaching each other from the corners of the room. She smiled, closing her eyes again. "I guess this time jaunt isn't for the most sane to begin with." She chuckled a moment, thinking of the second rule.

The scenarios scattered and reorganized in her head as she leaned her head back on the love seat, staring at the ceiling. Her chest slowly rose and fell with each breath as she watched the shadows battle on the ceiling.

"I guess I'll start comparing the historic documents starting with Charles II." Her fingers flicked on the crystal. Sure enough, the Honours of Scotland were used for the coronation of Charles II, at Dunnottar Castle to be the last stronghold for the royalists, but no word after that.

The dread of a long undercover investigation collected in her shoulders, building knots. Sometime within the nine-month siege, the Honours were smuggled out, and they never made it to the chapel. "Nine months." The knots grew as Johnston frowned. "That is even if the jewels were lifted from the castle or in transport. The outside history gets fuzzy on how they were smuggled out to go to the chapel. Some accounts say they made the trip. Some say that one or two of the three pieces made it, and the final accounts recall on ambush or that the jewels never made it out of the castle."

Johnston's mind paused a moment as she frowned with frustration. "The Honours made it out of Dunnottar Castle. Cromwell ransacked the place looking for them, with no luck. His thorough search would have found them if they were there."

A plan started to solidify from the chaotic spattering of historic notes. Her touch pen wrote furiously on a notepad. She still enjoyed the ancient tradition of parchment enough to insist on synthetic parchment. Her notes transferred to text on the screen in the field notebook.

Her pen flew across the page, drawing arrows from "Are there" to the next line and "Not there" to the following line. Her mind started to wander again as she sighed. The exhaustion of the trip to Warsaw caught up to her, and she decided to tackle this with some caffeine tomorrow.

***

Johnston ducked into the library to chat with Jen. The morning light had met her eyes already open. The night passed sleeplessly as the scenario passed through her mind as a bad movie played out on the ceiling in front of her opened eyes.

"Hello, Ms. Litwiller." Johnston stood straighter, rolling her shoulders back as she had been taught in finishing school in 1893. Another mission.

"Johnston, what brings you in?" Ms. Litwiller's eyes narrowed, her piercing glare analyzing Johnston, making her shrink a few millimeters under the scrutiny.

"Um…seeking Jen's consultation on a matter of an investigation." Johnston could feel her mouth drying and cheeks flush. "I'm, um, involved with." Johnston's voice trailed off, followed by a hard swallow as her face tried to smile.

"She is working. Save socializing until after hours." Ms. Litwiller stood as a beacon of resilience, like a piece of garnet, maybe a bit worn over time but still stone, standing undeterred.

Johnston cleared her throat. "No, ma'am. I am investigating a critical theft in history. The timeline must be set right. I need Jen's expertise in this matter to identify flaws in my plan of infiltration." She felt as sandstone to Ms. Litwiller's garnet. There was something about Ms. Litwiller that made her feel like she was in second grade again.

Ms. Litwiller stood studying her, looking through her for an intermediary. "Very well. Have coffee." She paused, turning to leave.

Johnston stopped in her tracks, pausing to look back at Ms. Litwiller, trying to decide if she knew about her assignment. Could she be testing her even now?

Jen's voice snapped her back to the archives. "Coffee? This must be an important mission."

"Yeah…" Johnston's voice trailed off, watching Ms. Litwiller round the corner, glancing back for that moment of shock from eye contact before disappearing behind the stacks. "Let's go to the coffee shop," she whispered.

Jen looked at the book stacks. "She is protective of her heritage and history. That is what makes her such a great guardian of the archives."

"I think this is the first time we have seen eye to eye, or maybe she just recognized me as an equal." Johnston tilted her head in contemplation. "I think…I think I'm honored, but that was odd."

"Caffeine…"

"Yes." Johnston looked back at Jen. "I need to pick your brain."

The two walked slowly to the coffee shop, talking about the last trip to Warsaw.

"Your quick notes are worse than a history book, dry and full of facts."

"Jen, I'm worried over the next mission." Johnston paused. "When this is all over, we'll split a bottle of wine and discuss my crush on Pilecki."

"I knew it." Jen grinned. "It is good to see you moving on from your ex."

Johnston sighed, closing her eyes and pushing out the pain of memory and betrayal.

"Sorry." Jen smiled. "We definitely have some catching up to do."

"Yes." Johnston paused. "I have a plan to visit Scotland for an investigation, but it is at a time where I really can't afford to fail."

"More than the trip to Warsaw?" Jen frowned, sitting at a table next to the window with her back to the door. Cupping her hands around the mug, she pulled it to her lips to sip the caffeine.

"Definitely." Johnston sat, glancing at the door then out the window, more out of habit than feeling unsafe in the café. "Imagine modern tech falling into the hands of a man whose obsession with power who already left a bloody path across the United Kingdom, or battle information falling into the hands of religious zealot who concurred all in his path, thinking his god encouraged his every step of the way." She glanced around one more time to note the faces of the people within listening distance. Leaning back into her chair and taking a sip of her tea, she continued in a lower voice, "I need your insight."

"Maybe we would be better back at my place." Jen leaned over, speaking in hushed voice.

Johnston looked around the café to those oblivious to the conversation and to those intently listening to the details while pretending not to be eavesdropping. Johnston leaned in. "Come by after work. We can split a bottle."

The day dragged on until the inevitable knock on the door. Johnston stepped forward, opening the door to hand Jen a glass of Merlot.

Jen quietly took the glass then wrapped her arm around her best friend, hugging her tightly for a long moment before stepping back and taking a sip from her glass. "Where is this assignment?"

Johnston smiled, walking over to the love seat. She picked up the field notebook from the end table and then handed it to Jen. She turned to sit on the love seat next to the lamp.

Jen's eyes widened as she blurred her way through the data: missing Honours, Cromwell's invasion status, Dunnottar Castle.

"There are so many ways this can go horribly wrong," Johnston commented with a sigh.

"I can see why you got this assignment." Jen scanned the crystal again, taking a sip from her glass. "How will you get in? Where will you start?"

"Well, I need to know if the jewels made it to Kinneft Parish. History outside of the PX shield is murky at best. They may have been stolen from the parish when they were buried in the floor, or the people who smuggled the jewels out may have been ambushed when they were in transit."

Jen sat back in her chair, setting down the glass to continue scanning through the data. She looked up at the ceiling, contemplating. "That is a lot to take in." She continued to look at the ceiling, studying the dancing shadows above her.

"I'm thinking I should jaunt in on the parish first. If they know where the Honours are, then I just stay to wait." Johnston picked up her glass for a sip. Sighing, she closed her eyes and shook her head. "That would be maybe seven years at most to wait until the theft. They were in the parish seven years before returning to Edinburgh."

"What happens if the Honours never made it to the parish?" Jen lowered her head, looking Johnston in the eye.

"If the Honours never made it to the parish, then I travel to Dunnottar Castle to make sure the Honours make it there safely." She shook her head. "That is a nine-month siege."

Johnston and Jen agreed in a glance. The worry and weight of the complicated situation, the risk of failure, and the impact to both history and themselves…and then with a heavy sigh, they sipped the glass of wine.

"I'm sure you realize if you visit the parish followed by the castle and you fail, you won't have a second chance. Additionally, the agency may think that you planned the theft from the beginning." She looked to the items around in the room. "For your personal collection."

"I know. There is no room for error on this one."

"What is the probability that a seasoned tested agent such as you would steal the Honours of Scotland and then set it up that you would investigate it?" Jen leaned it.

Johnston felt a stab of pain in the question. "Do you have your doubts?"

"No!" Jen leaned back in shock, appalled at the accusation. "We've been friends since we first entered the academy together."

Johnston sighed with relief. "I know you believe in me, but I need to know where you stand on this."

Jen smiled. "It still takes me aback when you start talking about your mission."

"What do you think of the plan?"

Jen closed her eyes as they fluttered. The possibilities flowed through her mind. "I think this plan is your best option."

"Thank you." Johnston sighed, sipping her wine.

"How long will it keep you out?" Jen opened her eyes with worry setting in.

"A couple weeks or maybe nine months, but here only a few days." The resolve of the long assignment was setting into the lines of her face. "I just hope it will not be seven years."

"Sounds like you have some research before heading out. Shall we open another bottle?" Jen perked up with a bright cheery grin. Then she let a bit of the cheer drain before continuing, "Besides, you look like there is more on your mind than just the Honours of Scotland. The past will still be there tomorrow." The smile returned to her eyes.

"Okay then. Another bottle."

Hajjar sat in his corner of his pub. The dark wood table and tall wooden chairs surrounded him. The ideas started flowing after the second pint of red. Hajjar took a sip, thinking this was the closest he had ever gotten to actual Irish red ale without jaunting back to nineteenth-century Kilkenny, Ireland. Of course, it didn't hurt that the agency sent students back to learn from the Irish brew masters themselves.

It hadn't taken long for the Time Agency to learn that agents needed a place to unwind under the safety of the Px-Shield and field notebook. The last thing the agency wanted was an operative to head out on the town to have a pint and be caught in a time shift or force them to take their field notebook for protection but lose it and the crucial data in it when blitzed. A few good agents and top-secret data were lost as the timeline shifted around them during a drunken night. Without their field notebook to extend the paradox protection and help them get their bearing, their memories soon shifted to the timeline they were in, leaving them stranded. When they were recovered, their memories were never recovered.

Hajjar enjoyed being able to review his case files in a relaxed place with a pint in front of him helping his creative insight. He pulled out his notes and the device. He placed the field notebook on the table in front of him, flipping to the back of the book, flicking his fingers on the screen. He pulled up the scans of the shoe tread. The tennis shoes worn by the girl were manufactured in 2408, give or take. That would make sense for the girl selling the tech. He pulled up the image of her from the video camera, looking hard for additional elusive details. The clerk had said she had greenish eyes, late teens. Hajjar looked hard at the image, pulling the image in to her face. The shadows obscured her eyes, hair, and the majority of her facial structure.

He shifted his attention to the other set of treads from a men's size 9 or woman's size 10 sandals. He looked at the result and resubmitted the search. The result came back the same—the tread was a tire tread. The tires were Goodyear tires dating to early 1960s, cut into the shape of a shoe sole. His fingers flicked, pushing this file back to the side to process this information later. It was important, but he didn't quite know how yet.

He pulled out the recording device, holding it in the palm of his hand. Leaning back in his wooden stool and smiling, he lifted the pint to his lips. Satisfied with his first successful solo recovery complete, he flipped the device over in his hand. *Such a big deal over such a little device*, he thought.

Leaning forward on the table, he uploaded the contents of the device to the notebook and started to study the contents. Flicking his fingers on the crystal, he skimmed the report. The content was in fact a first generation recording. The date stamp was clearly not reset after the jaunt. It said October 23, 2404.

He queued up the recording to listen to the entire thing. Hajjar slipped the earbuds in, turning up the volume. The clinking and chattering of the crowded bar filled his ears. The sounds of someone tuning an acoustic guitar flowed in from the background.

"Can I go up to put this on the stage?" a young girl's voice came over the background noise.

"Sure, have fun. I'll be here while you enjoy, Janis." Her youthful voice had a tinge of motherly tone sneaking into her Southern accent.

"Thanks." The girl giggled as the sound of the guitar tuning got louder. Shortly following the giggling, the clear sound of the guitar started playing, and a recognizable voice came through his earbuds. The next piece was a perfect recording of a live concert. He closed his eyes, leaning back, enjoying the music. The time passed too quickly. Soon his pint was empty in front of him, but he was enjoying the music too much to flag down his waitress. After a few musical sets, he again heard the voice of a young girl cheering and clapping. He could almost imagine pigtails bouncing in time with the clapping.

"That was amazing!!" The sounds moved around as the girl's voice said, "I love it here."

"I'm glad you are happy," said the motherly voice again.

Hajjar sat pondering a moment. That was definitely Janis Joplin. This was not sold to a record company; it was sold to a no-name pawnshop. What would the recording companies give to get a hold of this recording, even today?

The little girl is clearly the person who placed the device on the stage, but for whom? Then there is the girl with the blue hat. Did the blue hat girl take the device back to the 1960s and get the little girl to get the recording? Maybe the man and blue hat girl are working together? Maybe *he* jaunted to mug the girl with the blue hat to get the recording device to jaunt forward to sell it for money, and the girl didn't know what it was and sold it before he could get it.

Hajjar opened his eyes. Seeing his pint refilled, he leaned forward to take another sip. The next step was to find where this recording was made and when. He needed to intercept the little girl before she was manipulated by this size 9 men's or 10 women's shoe wearing person.

He called up the recording again to listen to it. With a flick of his finger over the sound waves hovering over his notebook, he removed the voice of Janis, the girl, and the motherly voice to listen to the background.

The sound of clinking glasses and scooting chairs was more prevalent now as the primary voices cut in.

"She said she wanted to head to San Francisco after this." It was the voice of a man, relaxed and mellow. Hajjar could almost imagine him taking a drag off a slender hand rolled cigarette or joint.

Hajjar flicked his fingers on the crystal, removing the ambient noise while bringing back the woman's voice. He remembered her saying she'd watch the floor. He hoped he would be right that she was the bartender. He listened closely to her as she took orders, made drinks, and talked to the group at the bar. "Hey, what can I get you?" "One bud coming up." "Bourbon on the rocks." "Here you go." "One Shiner, two Jack and Cokes, one…Cosmo." Hajjar noted the almost question of disgust at the idea of someone ordering a girly martini like a Cosmo. "Welcome. What can I get ya'll?" "Local beer? Shiner is good." "Right up." Drink…Drink…Drink…Close tab.

He listened to the bartender a while longer before removing the bartender's voice to focus on other voices again.

"Isn't she cute and helpful? She's new?" A voice carried from the other side of the bar.

"Yes, she is." Hajjar could almost hear her smiling with pride.

"What do you have that is local?" A man's voice.

"Local beer? Shiner is good."

"Mmmm, I'll take one of those."

Hajjar continued listening to the newcomer.

"That is good beer."

Hajjar flicked his fingers to listen to the rest of that conversation.

"There they go again, making a deal over Juneteenth, next week."

Another man replied, "It is not like the Emancipation Proclamation actually freed any of those…"

Hajjar cringed at the rest of the sentence.

The first man continued, "And now the march on Washington next year. What do those…"

Hajjar cringed again.

"…expect, equality? When they…"

Hajjar stopped that conversation. He had gotten the information he needed. A chilling shudder ran down his spine. He thought about how dangerous trips could be, knowing the prejudices some people had back in the day. He felt a slight relief that he was not traveling to the early twenty-first century, given his name and complexion.

He turned his attention back to the information at hand. The week before Juneteenth would be roughly June 12, and the march on Washington was August of 1963. And Janis Joplin would be heading to San Francisco by the end of 1962.

Hajjar opened his eyes with a satisfied grin stretching across his face. *I know where they are, and more importantly, when.* He leaned back in his seat, exhaling with satisfaction. His fingers folded behind his neck. He slowly blinked. "It looks like I don't need any help from

Johnston." He leaned forward, reaching to pick up the pint and taking a long drink. He would sleep well this evening.

***

The morning arrived, bright with excitement. It greeted Hajjar as he sprinted across the campus, his field notebook and folder under his arm. The sun was high on the horizon, making the shadows retreat.

This morning started much earlier than the sun for him. He was up looking into Austin 1962. What to wear? How to speak? What about a Texas drawl. No, not Southern. He couldn't be mistaken for Georgia or Missouri. It would have to be Texas. He looked into the culture around the university. He might fit into the culture as a student. He was young enough to be a student. He would have to be there in May to enroll in summer classes. Or better yet, he could be looking into grad school. Grad student would be more to his age. The University of Texas or UT had a great law school at the time. Summer before the start of the year would be the right time.

Johnston firmly placed where she was going in her head. The chill damp air with the Scottish Highlands tried to emerge from the grips of the winter siege into spring. She centered her thoughts. Inhale, chilled air, exhale. Cromwell's troops were leaving her homeland. Inhale. Little green buds of spring were starting to emerge from the cold winter. The dry chilled air from the jaunt pad changed into cold damp winds, sending chills down her spine. The winds rustled through the trees like children playing in the leaves, knocking the water droplets loose to fall to the ground or, on the next best thing, Johnston's head.

She slowly opened her eyes to see the gray somber blanket of fog that laid across the green plush carpet, surrounded by a sturdy platoon of gray stones standing tall against time around a chapel. The wrath of Mother Nature would never be held back. Just like she expected 1670s Scotland to be.

Johnston pulled the hood of her heavy dark gray cloak to cover her head from the artillery of water drops hitting her head. She glanced over her shoulder, past the edge of her hood, to the stone building to the right. The arched windows of color flickered with dancing light on the other side.

Johnston grabbed through the layers, lifting her deep blue skirts up to avoid getting them wet on the sprouting grasses. And then she turned to walk to the side entrance. The squishing of each footstep turned to splashing as she traversed from the grass to the stone entrance. The ornate peaked archway over the carved wood door made Johnston pause in awe before grabbing the handle of the door.

The wood and metal groaned as she pulled. The door yielded and opened a few feet, just enough for her to slip inside and turn toward the door, closing it behind her.

She paused at the door, letting the water drip from her cloak a moment before heading into the church. She lowered her gaze and stance in a curtsy a moment before standing again and continuing around to the back of the parish.

Silently she walked down the side alley to the kneeling bench. One hand rose to her hood, lifting it and letting it drop around her shoulders and back.

The flickering candles lit the way to the bench. No matter what time or place, those lost to the ages should be remembered. She knelt on the bench with the flickering sconces on either side. Folding her hands and bowing her head, a long moment passed before she muttered words of blessing under her breath in memory of those she remembered. Slowly, she opened her eyes and lifted her head. Sitting a moment longer with her hands folded, she smiled.

"You look just like her. You must be her sister. The resemblance is extraordinary." The cracking wizened voice came from the spot she heard footsteps a moment earlier. "Come to pay respects to her?"

"Good afternoon, Father. Why would you say sister?" Johnston slowly stood, taking care not to get her skirts tangled under her feet, and turned to the priest, lowering her gaze. "Respects? Did something happen?" She reached out with both hands to take his outstretched hand and bowed, touching her forehead to the back of his fingers.

"Extraordinary..." he whispered. "But I saw her die."

Johnston knelt, speechless a moment as her breath came back to her in a start. The words *saw her die* echoed in her head.

"Breathe. You will be all right. I must be mistaken, but you look exactly like Elizabeth."

The air escaped her lungs again as she felt faint in the head. *I'm sure there are so many others named Elizabeth in this time. Cursed corset!* she thought as she paused a moment to catch her breath. "I apologize, Father. I am..."

"Are you okay? Lady"—he paused—"what shall I call you?"

She stood, her thoughts scattered, finding their way to the first name to come to mind. Her mother. "Kathrine." She slowly breathed to steady her nerves. "Kathrine."

"I knew you had to be sisters." Father sighed. "You look just like her. Even the same eyes." He touched the corner of his eye. "I'm Father Granger."

Johnston clasped both of the father's hands and leaned in. "Please tell me everything."

"My wife knows more than I do. She is away at the moment, but I'll tell you what I know." Father Granger led her to a nearby pew. "They were ambushed when your sister stood against Cromwell's attack."

"Attack?" Johnston grasped her chest. "How many were there? What were they doing there?"

"They were trying to save the Honours of Scotland. She, Lady Douglas, and Christian smuggled them out of Dunnottar Castle to be ambushed by a small force. Four men ambushed them." Father Granger closed his eyes, swallowing back the tears. "She saved my wife, but the jewels were lost to Cromwell."

Johnston reached over to hold his hands.

"She fought, as a warrior. She took down two of them before she was slain. Christian took one of them, but the fourth made it out with the Honours." He paused to catch his breath, wide eyes damp with grief. He tried to smile though the pain. "She was run though during the fight. In the distraction of the moment, she left us to the Almighty."

His face was damp now, and his handkerchief was soaked. "She made us swear to never mention her contributions to the attempt to save the Honours. I have not spoken it to any one out of respect to her until now, with you. I thought you should know how your sister left this world."

Johnston laid her hand on his. "She would have wanted that."

"She saved my Christian's life." He looked up at Johnston with his eyes flooded with tears. "I just wanted you to know…what she did for me…what she did for…"

Johnston sat a moment with the yards of fabric keeping her legs warm, and the corset prevented her from breathing enough to clearly think. "I will remember this. Thank you. I will take my leave now, with comfort knowing my sister's honor, and I will remember her as a heroine." She stood slowly. "I am happy that she was able to save your Christian and would wish the return of the crown. I am glad to know her efforts were not in vain." Johnston tried to control her anxiety. "She would not want recognition for her actions. Thank you for remembering her memory by sharing this with me." Johnston embraced Father Granger tightly. "Please pass my words on to Christian." She lowered her head to Father Granger before leaving.

She stood straight, gliding to the door. She heard the sounds of a few sobs, followed by a gasp from Father Granger trying to hold his emotions together while she pushed out the side door.

Alone in the gray yard, she stopped. How could she die? Thirty-seven, too young to die.

She gasped. She was faced with her own mortality doing the right thing, doing the mission.

***

She didn't have to go back to recover the Honours. Her thoughts raced. Struggling to catch her breath, she leaned hard against the gray wall in the jaunt room. Her breath came in quick spurts. Desperately, she reached behind her to untie the corset. Her chest started to tighten, and the tingling slowly made its way down her arm as the pressure and anxiety collapsed in on her.

Dizziness set in, turning her knees to jelly, and she fell into a tangled net of silk and embroidery around her as she sank to the ground.

The words surrounded her as fingers started tugging the laces of her corset. "What happened?"

"Never saw Johnston faint…"

"Is she okay?"

"Is she injured?"

Johnston leaned forward, her hands on the floor, and she closed her eyes.

The voices faded in and out of her mind, mixed in with the "She was run through" and then "She returned to the Almighty."

She forced everything from her mind and started counting her breaths.

In…the rush through her nose

Hold…two three…

Out…slowly between her teeth…

In…focusing on calming her heart rate the corset loosened.

Hold…two three…her body screamed for air, mistaking anxiety for oxygen deprivation in a heart attack.

Out…the light-headed feeling started to lift.

A few more repetitions of this and she lifted her fingers on her right hand to her neck to count along with her heartbeat. A few long minutes passed as the tingling and light-headed feeling passed. Slowly the world came back into focus.

The Honours of Scotland were never truly lost to history. Worse, she would die in the attempt to protect them. All she had to do was prevent the Honours from being taken. She would correct history and save herself. Her thoughts seemed like a desperate attempt to trick her body that all was okay.

Standing slowly, she took another deep breath.

The voices around her suddenly came back as a tidal wave crashing over the beach. "Are you okay!"

"What happened?"

"Do you need a doctor?"

"Should we contact TDCI Stewart?"

The gray of the room came back into focus as Johnston opened her eyes to the crowd of people around her. The strength in her legs returned as she convinced herself that this was a history that could be changed. It worked its way from her head, and she willed to the rest of her body.

She slowly stood with the weight of the skirts adding to the gravity as she rose to her feet. "I'm…fine…fine." The finality in her voice made the technicians step back as she left the room to return her dress to the closet in the archives.

***

She looked out her window to see the dim yellow and orange hues from the window shifted to deep fire red. She looked to the sky to see the last shades of reddish purple drift to midnight blue with flecks of starry glitter. She imagined they were sparkling stars, but she knew better. She had seen the night sky with the trillions of stars following as a river across the sky. These flecks of glitter were merely bugs, birds, or dust passing through the PX-Shield.

She walked to the glass flowered lamp by her love seat. The soft light cast from the lamp was perfect to bathe the room in a warm yellow glow, yet it gave soft white light for reading at in her favorite spot.

How would she survive this? How could she prevent the Honours of Scotland from being lost to the recesses of history without becoming a casualty of them herself?

The details pulled her deeper, looking for a place to jaunt in. Maybe a landholder to represent a family with influence. Yes, that is strategic, but where should she jaunt in? Maybe right before the siege, or during? How to gain the trust of the…

The rapping at her door shattered the peaceful silence.

"Who is there?" Johnston sighed, breathing slowly as she rose from the seat to answer the door. "TDCI Stewart?" She stepped back, holding the door. "What brings you here?"

"Seriously?" His face looked both annoyed and insulted. "You collapsed coming back from the recon of a mission that I sent you on, with no word on your well-being, and you wonder why I am stopping by." He paused. "And for the record, I am John when I am off the clock." He held his ground at the door with arms crossed and a concerned smile.

Johnston took a moment. For all the times she had been in TDCI Stewart's office, she never saw him with that concerned look on his face. He was five or so years her junior but kept a persona of confidence the whole time on her entry to the agency.

"I only have a few moments before I need to be home. May I come in?"

Seconds stretched to minutes. "Oh, um, yeah." Johnston opened the door and held it open for him to pass. "I've got this. I know what I have to do."

"I don't think you do." He looked into her untelling eyes. "You know you are one of my best." He paused. "No, my best investigator. I do not want to lose you in an assignment."

"That is because you aren't Scot." She glared at him. "Because you…" She closed her eyes, clenching her jaw.

"I value you more than your mission." He leveled an eye at her. She held his gaze. He studied her a moment, and then he frowned. "It is not just the Honours of Scotland? There is more." He walked over to the chair. "Or I wouldn't be worried. I wouldn't be here." And he turned to look at her, studying her response.

The reality caught Johnston. Why now? "Have a seat." She gestured to the living room with the love seat and the chair. "Can I get you a glass of something?" The bottle of Chardonnay in the kitchen beckoned her.

"No, thank you." John called from the living area.

Johnston returned to the room with a glass. The clear crystalline liquid glistened in the warm light. She curled her leg under her on the sofa across from the love seat. Slowly taking a sip, she continued looking into the glass, hoping it would show her a different future. "The jewels left Dunnottar Castle and were intercepted in transit. According to Father Granger, I was there in the transit, and I was killed in the ambush." She continued studying the light playing in the light liquid of her glass.

"Oh, maybe I will have a seat," John continued as he sat next to the lamp. "According to the history recorded in the Px-Shield, the Honours were never taken, and you didn't die. If you correct history, you didn't die in the process."

"I know, I know…" Her head shook slowly side to side, then she raised her eyes to meet his, taking a deep breath.

"You have been in much more dangerous situations than this on previous missions. You know what the possibilities are and can prepare for them."

"I know." She closed her eyes. "I've just never had my death... predicted." The reality was still hard to say aloud. "Witnessed." She opened her eyes again. "I'll be fine tomorrow."

John shook his head then looked back at her. "Really? You have been an agent almost twenty years and never had your death predicted in the field?"

"No," she whispered. "Not yet."

John leaned forward, placing his arms in his knees. "I hate to trivialize this jarring event, but it happens to everyone at some time in their career. I'm surprised it took this long for you." He emphasized in each word. "You need to save yourself." He leaned back again. "This history is not yet written. You can change it and survive to tell the tale. In fact, you are so focused on detail that you can and should be able to prevent this from happening, and I expect you to." John looked at the flickering of the fire in the fireplace dancing across the room. His voice seemed young for a moment. "You are more qualified than anyone, than any person I know. I know you will figure it out."

Her gaze relaxed as she smiled. "I guess you are right." Her breathing slowed. "You are right." A slight smile crossed her lips.

"Where did you get the wine?"

"France, 1886, but I picked it up in 1899."

"Souvenir?"

"Yeah. I bought it while I was there and brought it back to enjoy. When I drink it, I remember the journey, the creativity or..." She smiled, thinking of the trip.

John smiled. "I miss the adventure."

"Then why did you accept the position of chief?"

"The department needed direction, guidance. I had to leave the investigation."

"You are a good chief. We need you."

He smiled. "Oh well, doesn't mean I can't travel...Just not the excitement of a case."

"If you regret it so much, why don't you take the odd assignment?"

"What would happen if I die? Is the desire for adventure more important than my wife, my little boy? I would love to do it again. Some people crave the investigation…" John trailed off.

"We need to get together more frequently…as friends."

"I agree."

"I…" her voice trailed off as her mind drifted back to her impending death. She couldn't decide if her fate had been written.

"You will know what to do when the time comes. I know you. You will return to us when all is done. This is not your last assignment." He looked around the room. "Wow, your collection keeps growing. These mementos are amazing."

"Yeah, there is a story with each one." She leaned back onto the sofa. "Is your son jaunting yet?"

"Yes." Stewart's eyes brightened. "The jaunt school said he is the head of his class at six years old."

"He'll be time jaunting before you know it and taking your position in the force." She smiled, thinking about what it would be like to have a child, a person to pass on her knowledge. She looked at each memento of her life, the breakable mementos that would not last long with a kid, and tried to hide, cringing at that thought.

"I don't think so." John smiled. "He seems to like building things. He'll probably be an engineer or something." The expression of confused pride crossed his face, admitting his son would probably not be following his footsteps in the prestigious field as a time investigator but remaining proud as a father looking at his son through rose-colored glasses.

"Then he'll be monitoring the PX-Shield. Those engineers are amazing at what they do." Johnston smiled. "And he has proven that he is amazing already."

"I'm his dad." John grinned, and his chin rose a few millimeters with a dose of pride.

"That you are," Johnston agreed.

He glanced at his watch. "It was important for me to drop by, but I also don't want my dinner to get cold."

Johnston smiled and nodded.

"I know you will find a way." He smiled, chuckling as if to a joke in his head. "Just like Ryan, um, Agent Hajjar."

She smiled with the seed of curiosity. "Why?"

"He is on a particularly difficult assignment, and it is his first," John emphasized.

Johnston quirked her eyebrow. "Do tell. I did tell him to come to me if he has any questions."

"He won't." John quirked a smile again, same as that joke Johnston now felt she was being left out on.

Johnston closed her eyes, shaking her head. "I was hoping he would have learned by now when to ask for help."

"I think he has…but this is the assignment that he can't ask for help, not from you." John smiled and chuckled with the inside joke turning into one of those naughty jokes that you shouldn't tell in public.

"His first assignment out?" She paused. "Well, trial by fire, I guess." She paused a moment, searching introspectively. "I hope you haven't miscalculated."

Johnston sighed disapprovingly then got up to refill her glass as John rose in turn.

"I know what I'm doing." John inserted one arm into the sleeve of his coat. "He can figure things out."

"If he doesn't?" Johnston looked up at John.

"Well, we won't have to worry about your trip for Scotland." John smiled. "Really, he'll work it out."

※

The warm Austin air hit Hajjar in the face with enough humidity to make him appreciate Sarah's suggestion of lightweight cloths, though the sandals made his feet feel naked. The clear blue sky dotted with clouds left him squinting at the tall walls within arm's reach of the buildings around him in the alley.

The short walk to the front of the hotel still left him sweating. It gathered on his skin from too much humidity. The red dome of the capitol loomed half a mile away. The subtle gurgling of the Colorado River behind him would put Sixth Street in front of him a couple blocks, close enough to walk and even a longer walk to the University of Texas campus.

The small brick building with two layers of rooms side by side stretched along the two far sides of the square parking lot. A covered awning wide enough to fit a car extended from the lobby. Hajjar smiled, enjoying the classic motel. The short building had actual rooms, space enough to live for the night. This was not the hole-in-the-wall from his time, allowing one person to slide into their bunk with little more room than a crypt to sleep for the evening.

"I'll be right there," the voice cheerfully called from the back room.

Hajjar turned, looking out the window at the cars on the street, leaning back onto the counter and resting his elbows behind him on the wooden top. This was the period when vehicles were artwork. Wings on the back end, multiple colors emphasizing the curves and style of the car, and then there was under the hood. He sighed as an original T-Bird rolled by. Beauty in motion.

"Okay…I'm here…Hmm." A woman scuttled out from the back room. "What can I help you with?" Her brown eyes were covered with clouds of gray hidden behind half-moon glasses with a red chain connected at the hinges dropping behind her neck. She seemed to smile at the prospect of a visitor.

"Yeah, I'd like a room for a few days." He turned back around to face her.

"What brings ya to Austin?" Her sweet voice came from behind the reservation book.

"Visiting the University of Texas. Looking into grad school."

"Oh, UT is a great school." She laid down the book. "You will like it here. How long are you here for?"

"Umm, what day is it?" He looked up from his wallet.

Confusion crept over the woman's face. "June 10. You don't know what day it is?"

"I'll be here for the week…I…umm." Hajjar paused, looking at his feet. "I am…umm…I just finished a very consuming research project."

The woman smiled sympathetically. "I know the feeling. My grandson just finished his master's. Days on end in the library. Sometimes he wouldn't even remember what year it was but could remember all of the Texas Supreme Court rulings for the last hundred some years. Here you go, young man." She handed him a key after getting the money. "Room 21."

"Where is Sixth Street from here?"

"Out this door, one block over to the sidewalk that is in good condition, and then left five blocks to the nightlife."

He thanked her and then walked out the door to find his room. The shade from the drive-through gave him pause to enjoy the "21" on the big brown plastic shaped key chain attached to a key. He continued to walk through the parking lot along the L-shaped building to the red door with a gold "21" on it. Again, the nostalgia brought a smile to his face as he heard the clicking of each tumbler in the door lock fall onto the key. Then he twisted it clockwise with a giggle to feel the dead bolt slide.

The dark room was exactly as he imagined the sixties to be, with a big print on the wallpaper and the khaki green carpet and bathroom fixtures.

He studied the room, its colors, patterns, aromas. He wanted to memorize how it felt to him to ensure he could jaunt back here in case he needed to return unexpectedly. Finally, he flopped on the stiff bed to rest a bit before going out on the town. His best intentions for rest were thwarted by excitement which kept his eyes open, running scenarios in his head until the glowing brightness through the curtains faded. As the searing white light turned into hues of gold then orange, he rose from the bed to comb his hair and got cleaned up for the evening. He pulled his long hair back and then headed out into the town.

He would be looking for a girl in her late teens, about six feet tall, green eyes, possibly with a partner, a guy or girl with a deep voice, and…well… not much more to go on.

Two blocks to the sidewalk in good condition, then he turned to face the glowing light of the nightlife.

He first headed to the club in the recording. He wouldn't have to be there for another couple days, but he wanted to see the place and the people there to get to know the regulars.

The pinks, blues, and whites from the sign glistened off the oils on pavement. Looking up the street, he walked to the door, giving it a tug. Surprised at the heaviness, he pulled on it again. Clouds of smoke curled out from the open door surrounding him, beckoning him in. The door groaned, closing behind him as he stepped through. The crisp lines of the beer signs behind the bar were hazy swirls of smoke lifting lazily through the air. The smell of stale beer and old cigarettes were a welcome change to him after the sterile pub on the campus.

Hajjar waded through the moderate crowd toward the bar to sit on the stool next to the oak top. He turned with his shoulder to the bar so he could watch the people.

"You're new here." A woman's voice made him turn. "What can I get ya?"

He leaned in on his elbows to study her face a moment, meeting her brown eyes. He cocked a smile and said, "Shiner, please." His voice cut though the noise enough for her to nod and pull a bottle before popping the top and passing the damp bottle to him.

She smiled at him and then walked down to the other end of the bar to lean over to speak to a patron before reaching into the well to pull a bottle of dark amber liquid. And then she poured it over a handful of ice cubes in a short rocks glass. She passed the glass to him and then handed two beer bottles to a pint-sized girl in pigtails, who ran the bottles out to a table with two young girls. The two ladies giggled and handed some money to her. The lady with the black hair leaned in to say something to the ear of the blond friend before looking back at the little girl skipping back to the bar.

Hajjar looked around at the groups of people scattered throughout the room and some trickling in from the street. They were mostly college students around discussing…whatever they found interesting at the moment—politics, music, the war…

"So what brings you into town?" The woman leaned in to Hajjar. "I'm Bridget, by the way."

Hajjar pulled his attention away from profiling and turned to face her. "Grad school." He leaned in, resting his chin on his hand while lifting the bottle to his lips. "I'm checking out the law school and the area to see if I really want to live here while I get my degree."

"I like the area. We have a good music scene, and the area seems more forward-thinking than other parts of the state."

"Yeah?" Hajjar raised his lips into a slight smile.

Bridget stood up with a wide smile, shaking her head. "Won't work on me."

The other side of Hajjar's lips turned up into a full smile. "I'd guess not, but it is fun to try."

"To the chase." She lifted a clear bottle from the well to clink his beer, then poured a small stream of liquid into her mouth for half a second without touching her lips to the pour spout. She returned the bottle to the well. "Good luck to you. You should come back in a couple of days. A local talent is scheduled to perform here. You might like her. I think she's got a real future in music."

"I think I will." Hajjar smiled.

The little girl ran up to the bar and crawled onto the stool. Bridget leaned over. "What da ya need?"

"A Shiner, a Miller, and a Bud." Her Texas accent carried over the bar.

Bridget popped the top on the three bottles and then set them in front of the little waitress. "Here you go."

The squirt slid off the stool, landing on the floor as a bit of foam rose to the tip of the bottle. And with a bounce, the beer foamed a little out of the top, and she ran to the table.

"She your daughter?" Hajjar asked.

"Yeah, one of the family." Bridget smiled, looking over at the cute bobbing pigtails with a motherly smile.

"What can you tell me about that group?" He pointed to a cluster of two girls huddled around a guy, discussing something enthusiastically.

"They love their government conspiracy and alien abduction." She looked at them over his shoulder. "But they are harmless. Entertaining at most."

"I'd love to see them, actually meet an alien."

Bridget smiled, shaking her head, and then walked over to a patron beckoning her at the other end of the bar.

Hajjar swiveled his chair, looking out to the floor over the sparsely populated tables. His arm relaxed on the bar with his fingers touching the bottle.

Two men sat in the dark corner with a single light hanging above, illuminating the parchment between them. They leaned into the center of the table, nefariously plotting. They looked like conspiring agents, except for the long hair, bright blotchy T-shirts, shorts, sandals, and the animated way they threw their hands about. Hajjar chuckled, imagining a conductor's baton in their hands and watching them flail about. "There is noooooo reason we shouldn't travel to space. There could be *aliens* out there," he imagined the one saying. Followed by the reply, "Well, they would be more accepting to your wardrobe and hair than your parents!" Hajjar leaned back on his stool with his back on the bar. His smile dropped as he noticed the guy with his back to the corner lift a small rectangular white card, and then he threw it down on the table. Most likely the conversation was over that draft card. Neither of them would adjust well to military life.

His attention quickly moved on to the table just left of the stage in the corner. The two ladies sitting there each held a moist bottle and were leaning in to talk intensely. The blond sat, twirling her hair in her left hand as she continued talking intensely. "Oh, isn't he so cute, the one in the Hawaiian shirt." Hajjar continued making up conversations for them. "You are too good for him." "You are just jealous of his silky hair." The blond leaned back, lifting the bottle and taking the last drops of beer. Her dark-haired friend leaned forward, smiled, and laughed. Hajjar paused a moment, catching her face and bright green eyes. Hajjar imagined what she would look like in a blue baseball cap. The two ladies continued laughing as they caught the eye of the little girl and held up two fingers. They nodded and continued laughing. He glanced down at the floor, hoping to see their shoes hidden in the shadows. Maybe their intense talking was actually from planning future tech heist, and their laughter was over their confidence in pulling it off.

Another group sat at a table near the bar. The gray-haired man sat with a notebook and pen. Hajjar took a second glance to confirm it was not a Field Notebook. The man's salted hair was pulled back into a ponytail, and his neatly cut beard had flecks of white. He sat observing, taking notes, entering the conversation every few moments now and again. The group of one girl and three guys around him was half his age. They were all sitting around the elder man, doe-eyed and hanging on his every word before breaking off into lively conversation, gesturing and note-taking.

Bridget returned as his bottle dangerously approached empty. "Another?" she asked.

"Yeah." Hajjar nodded toward the two at the table. "What can you tell me about those two?"

"Are you an investigator?" Bridget asked sarcastically with a tinge of accusation.

"Yeah, wanted to know if they were together." He winked at Bridget. "Or if I can pick one or…" His grin widened. "Both for an evening that will live in infamy."

Bridget sighed with both amusement and disgust.

"Well, they are both drinking Shiner, if you want to get them around and try your luck." Bridget smiled.

"Maybe I'll do that." Hajjar grinned, lifting his bottle to take a slow drink.

Bridget said something to the pigtailed girl, who giggled and passed the message to the ladies at the table. He realized he didn't know the girl's name and made up one for her. Maybe she was… His attention shifted back to the two girls at the table.

Both of the girls looked over their shoulders back at him and then turned their glances to each other, giggling. They both looked back at him with desire in their eyes and beckoned him over.

The confidence of a young time travel agent brought him to his feet. He grabbed his fresh bottle of beer to make the journey across the floor. Gracefully, he danced his way through the tables, not jostling the bottle and coming to stand at the table. Both ladies looked up at him, leaning over on their elbows toward each other with an amusing grin.

"Have a seat." The dark-haired girl probed at him with emerald eyes glinting in the low light.

"Thanks for the beer." The blond girl smirked. Her sapphire eyes either beckoned him to join or were annoyed with his intrusion on their *private* discussion. He couldn't quite tell the difference.

Bugger that! I'm either here to thwart their best laid plans or be the time traveling adventurer that will make them cream in their seats. Sitting down with his smile quirked into a mischievous grin, he cocked his eyebrow. The two girls grinned. He knew he could either get a lead talking to them, fitting the profile of the girl outside the pawnshop. Or if it was not them, he might just have a fun evening.

"You two look like you are quite intent on an enthralling conversation."

"You are." The green eyes flared a challenge and then settled down with a smirk. "Join us." She flicked her eyebrows.

Hajjar met her challenge by pulling out the chair, turning it around. He straddled it and sat, then raised his bottle with a satisfied conquest almost achieved. He crossed his arms in front of him on the chair, taking a swig from the Shiner bottle, lowering his eyes to meet the sapphire-eyed blond. "I'm Ryan."

"I'm Tricksey," stated the dark-haired girl with the piercing green eyes. "And she is Bambi." She pointed to her blond friend.

Hajjar smiled. "Pleasure to meet you both." He was convinced these were names they gave to throw him off. "What were you two discussing before I intruded?"

The two girls swapped looks of brazen offense at his abrupt presence.

"Time travel..." Bambi leaned in to urge him on while her dark-haired friend nodded. "Where would you travel to?"

Hajjar's mouth quirked into a smile as his eyes looked up to catch their reaction. "Ground rules first. Are we observing only or making changes?"

"Making changes, of course. How could you not try to prevent the death of six million Jews, Gypsies, and other innocent people at the hands of Hitler? In standing by without trying to make a difference, how are you no better than the people responsible?" Tricksey's green eyes pierced into him.

Rookies, he thought. "Assuming you stop Hitler, kill him, who is to say there isn't someone worse sitting in the sidelines? First you have to be sure that you have a hundred percent confidence that your attempt to kill him will be successful. Otherwise, he becomes more paranoid, embedding himself in the bunker as he did after the attempt by Stauffenberg," Hajjar stated.

"Additionally, Hitler pulled Germany out of the Great Depression. The unemployment rate was less than seven percent while the rate in Europe and the US was still hovering above twenty-five percent. Most of the German population were oblivious of the employment rate connection to the absence of a large portion of the population. Point is, if he was killed during the war, he becomes a martyr, and his top generals take over the crusade. The outcome is far worse than we all could imagine," Hajjar continued.

"He had to die, but at the right time and circumstance, suicide discrediting him when the end was inevitable in the only way that he would not be followed by obsessed cohorts. Most of Germany was obsessed with maintaining their way of life; most had no idea the destruction of the Jewish population was occurring at the time."

"Once the head is destroyed, the rest of the command would fall, and the population would have their eyes opened to the atrocities." Tricksey sat up, taking offense.

"Don't you see? He had to be destroyed in the downfall of his conquest, or he would be made a martyr, and his top generals would take over the crusade. He had to die the way he did as a suicide disgracing himself and those around him," Hajjar stated as fact. "You can't change history, because it will have irreconcilable changes to time itself." Hajjar leaned in, taking a drink of Shiner.

"What are you, a *historian*?" Tricksey's green eyes frosted over, cold.

"No, I'm here to parse my l…cough…degree." He smiled. "But I like history."

"She doesn't like being shown up. I'm actually Chris." The blond-haired Bambi met him with a smile on her blue eyes.

"History is currently misinterpreted enough as it is," Tricksey continued. "If I can't try to save millions, then I might just visit the people and observe the events to record them untainted. Maybe like Guy Fox, London." She paused. "What is history versus lore?"

"I see your point. At the same time, I can't just stand by when I could make things better, but the road to hell is paved with good intentions. Maybe good deeds could be catastrophic in the long term." Chris blue eyes smirked.

"So what inspired this conversation?" Hajjar grinned and leaned in.

"Science fiction class we are taking." Tricksey sipped her beer. "It's fun fantasy. I'm actually Bethany." Her voice softened, letting go of the defensive posturing.

"I'm still Ryan." Hajjar's first name was still Ryan. "But back to the point, science fiction is the dreams of science, the inspiration." Hajjar leaned on the table. "The inventions of the future are inspired by science fiction of today."

"Good point," Chris said. "You ever read *Stars My Destination*?"

"Bester?" Hajjar smiled.

"Yeah?" Bethany sighed. "I loved it."

"Imagine transporting through space in the blink of an eye of thought." Chris smiled.

"Yeah, nothing quite like *Star Trek*," Hajjar muttered.

"What?" Chris dropped her smile, looking straight at him.

"Nothing, well, not for a while…" Hajjar didn't see her smile return. "Engineering problem, need a recombinator." His eyes continued to study her as he continued, "Where would you visit or try to change?" He leaned forward with a grin.

"Yeah, Chris? I answered. Where would you go?" Bethany added sass to her voice.

"I'd go to…" She paused. "To meet Jesus."

"I never thought you were religious." Bethany grinned, sucked into the conversation.

"I'm not, but he is the focal point of multiple religions. Christians would be Jews without him, and Islam includes him, but as a prophet and not as son of God. Did *he* know how much theological turmoil would be surrounding his existence? Many other men were alive at the time, getting through their lives but not provoking this level of debate. I'd want to meet him. See if he is who he is or just in the right time and place to be caught in the religious crossfire."

"But." Hajjar pondered what he was about to say without being blasphemous. "How would you confront him to ask the questions you are seeking the answers to? How would you ask the question or questions to him to get our answers without altering his attitude of the subject, and ultimately the entire history? What if he was really going to be a common carpenter set to live his life, satisfied and happy making creations out of wood, until a time traveler gave him delusions of grandeur, saving all of the religious problems. So as the time traveler, you end up unknowingly starting the religious factions that caused genocides and crusades." Hajjar paused to take a breath before continuing, "And what if you got your answers you were looking for? The answers to dissolve all of the theological questions. What would you do with them?" Hajjar leaned in, tilting his head to the side to look at Chris, and raised his eyebrow inquisitively.

"You know, I don't really know. The truth would probably result in more bloodshed, or even society reinstating witch burning for heretics, just especially for me." Chris laughed with the sad reality that within her nation, especially her state along with the neighboring states, people burned and were killed by men in white sheets for far less. "I'd probably just get his autograph and maybe a lock of hair to incorporate it into a wine glass charm to ensure I would never have a bad glass of wine." She looked to the ceiling. "You know, after a bad day, fill your glass with water and drink wine made from God's son." She sighed and chuckled, looking over to Bethany then to the confused stare of Hajjar. "You know one of those things that you put around the base of a wine glass to distinguish them apart at a dinner party. God, you need to get current of new items. It is not as funny if I have to explain it."

Bethany met her grin, chuckling. She raised her bottle to meet Chris's then lowered it to take a drink.

"I never heard yours." Hajjar looked at Bethany.

"I mentioned Guy Fox, but…" She looked at Chris. "Leonardo Da Vinci. I would love to witness his experiments and artwork. Knowing what I know about science, how did he figure out what he did? And maybe have him draw me a souvenir."

"Umm…" The squeak broke the conversation as all three looked down at the pint-sized waitress. "Another round?" She gave an infectiously peppy smile.

"Yes." Hajjar quirked an eye with amusement, then looked back to the two ladies sitting with him at the table.

"Sure." Pigtails turned and bounced away, returning a moment later with three bottles.

"What about you? You never answered." Bethany leaned in, resting her chin on her hands.

"Yes, I did."

"No, you just gave the rules, which are that we witness and make no changes to history." Bethany leaned closer to look into his eyes with a grin. "Where would you go?"

Hajjar sat pondering a moment. "I'm not sure, really." He sat a while, thinking. Where would he travel to? "To ten years ago. To meet some of the science fiction authors as they were getting the inspiration for various stories." They seem to be less fiction and more science in his timeline. He often wondered if the future was told to Bester, and he wrote it and called it sci-fi, or his writing fiction influenced the path to the future events to come to pass.

"Really? Ten years ago?" Chris sat a moment with a bewildered expression. "How unimaginative. You could just go find them and ask them now."

"Well, it is better than traveling ten minutes ago…to pay the bill on time." Hajjar placed his head in his hand, muttering under his breath. "Not a Weird Al fan…well, maybe in thirty some years."

"Would you travel forward?" Bethany asked. "Would you want to see the future?"

"No." Chris leaned back on her chair. "I like to be surprised."

"That's no fun." Bethany sipped her beer, enjoying the conversation. "You could see if you even make it into space, or we get taken over by the communist revolution."

"The future cannot be traveled to. Well, that is in my favorite books. Traveling to the past would be easy. You can do research on where you are heading in order to make it safely, but the future is not yet written, so how can you get there?" Hajjar looked at the two and then quickly added, "Or so I have read."

"Not a time machine, George Orwell fan?" Chris commented with a quirked eyebrow.

"I like him, but he is just not my favorite." Hajjar tipped his bottle up to drink and continued, "Would you ever think about going back to save an artifact before it is lost forever or destroyed?"

"Like what?" Chris smirked, leaning back in her chair and furrowing her brow.

"Like trying to save the scrolls from the libraries of Alexandria before they all got destroyed in the upheaval. Maybe music from an artist before she dies far too young?"

Bethany sat up, taking a drink. "But wouldn't that rewrite history? The item shouldn't exist because it would have been destroyed."

"What would you hope to do with it? Remember, don't rewrite history. The item shouldn't exist because it would have been destroyed."

"You can't put it into the population. Historians would eat it up, and then there is carbon dating." Chris shook her head.

Hajjar leaned back, having planted the trap and now enjoying where this conversation was going.

"What?" Bethany frowned.

"The item would be taken from 800 BC to present. Any carbon dating would show it to be new, not 2800-ish years old, because that is the linear path that it would have taken." Chris paused. "Or would it artificially age? Like the things taken from the bottom of the ocean to the surface. They fall apart at the top with less pressure. You get a scroll, trying to save it, only to have it turn to dust in your hand as you get it there."

"I would love to record Mozart or Beethoven playing piano." Bethany leaned her head back and looked up at the ceiling with a smile. "I love music. That would be appealing to me."

"You like music?" Hajjar asked.

"Oh yeah!" Bethany perked up.

"What about in a couple days? Janis Joplin will be here."

"Why, Ryan, are you asking me on a date?"

Hajjar paused, blushing a bit, and then answered, "Well?"

"Well." Bethany paused with temptation. "No, Chris and I have a final exam for a summer sci-fi class to study for," Bethany said flatly. "Maybe some other time?"

"If I'm still in town." Hajjar tilted his head. *Bust*, he thought. Both of his best leads were not panning out. Neither of them were suspects now, but he would still keep an eye out for them on Tuesday.

"How long are you in for?" Chris asked.

"A couple more days."

"That's too bad. I kind of like picking your brain on this subject."

"You seem very knowledgeable on the time travel thing," Bethany chimed in.

"I'm a fan of the doctor." Hajjar smiled.

"*Doctor Who?*" Chris frowned.

"Exactly..." He paused as the timeline hit him. Ouch, he was in 1962. *Doctor Who* started in 1963. "British broadcast, television show." Hajjar smiled. Maybe he should have referenced Rip Hunter in the DC comic series *Time Masters* that came out in print in 1961, ending its series two years from now. He smiled, wondering if they were comic book fans.

"You go to England?" Chris asked.

"Yeah, on a trip." Hajjar smiled and then looked at his watch. "I have a meeting tomorrow with the adviser, but it won't be until late morning." He smiled at Bethany and Chris. "We could take this debate back to my place."

Sarah perked up hearing someone enter her giant costume archive. "Hi." Sarah's voice waded through the racks of clothes before her head peeked over the top of a rack. "Oh, Johnston."

"Wow, glad to see you too, Sarah. Who were you hoping it was?" Johnston remembered her swooning over her partner, former partner. "Hajjar?"

Sarah hushed, looking at her feet as shades of embarrassment danced across her face.

"I think you two would make a cute couple." Johnston smiled, enjoying the youthful optimism of a crush.

Johnston paused and refocused on the next part of her mission. Slowly she stepped into the open room. Typically, she loved the dress up portion before heading out, especially the dresses of the 1650s. The gorgeous corsets, yards of skirt made of luscious fabrics, and hair designs made her truly feel like a lady, not the time warrior she was.

"You look like you are expecting bad news." Sarah placed a hand on Johnston's shoulder. "What's up?"

Johnson's eyes focused back from her thoughts to Sarah's worried smile, and then Johnston shook her head, slightly returning the smile.

"Agent Hajjar was in here yesterday. Hippie clothes for a trip to Austin." Sarah's lighthearted voice barely reached Johnston's ears. "His first solo mission. How exciting!"

Johnston didn't have to look hard her to see Sarah glowing. Johnston shook her head and closed her eyes, allowing an amused smirk to lift her frown. "You know, there were no hippies in Austin 1962."

"How did you know...when?" Her voice trailed off as she decided she really didn't want to know the answer. "I know, it is my slang for loose-fit relaxed clothes for the nightlife. I would not send him at that time with rose-colored John Lennon glasses, knowing that wouldn't be a fad for another four to five years."

Johnston smiled, not revealing her thoughts.

"What can I *get you*?" Sarah bubbled. "Wow, I sound like a bar wench."

Johnston shook her head again, amused. "England 1651. I will need at least two outfits."

"Two? Umm…that only leaves the one you used for your last trip." Sarah's eyes widened, surprise in her voice reflected in her face.

"Hopefully it will not be the entire nine-month siege, but I will be packing for it." Johnston sighed.

"You will need a chest to pack your belongings into. And jewelry?" Sarah paused. "So…you may not come back with both dresses you head out with?"

"Yes, you need to expect them to be lost to the times." Johnston sternly looked at Sarah, knowing that losing the dresses were the least of her worries. "I will need jewelry. I will need to infiltrate a castle before it is under siege." Johnston paused, looking at Sarah somberly. "If they find me out, it will be my death before the mission begins."

"I know that. It's my job." Sarah stepped back with concern settling on her face. "Are you okay?"

"I have a bad feeling about this mission." Johnston sighed.

"No! You can't let it get into your head or the mission is already lost!" Sarah gasped, stepping back to grasp her hand. "No, you are not intended to end this way."

"I'll be okay." Johnston exhaled, trying to force a bit of worry from her mind. "I just need to figure out my persona. I'm sorry to dump my worries on you."

"It's okay." She paused, looking at Johnston wide-eyed.

"That's my job. I get people the outfit to fit their personas. I don't want your cover to be blown because I accidentally gave you a dress from France in 1852 instead of England 1852. That would be the difference between you being welcomed openly and being strung up as a traitor."

"I'm sorry. I guess I'm overly worried."

"Well, of course you are. You are heading to a turbulent time when a woman can be beheaded at the whim of her king on false charges and then tortured to death." Sarah's feminist opinions started to get her excited.

"That doesn't really help calm my nerves." Johnston looked at Sarah. "Thank you though." She slightly smiled.

Sarah paused, looking at Johnston as the long moment of silence sank into Sarah. "Two or three dresses." Sarah smiled. "What is the scenario? Are you fleeing with time to run or are you fleeing with no warning, the clothes on your back, and what you can throw into a backpack? Okay, they didn't have backpacks in that time, but you know what I mean." Sarah shrugged.

Johnston pondered the plan. "The castle is northwest of Edinburgh in 1651 during the invasion, but right in the path as the English army crossed the Furth and moved up to Perth. I would have a day to pack and leave the area with haste."

Sarah sighed, closing her eyes and allowing the gravity of the assignment to flow through her, focusing on her knowledge of the time and area. Slowly, she opened her eyes, staring into her thoughts. "Are you escaping with the help of the chambermaids to pack?" The question was more to herself, and not to Johnston. "I doubt it. You would want to give the persona of a woman fleeing on a horse with what she can carry. That gives you one dress max, and no trunk." She focused her gaze back to Johnston. "How long is the ride?"

"Um, a day or two?"

"You will need good clothes to show your status, but not too flashy to advertise your status if you are caught." Sarah walked down to the shelf with the dresses, pulling out a long thick orange box with a handle. She then pulled a second blue box with a green handle. "This will be a start." She carried the long sturdy orange box with red ribbon handles at both ends and lifted the lid. Setting the lid aside, she lifted the tissue paper from the top of the dress. "I think this will do for the more dressy events that you may want to show your status." She lifted the dress from the box by the corset, the skirt following, allowing the light to catch the facets of sunset layered in the weave. "The chemise is in the box with the dress. This is designed and made in Edinburgh around spring of 1650, with design inspiration from Italy, Venice, and Paris in the bodice. We will be able to wrap this into a roll that can be placed on the back of a horse." Carefully, she lowered the dress back into its case. Walking over to the blue box, she lifted the top, revealing a turquoise bodice with ripples of sea blues and greens woven on the threads. "This dress will be your riding dress. The design is early 1649. It will work as a dress that can be travel attire. Concealing your status with a design of maybe two years old could be work attire for a lady of stature and affordable for a chambermaid at that time. This should work, as long as you treat the dress as an old, out-of-date item with little importance to you."

Johnston took a step back. "Beautiful! Will they fit?" she asked, remembering the breathless binding of the last dress she wore.

"Give me a day for tailoring," Sarah stated. "It will fit like your corset in 1651. Exactly what a lady of your stature would be wearing at that time." Sarah smiled with confidence.

"Good job, Sarah." Johnston smiled. "I will need the other wrapped tight enough to put on the back of a horse. On second thought, the jewels were hidden in the castle. I will need a dagger or three to protect myself. Whatever I can conceal on myself."

"That will be in the armory. I don't handle those." Sarah paused. "I deal with props, not the ones you will want to use to defend yourself."

Johnston paused, looking at the dresses. "Thank you."

***

The cool dry central air filled Johnston's lungs. Her eyes closed, feeling the air become mildly humid. Her thoughts focused on the smell of grass and damp trees from north of Stirling. As she inhaled, she felt the air change around her. As reality slipped like falling into a dream, sounds of people on the other side of rustling leaves reminded her that she was outside of a battle. Johnston opened her eyes to see Scotland in 1651.

She slowly inhaled and gazed at the sun dipping low behind the string of clouds, finishing its march across the sky. A small open field reached ahead of her, ending at a line of trees reaching out to pull her into hidden cover.

With the heavy bag hefted over her shoulder, she staggered a step before trudging forward. Steadying herself a second time, she lifted her skirts to leave the cover of the trees.

Everything around her was distantly familiar from her memories as a child. The size of the field was a fraction of its size when she visited Kinross as a child with her parents, but she felt like she was still a twelve-year-old running through these woods, looking for the spirits her father told her about. A tear of bitter joy wet her eye and ran down her cheek as she remembered the heroic stories her mom and dad told her of Scotland.

A grimace crossed her face as she stepped into the stream with her skirts draped over her arm, showing leg and knee as she submerged her shoe and ankle into the icy brook. The hiss of shock broke the quiet as the prickly fingers of cold water penetrated her socks and shoes. It always amazed her how cold the water was in Scotland, even in midsummer.

Slowly the woods parted, revealing Huntingtower Castle in the clearing beyond. The stone walls reached high on all sides of the quarters with a meadow stretching out from the main entry. Her heavy bag dropped to her feet. She was taken aback by the majesty of the castle. The images she remembered in the visitor's guide now lay in front of her in the full glory of this time.

The castle now stood tall in front of her, in the prime of its life, not like when she visited in her childhood. Then it was in ruins. It was a child's perfect playground for the imagination, pretending to be a princess in one moment, and in the next an archaeologist uncovering a thousand-year-old civilization. Now to be standing here, looking at Huntingtower Castle the way she imagined it as a child was brilliant.

Her eyes followed the top of the walls of the castle where the small glass windows looked over the meadow to the tree line, where a small group of weary refugees carried only necessities, along with the weight of not knowing if their home was left to return to. Each burdened was carrying as much anyone could handle. Baskets with food and belongings draped them, almost hiding their clothes. Their skirts were damp and muddy with rips and tears fresh from the journey.

Johnston looked at the small clusters of people struggling for safety. The reality of the refugees fleeing the fight dampened her happy reminiscing and snapped her back to the present danger.

With a count of three and a heave, the heavy bundle returned to her shoulder. Steadying herself and adjusting the balance of her load, she started the long journey to the entrance. Her hair fell from its bun in red and white streaked curls down her shoulder, and there were scrapes from the limbs on her neck; she lifted her chin high and continued her march to the castle.

Two solders briskly walked out to her. After bowing, one rose. "May I take this?"

"Yes." Johnston heaved the bag to the first boy.

A groan slipped his mouth as he stepped forward to catch himself. "Where are you from?"

"Castle Campbell."

"That far? Where is your horse?"

"He fell lame a mile or so back." She looked sternly at the boys too young to be in battle, left behind to guard the castle as best they could. "You should return to your post." She looked at the second boy. "My guards would be flogged for such insubordination. Especially now."

"I apologize, my lady." The boy's voice cracked as he turned back to the castle as quickly as he could.

She silently walked across the meadow with planted bushes creating an organic outer wall that opened onto an inner meadow. She could see the tall stone wall guarding the dwellings inside. It seemed larger than she imagined it when she was a child, looking at the drawings and 3D projections in the visitor's center. The wall surrounded the additional buildings and pillars of smoke from their chimneys and shadowed the tall main keep. The interior was filled with displaced families. Groups of people were holding each other, weeping and happy to make it to safety. Others walked numbly, worn with worry and overwhelmed. Johnston's eye fell on a lady standing tall, talking with her hands while directing people to where they should be. Johnston noticed one thing missing from the groups—men, even young men. All men of an age to fight were noticeably absent.

She and the young guard walked to the woman in the center of the courtyard. "Lady Murray."

"Yes?" The lady turned with a quick glance. The redhaired freckled kid slunk back a step, dropping Johnston's bag.

"Yes, my lady. I should not have left my post." His voice cracked as he continued his bow. Then he turned and ran with the energy of a boy not yet wise in the dangers ahead.

Her eyes followed him as he scampered off. Her eyes swung back to rest on Johnston. The lines around her eyes and cheeks told stories of joy from the past within these castle walls, but the weariness in her eyes told the present story of sleepless nights, battles, and loved ones lost.

Johnston held her gaze steady. "Lady Murray." A slight bow with a curtsy as Johnston's eyes rose again to meet her gaze. "Elizabeth Ogilvy from Castle Campbell. My horse fell lame trying to stay ahead of Cromwell's advancements."

Lady Murray's eyes widened a bit. "That is near Fife. Come, there is a room near my own. You can give me all the news this evening." Lady Murray beckoned another boy over. "Take her bags to the corner chamber near mine." She clasped Johnston's hands. "We will talk this evening. My maids will help you freshen up."

Lady Murray pursed her lips and looked around at all the people gathering around the castle, huddling in fear and relief, then to the sun lowering below the horizon, leaving fire streaking across the sky. "There is little time to continue your travel today. You are welcome here. I welcome you join me by the fire this evening to discuss the news of the day."

Johnston could see the glistening of tears in her eyes before she blinked them away. The hope that her family might still be well, yet knowing if Johnston were here, then there was less hope of their safety. "Thank you, Lady Murray Ross. We will discuss the best or the worst that it may not come to pass." Johnston turned to follow the lad with her bag.

The maze of hallways led her to a quaint room at the corner of the hall, lit with intermittent sunlight through the few windows and clusters of candles along the walls. She paused at the door and looked in.

The boy dropped her bag, bowed, then scurried out the door. Johnston stepped in, looking around.

"I gather this will suffice for your stay." Lady Murray's voice broke the silence behind her.

Johnston turned to face her. "Yes, my lady. You are more than gracious." She continued on setting her smaller bag on the table near the fireplace.

"My maid shall attend to you shortly."

Johnston sat on the bed a moment, letting the reality that she was in 1651 sink in, reminded by the tightness of the corset. Wanting to take a full breath again, she reached behind her back, untying and loosening the laces. Finally, with patience waning, Johnston lowered the dress to the ground, stepping out of it. Then she gathered up the dress, taking it over to the bed near the window to see if it needed cleaning and mending. A dark glee overcame her as she laughed, wondering which would be worse, death on this mission or Sarah killing her when she saw the wear on this dress.

Johnston spotted the basin and the kettle, curls of steam lifting out of it near the fire. She lifted her underskirt off, setting it aside, and then she set the basin next to the rug on the floor in front of the fire. She checked to see if the water was boiling before kneeling on the rug. She poured the steaming water into the basin. Dipping the rag into the basin, she wrung out the majority of the wetness back into the basin until it was merely damp. Then she ran it over her face and shoulders, feeling the warmth of the water and small few droplets start to roll down her back, cooling along their path over her shoulder blade and down her spine.

She sat, enjoying the warm rag yet wishing she were at home in her own bath. A soft knock broke the quiet as a young lady entered and started busying herself on the other part of the room.

Johnston finished washing her legs and toes before sitting the basin aside. She pulled the chemise over her head then sat back in the chair. "I am Lady Ogilvy. And you are?"

"Jane." She spoke softly as she bowed quickly then walked over. She reached for the brush and paused for a second, looking at the sharp dagger sitting next to it, before picking up the brush to detangle Johnston's hair. Now *this* Johnston could savor—someone with a light and firm touch brushing through her hair. She could fall asleep with this pampering.

She felt Jane's fingers pull pieces of her hair on the side loose. She then wrapped the remainder of her hair into a knot and finally pulled those side strands of hair crossing in the back, holding the knot of hair steady.

"There you go, my lady." Jane stepped back, handing her a mirror.

"Thank you." Johnston sighed. "I feel so much better." She stood, stepping into the dress of sunset with gold highlights around the sleeves and embroidery across the front.

She turned to face Jane, looking again in the mirror with the long handle that matched her brush. Holding it aloft, she swiveled her head side to side. "Beautiful indeed."

Jane's hands worked quickly, lacing up the dress. "I will have your bed turned down when you come back."

"Thank you." Johnston walked over to her bag, pulling out three more blades of various sizes, and then set them beside the small dagger she had pulled from her hair.

"My lady?" Jane's eyes widened.

"These are dangerous times." Johnston turned to the door. The sun was now gone below the horizon, leaving a fiery light through the hallway, amplified by flickering candles. Johnston instinctively headed to the balcony overlooking the dining hall. The woman from the kitchens bustled around, setting the long tables. She marveled at the fluidity of the workers as they prepared the hall for the evening.

"Will you join me in my chamber until dinner?" Lady Murray stepped beside Johnston.

"Seeing them preparing dinner reminds me of home." Johnston looked over to the lady and smiled grimly. "Yes, we have much to discuss." She turned to follow Lady Murray down the hall to her chamber.

Once there, Lady Murray picked up the sconce and poured two glasses, handing one to Johnston. "What did you think?"

Johnston sipped, closing her eyes and remembering her father slipping her sips of the local wine when they visited so many years ago in her youth. "Mmm." She took another long sip, tasting the wild berries from around the castle. "Smooth with unique flavors. Quite good." Johnston opened her eyes, setting the glass aside. She lowered her gaze and her smile, pushing the fond memories to the back, and focused on the current mission. "The Scots fell and were pushed to Sterling." Johnston looked down awhile before looking back at Lady Murray. "They thought they were fortified. Cromwell came across. The battle was over so quickly." She shook her head. A tear trickled down her cheek. "So many died. Hundreds, maybe thousands." Johnston picked up the glass to take a sip. "There is so much death," she whispered then took a deep breath. She pulled herself to the resolve. "I am sorry, Lady Murray…I am…my husband was in the battle at Invasion, and my home fell under siege." She spun her story to fit history. "Then Cromwell took my home, Castle Campbell."

"I am sorry. I, too, fear for my husband. He and our sons." She refocused, setting her personal grief aside. "Our men went to help in the fight. I will see him again." She smiled with resolve. "I fear more for the people here under my care. You said you were staying ahead of Cromwell's advancement?"

"Yes." Johnston lowered her voice. "The army was, maybe, only half a day's ride behind me. I would not be surprised if they made Perth within the day."

Lady Murray gasped, whispering, "What will we do if they advance forward?" She stood, holding the glass in her hands with anxiety. "What if they come here?" Taking a moment to regain her composure, she looked to Johnston then sat back down. "What can I do for you?"

"I am merely passing through, my lady." Johnston paused, taking a sip and wondering what of her mission she should divulge. "I am headed to a cousin in Dunnottar Castle. I have family there."

"How will you get there?"

"I am not sure. My horse fell a ways from here. I will walk if I have to, but I was hoping to negotiate getting a horse if you have one available." Johnston held her gaze. "I know these are hard times. I would expect to compensate you generously."

Lady Murray sat, quietly contemplating a moment. "What compensation do you have in mind?"

"This." Johnston reached forward, holding a locket in her hand. "And a portion of gold that I brought with me."

She took the locket from Johnston's hand, looking over it carefully and turning it over and over again. "This locket has my mother's crest. Where did you find it?"

"We met once a few years ago. Your mother spoke well of you." Johnston leaned back in her chair, looking to the fire. "Your mother gave this to me in gratitude for a favor, and now I pass it on to you."

Lady Murray studied the crest closely as a tear welled in her eye. Then she looked to the fire. "We have only one horse. It is my husband's. The rest are our with the boys in the fight or belong to those seeking refuge."

"I do not want to create tension between you and your husband."

"Nonsense. I have more pressing matters with the threat of Cromwell nearly on my doorstep." She took a sip of wine. "Besides, that is the least of your troubles. The horse is arrogant and will not let anyone ride him. My husband is still breaking him. He would not take this petulant horse into battle." Lady Murray looked to Johnston.

"I have some experience with headstrong horses."

"I will not take any compensation if you are not able to ride him."

"That sounds fair." Johnston continued within the next breath, "The locket is yours. You deserve it for your hospitality. I wish it to give you hope and remind you that you are not alone."

Lady Murray looked back to the locket. "Thank you."

***

The next morning greeted Johnston with a beautiful sunrise through the cloudless sky. Her blue dress seemed to match the blue of the sky. Her explorations of the castle led her back to the courtyard and into the stables. She looked in on a line of various colored tails of browns, reds, and blacks, each diligently shooing away the flies. A few of the horses' turned their heads to her as a greeting when she entered the area. A few younger horses leaned toward her, excited, hoping to see one of their family members, but Johnston or any person with an apple would do. A few of the older horses peeked around, hoping for a person with oats or hay. And with disappointment, they returned to ignoring the world.

Johnston smiled with the satisfaction of finding a place to hide from the expectations of her persona, out of the way of the choreographed dance of the castle yet surrounded by familiar friendly faces, even if they were equine. She walked past the open stalls to the closed stalls near the back.

With the sun rising above the horizon, her next stop was the orchard. The shadows of the trees retreated; Johnston stepped out to find the apples and pears left at her feet beneath the tree. The trees' limbs drooped heavy with early ripening fruit and no sign of picking except from birds.

The trees were neglected with the majority of the people absent from the castle. She selected a handful of fruit, placing them into a basket. She paused to look at the glistening sunlight through the trees across the orchard and back at the shadows reaching to the castle walls.

Johnston carefully picked a basket of fruit not quite fit for people but perfect for the others she just met who would welcome a treat.

Returning to the stable, she quietly slipped in the door. Again, the younger horses greeted her, but this time the older ones also perked their ears, keeping their attention to Johnston, fixated on the aroma coming from Johnston's basket.

A smile brightened her face, knowing she would be improving the day for at least a few. One by one, she worked her way to each horse and through the stalls. Each horse took two delectable treats from her hands. Some impertinent youths tried to search the basket across her back for just one more.

"Not today." She laughed, stepping back yet continuing to place one hand under their jaws and rubbing their noses and foreheads. "We need enough for everyone."

The more worldly horses graciously received the treat, nodding thanks then returning to their personal room once it was clear. They had received their ration. They were grateful but knew better than to get greedy.

Suddenly, a loud thumping sounded as a hoof hit a wooden stall door followed by a snort shattered the peace in the room.

Johnston tilted her head at the rudeness. "I will get to you when I get down there!" She sighed. "Prince or not, you are still here!"

She walked to the next stall. The horse with the dark brown coat kept looking to the end of the stable, then flinched when Johnston caressed his nose. Laying his ears back, he paused and continued to look in the direction of the disruption. "We are all taking this in different ways," Johnston told him. The gelding sighed, turning his attention to her. "I know you wish you were in the battle too."

He bobbed his head up and down then exhaled, letting his lips flutter a bit, looking down at the end again. Finally, he exhaled and looked at Johnston.

She chuckled, smiling. "I completely understand. Why should a young upstart be allowed to have tantrums when you are in the same predicament? Yet you carry yourself as a gentleman."

One last low bowing nod as she held out an apple to him.

"Shhh. These were going to waste in the orchard. Just sitting on the ground." She looked at him, shaking her head. "Why let these"—she held out an apple to him—"go to waste when you and the others can enjoy them when we all are waiting and tension."

He nodded then looked down at the closed stall.

"Oh, I got some for him too." She sighed. "He may not want them." She sighed then held up the pear to the horse with maple eyes. "Oh, youth in the spring with love in the air."

He nodded again and then took the pear, munching it happily.

Smiling, she walked in the end stall. The door was too tall to look over, so she pulled a stool over to climb on top. Her fingers hooked over the top of the door. She pulled herself up just a little bit further to peek over the top while keeping one toe over the stool to remember where it was when the time came to lower herself back down.

The sleek black horse with a white stripe between his eyes down to the snip at the tip of his nose stood and glared at her. He reared up then shook his head when his front hooves hit the ground.

"Oh, please." Johnston's teacher voice came out. "If you don't want an apple and pear, then I can just give them to someone else out here who can behave."

The youthful horse laid his ears back then stood still, twitching his muscles and wanting to act out but desiring the treat even more.

"Very well." Johnston gestured at him. "I'm coming in. You have to behave." She paused for a response from the hotheaded stallion.

Johnston slowly lowered herself, hoping the stool was still firmly where her toe once was. Much to her relief, her foot rested firmly on it. Carefully, she lowered herself to the ground, trying not to fall. The wooden latch twisted easily, releasing the door to swing open an inch or two. Silently, Johnston slipped inside, clasping the hook behind her. She turned to face the horse in front of her.

He stood, holding back every urge to release all his energy. He pranced, giving in to the temptation a bit.

"Very well. You earned this." Johnston held out the apple to him in the palm of her hand.

He devoured the apple almost too quickly to enjoy it and then looked at her with anticipation, prancing a bit.

"Oh, you like pears even more?" She smiled.

His head bobbed up and down as he started to sniff on her, looking for another precious prize. She held the pear in one palm, reaching to his neck with her other hand. She stroked his neck gently while he inhaled the pear, crunching and slobbering bits of pear onto her hand. An odd sensation of relaxation rippled through his tense muscles as her hand continued to stroke his neck.

"I'll try to take you out to the meadow to let you release some of this energy and spring fever and pent-up frustration." She turned to leave the stall. Suddenly, a nose pushed her elbow. Turning, she stroked his muzzle and his jaw. "I'll be right back." She slipped out of the stall, closing the door behind her.

She turned to the building on the end that contained the rope and tack and came face-to-face with two boys. She could not tell if their cheeks were covered in freckles or pimples. Their eyes were wide with surprise.

"What are you…?" One sprang up from his stool near the door. "My lady," he stammered before looking at her feet.

"I am taking the black horse in the end stall out." She grabbed the long rope then turned back to the end stall.

"Oh, of course." Realization and shock flooded over his face. "You don't mean…"

"Warn her about Ingwe." The small blond boy's hand tugged on the shirt of the taller boy. "She might get hurt!"

Sucking breath, the tall brown-haired boy ran up to her. "You might want to let us take care of Ingwe at the end." His eyes were wide. "He has a temper."

"Ingwe. Is that his name?"

"Yes, my lady," the blond boy eagerly said.

"And what are your names?"

"I'm Mathew, and he is Charles," the blond boy piped up excitedly.

"Tell me, Mathew, why is Ingwe such a menace?"

"He tries to attack anyone other than Master Murray. His eyes burn with hatred," the little blond boy piped up.

"I think I'll take my chances, thank you." Johnston continued knotting the rope into what she would need. "Charles, can you and Mathew see that all the horses get an apple or pear from orchard?" The long walk to the end stall was interrupted with Mathew pleading with her not to go in.

She reached the door to the stall. Suddenly, the sound of the hoof slamming into the door made Johnston pause.

"See. I told ya," Mathew whispered, his eyes wide and looking up at Johnston.

She frowned, pulling her teacher voice again. She scolded the horse. "Do you want to get out or not?" A long moment of silence was followed by a low sigh on the other side of the gate. "Very well then." Johnston twisted the wooden peg, cracking the door open. She slipped in, hearing two gasps behind her.

Ingwe paused a brief moment before stepping closer, poking his nose to the hidden fruit. Johnston pulled out the first pear and handed it to him.

He munched it happily as she knotted the rope into a loop. Reaching her arm through the loop, she started rubbing his nose with her hand. And then slowly she lifted the rope over his nose and over his ears. He jumped a bit, realizing he was snared, and then pulled his head away. Johnston loosened the slack of the rope then rewarded him with a second pear. Again, he munched happily as she looped the rope around his muzzle. Again, he pulled back. Johnston stepped to the side. "I thought you wanted to let out some energy?"

Ingwe shook his head a moment left and right then paused, shaking it up and down.

He stood with his ears laid back and stomped the ground.

Slowly, Johnston opened the door. The young black horse reared and started to run as Johnston anticipated his excitement for freedom. She pulled down on the rope. The rope tightened around his muzzle, surprising him. Shocked, he stepped back. "Shall we?" Johnston walked out of the stall. Ingwe pranced, almost jogging in place as the two headed out the door.

The two boys stood, jaws gaping, unable to put words to their amazement.

With her head held high, she walked from the stable through the entrance and out to the open meadow. The excitement of Ingwe overflowed as he reared up to start a run. Johnston let loose about three yards of rope, slowly leading the horse around into an arc, starting a canter around her. She released the rest of the rope. Using it like a whip, she snapped his heels, spurring him into a gallop. She loosened the rope to six yards as he started kicking with excitement while galloping around Johnston.

She relaxed a bit, watching the black mane toss freely in the wind and the white feathers around his large hooves flow in the breeze. She empathized with the need to let loose, to head out from captivity of her responsibility to continue her mission to Dunnottar. As Ingwe continued his exuberant run, she felt her own captivity drift away. The knots in her shoulders loosened slightly.

After a therapeutic run, Ingwe slowed to a canter. Then he bobbed his head and walked to her. His skin glistened with sweat. He sighed before nuzzling her arm.

"You smart boy!" Johnston reached for the third pear she kept hidden from him until this moment. Palming the pear, she reached out. This time, he slowly savored the sweet juices, munching the yellowy brown fruit. Johnston wiped the pear slobber from her hand.

"You don't seem like an Ingwe," she mentioned, looking into his brown eyes. "Ingwe was a member of a horrifying tribe." Her thoughts wandered to her own time and the tribes living out in the ice belts past Uranus and Neptune. "But that was a different war in a different time." Johnston looked into his eyes. "You seem more like a Liam. It means strong protector."

His ears perked excitedly.

"Now let's get you cared for. Don't want your muscles to lock up due to the temperature and the wetness from coat." They walked to the orchard to cool down and get another treat. The walk back to the castle was relaxed, but he stepped high with a happy and tired feeling.

The two walked back toward Huntingtower Castle and were met by Lady Murray. Her mouth opened and eyes widened as the horse with white feathers pranced into the yard. "I had to see it with my own eyes. He won't let anyone but my husband touch him."

"That explains his pent-up energy. He is rather reasonable to a person with a firm hand." Johnston smiled. "I used to drive Father crazy being the only other person, besides him, that the horse would obey." She paused, looking down as the smile dropped a bit. "Well," she continued, "I am happy to be of assistance with him." She reached over to stroke Liam's neck.

"That is amazing." Lady Murray continued shaking her head in disbelief "My husband was still having trouble with him. That is why he wasn't taken when they rode off to battle."

"I haven't tried riding him. I only took him out on the lead. Hopefully, the stable boys have had enough time to clean out his stall. It looked a bit overdue." Johnston continued to lead the cocky stallion into the stable.

Lady Murray walked alongside them. "Do you think you will take him out tomorrow?" she asked.

The two boys stepped out from the stall, bowing deeply as the two women approached.

"I think I will try a saddle on him tomorrow, see how he reacts." She looked over to the taller boy. "Charles, will you help me brush him down before he goes back in his stall?"

"Yes, my lady." The boy's eyes widened with excitement.

"I look forward to our evening chat." Lady Murray smiled. "It seems we have much to discuss."

"I look forward to it." Johnston lowered her head in a bow.

"Boys, be mindful of Lady Ogilvy. You can learn much from her mastery of equine." Murray turned to Johnston. "This evening."

Johnston replied, "Of course, Lady Murray."

Lady Murray turned, leaving the stables as Johnston continued to lead Liam down to the end. Charles followed, watching her every move. She tied the rope in the slipknot around the wooden base. The two worked together to towel off the remaining sweat and brushed him down before returning him to the stable.

Exhausted and happy to be in a cleaned stable, he rolled in the fresh straw. Johnston shook her head, chuckling.

***

Jane continued to brush Johnston's hair. She closed her eyes, relaxing. The work clothes were draped over the back of the chair with dirt caked on them. The evening ritual of cleaning up and getting her hair brushed and put up before joining Lady Murray was relaxing. Johnston was looking forward to this time to herself as Jane removed a bit of stress with each stroke of her brush.

Jane took cue from Johnston not to pester her with a thousand questions.

"There you are." Jane stepped back, setting the brush on the stand. "I am sure Lady Murray is waiting."

Johnston sighed. "Thank you."

"You are very welcome, Lady Ogilvy." Jane took her leave.

The name Ogilvy reminded Johnston of the mission. Worry and uneasiness settled back into her shoulders, and she started feeling a bit guilty over her level of comfort and enjoyment in her new evening ritual.

Slowly, she rose from her chair. Reaching over, she grabbed the loop on the candleholder and made her way to the door. The light created eerie wavering shadows along the stone walls. The rafters gained a lot of character with the deep shadows in the features of the rough beams. The door to Lady Murray's room looked so much more dramatic with the flickering candlelight than it had been five days ago. Johnston still marveled over the craftsmanship and wonder of the castle, fully functional and relatively new at roughly 150 years old.

The echo of her shave-and-a-hair-cut, two-bits knock penetrated through the door and was answered by the voice of Lady Murray, muffled by the door. "Come in."

Johnston pushed the door open, gliding in gracefully over to her chair as Jane poured wine in the glass, setting it next to Johnston.

Lady Murray continued to gaze at the fire, smiling and slowly opening her eyes. "I want to thank you," she said as Jane stepped away silently.

"Thank me?" Johnston quirked her head.

She looked up at Johnston, changing the subject. "Your mastery of horse training astounds me. Where did you learn this?"

"My father acquired a trainer from France who trained many horses for the DeJauns. I loved working with horses for the beauty and pure loyalty once their trust is gained."

"Quite astounding. I am curious how he handles for you and a saddle tomorrow."

"I don't plan on being in the saddle at first. We will see how he reacts with something on his back before I take to the saddle."

Johnston sat with her thoughts and reached over to take a sip of wine. She returned her gauze to Lady Murray, who was calmly stitching.

The time continued to pass silently. Johnston wished she had brought her field journal to study while Lady Murray stitched to the broken rhythm of the crackling fire.

The fire dwindled over time to mere flickering embers by now, red and gold peeking out from behind the black burnt coals.

"I think I will retire for the evening." Johnston reached over with a lighting stick, placing it into the embers, lighting it then lighting her candle. She stood, nodding. "It has been a pleasure as always."

Johnston quietly padded through the hallway back to her room. Once in the privacy of the room, she loosened the corset and removed her dress. Keeping her floor-length chemise on, she climbed into bed to drift into dreams.

Johnston settled her racing mind by focusing on how to finish training Liam.

***

The late morning sun beamed into the stables. Johnston walked in, stopping near the tack. Mere second passed before Charles ran to her. "Can I help?" His eyes were wide with eagerness.

"Can you help me select a saddle I might be able to use?"

His eyes widened even more. "You're going to ride him!"

Johnston smiled. "Come, young jauntling. Let me teach you."

"Young what?"

"Trainee. The word is like apprentice." Her thoughts wandered back to the academy.

Charles's face glowed with a huge smile. "You will teach me!"

"And Mathew." She leaned in to say softly, "Though I think you may learn faster than him. You are older, with much more experience."

"Yes, my lady."

"Which tack"—she sighed—"is he accustomed to?"

Charles pointed to the saddle and bit. "That one is what he was being trained with."

"I think I want to call him Liam. The name Ingwe invokes memories of fear and savagery." She walked over to the tack, remembering the savages in the depths of space with tribal tattoos like leopard spots covering their face. She made sure all straps had no rough edges to rub soreness on a long journey. Johnston explained this to Charles. Carefully, she selected the tack to be used. "Can you take this outside the wall where we ran off his energy yesterday?"

"Well, yes." Charles asked, "But why?"

"I'll explain when we get out there." She grabbed the rope. "Get Mathew to help you carry all of this."

Charles hustled off to get Mathew as Johnston walked to the end stall. She knocked the same rhythm she used before opening the stall on the three previous days. Excited, Liam nodded, acknowledging Johnston as she stepped in. He pranced a moment before Johnston stepped in. "Do you want to go out? Then hold still so I can get your lead on."

He sighed impatiently.

He huffed then lowered his head to the level of her elbow to be roped. The two walked out to the meadow to the castle. She grabbed the lead firmly before rounding the corner, but to her surprise, he didn't react when he saw the two boys. At this, she improvised her original plans and walked him over to the pile of tack. He recognized the items and got fussy before Johnston pulled his lead tight and placed her hand on her neck.

"Go ahead and put the gear on him." She looked into his eyes, thinking of her impending mission, and he was her best hope to accomplish this. "Don't run. Walk. Talk calmly to each other while you saddle him."

"Yes, my lady," the two said in unison.

Liam's ears turned back, noting their location.

Johnston continued advising them on what she was found and why. When Liam had the saddle on him, she stopped them short of placing the bit in his mouth. "We need to let him run a bit to see how he reacts with the empty saddle." he looked at them. "I will find out now if he will throw me before I take a seat."

She saw a light flare up in a dark castle window as she walked Liam to the meadow. Just like yesterday, she started a trot, then canter, and into a full gallop. Liam enjoyed the freedom and running, though short-lived, as she reined him in.

"We will try the bit now," she said to Liam. The boys continued to hang on her every word.

Together they walked over to the wall, and she loosened the rope from his muzzle and neck. Gently, she guided the bit into his mouth behind his teeth and guided the reins over his neck. He watched her, turning his head back toward where she now stood.

"We have a ladder." Charles lugged the wooden stool almost as big as him over to them.

"Thank you, Charles, but I will need to teach him to accommodate me. I will not have a ladder with me everywhere I go." She secured the reins on the saddle horn then walked back to his head, placing the rope around his muzzle. "We are going to learn something new today." She locked eyes with the dark chestnut eyes of Liam. "Down," she stated, and then she applied firm pressure on the rope still looped around his muzzle toward the ground.

Liam shook his head in defiance.

"Down." Johnston continued the constant pressure, imagining him in the process of lowering himself for her to sit upon his back.

Liam looked up at her, holding back the look of insult to his pride. Johnston could imagine the thoughts running through his head. *What the hell is this crazy woman doing?* But she remained firm.

"I need you to kneel down." She imagined the action again in her thoughts as she firmly spoke the words. "Down." She lowered his head a little more with a steady pressure, not hurting but unrelenting discomfort.

Slowly, he bent his front legs, lowering his body to the ground. Johnston immediately released the tension, stroking his neck and producing a pear. She loosened the rope around the muzzle so that he could enjoy his reward.

Liam munched happily as Johnston stroked his neck. She let him stand again before proceeding through the same ritual. Again, he ended kneeling on the ground, happily munching another pear.

On the third try, Johnston only said the word once before Liam knelt to munch on a pear. She stroked his muzzle and neck lightly.

This time, she walked alongside him, placing one foot on a stirrup. Liam looked behind him to her as she settled herself onto the saddle. Once settled, Liam stood with a slight uneasiness and pranced a bit, getting used to the added weight to his back. Johnston adjusted her skirts and then gripped the reins tightly, one in each hand. With a slight nudge of her heels, he started to canter onto the open field.

She pulled down and back on the reins gently. He slowed into a trot and then walked. She continued to test his training until she was satisfied. Finally, she loosened the reins and let him run. Leaning down and lifting herself up off the saddle, she felt the wind start working its fingers, taking down her hair lock by lock.

The meadows turned into trees and hills as the path took them to the overlook. Johnston reined back Liam as she ran her hand over her hair, guiding the loose strands behind her ear.

The path led down the slope into another large meadow and then through trees and grass until Johnston knew playtime was almost over. They needed enough energy to get home. Johnston pulled her reins, turning Liam back to the castle. Liam slowed a bit when his excitement settled in his muscles, leaving them heavy. Johnston let him walk to regain his breath. The return took much longer than the trip out. A long hour later, they reentered the meadow overlooking the line of trees, with the roof of the castle peering over the treetops.

Three horsemen rode along the tree line then ducked into the leaves toward the castle.

Johnston spurred Liam into a canter to follow them, but she was too far behind. By the time she reached the courtyard, the riders were two strides from the castle entrance, and the horses were being led to the stables. Johnston slid from the top of the saddle, sighing, disappointed that she had just missed the excitement. She gathered up the reins, leading Liam into his stall.

Her excitement was overwhelming. She wanted to run into Lady Murray's chamber to hear the news, to live the experience. She calmed her childish impulses and walked into the stables. Watching the two boys bustling to take care of the rider's horses, she decided to spend the time taking care of Liam herself, brushing him and wiping him down.

She found herself talking to him or to herself. She really didn't know at this point. She remembered the hills behind her parents' home and the gardens out front. The image of her parents' house came clear in her mind as she spoke to Liam. She wished she could take him there and ride through the hills and trees. If only. She rubbed his nose one more time before leaving the stall and heading to the castle.

Late into the evening, Lady Murray approached Johnston. "Lady Ogilvy, the evening is getting late. You were correct. The army has made it to Perth." Exhaustion filled her eyes. "We may have to table our nightcap until the morning."

"Very well, Lady Murray." Johnston paused. "May I inquire if you intend to send any scouts to monitor the progress or movement of the English army in the morning?"

"Yes. William is trusted. He was too frail to join the battle, but his knowledge of the obscured paths will serve him well as it already has today. I wish you to be in my chamber shortly after sunup tomorrow. I should like your insight after I receive his news on the troop movements."

"Then sleep well this evening. I shall join you at sunlight." Johnston lowered her head then watched Lady Murray head down the hallway to her chamber. The lives within the castle weighed heavily on her decisions.

Johnston wished she could lay her head on the pillow and drift into her dreams. She was no longer a teenager with insomnia. She knew remaining in the hall to be vigilant over the activities would be painful at first light, but she did not want to be blindsided by any turn of events. Though she doubted an allegiance between any of the guests seeking refuge might turn into an opportunistic takeover, she could not risk contributing or changing history by going downstairs. She knew her actions may have altered the timeline already; she had to minimize the potential damage.

She laid in bed, staring at the darkness. Threads of worry wove webs in her mind, preventing the depths of sleep from coming.

***

Despite trying, sleep did not come to Johnston that night. The hours crept by. Without a clock, the ticking was within her head, echoing through her attempted dreams. The fire in her hearth dwindled, once a party of dancing scarlet wisps upon the logs. Now merely one or two wisps remained over the glowing embers, and finally no wisps remained. The logs popped lethargically with glimpses of glowing red from within the cracks. With the retreat of the fire, the slight chill that came in early morning July had taken over the room, along with the darkness. Still, tick…tick…tick…

Finally giving up on sleeping, Johnston decided to venture into the chill. Wrapping her dressing gown with a thick blanket, she lit a candle from the glowing embers before adding a couple logs to the fire. She poked the embers to expose the heat to rekindle the flames, then she retrieved her field notebook. The prickle of electricity was invisible to most and unnoticed, but to those outside of the agency, the scan ran over her fingers. She opened the book as she sat in the chair, wrapped in blankets with the candle on her right. She curled up in the chair near the fire to review her journal and make notes. She had been diligent on marking off the days but became complacent on making notes on the daily activities. In the candlelight, she sat remembering the previous day's events.

She knew the importance for two reasons. Journaling and reviewing her notes would keep her focused and prevent her from going native. Second, the updates would instantly transmit to the agency, keeping them from sending agents after her for going rogue.

The slow clatter of hooves on stone caught her attention outside the window. William must have been heading out on his mission. She walked to the window, looking to the courtyard below. The old man teetered, leaning heavily on his staff and walking over to the horse being held by a small boy, Mathew. Johnston recognized the tussled hair of his silhouette. The man slowly and carefully climbed onto the back of the horse. The transformation was almost astonishing. Though his leg might betray him on the ground, he was released once he sat in the saddle, sitting tall on the back of that horse. With a smooth gesture snapping the reins, the two galloped into the tree line.

A tinge of jealously crept through Johnston's thoughts. She did want to be out there heading back to Perth, finding out the position of the troop's firsthand. The sitting and waiting were more than she could bear. She pushed those thoughts away and returned to her journaling.

Each minute dragged by as she watched the hours pass. The dark indigo of the window warmed into a deep purple. She set her book near the bed stand and then turned to the window, looking for the sun peaking above the horizon, and it started its morning advance with feathers of crimson stretching across the sky and lightening to a fiery orange. It announced the arrival of the sun as it peaked over the horizon.

A soft knock echoed through the room, bringing Johnston's attention back. "Come," Johnston called, not moving from the window.

Jane crept in the room without disturbing the peace of the sunrise. Johnston wondered how she managed to get through the door without the obnoxious creaking and latching sound.

"Shall we get you dressed?" Jane soundlessly crossed the room.

"Yes." Johnston sighed, not wanting to leave the window for the still dark room. "Let the day begin."

In mere minutes, Johnston found herself synched and tied into her proper dress, the one that matched the fire of the morning sky. She followed Jane up the hall, their dresses rustling across the floor past Lady Murray's chamber, continuing down the corridors into the study.

"Good morning, my lady." Jane paused at the door.

"Enter." Lady Murray looked up from the pile of papers in front of her. "I expect William back any time." She looked over to Jane. "Thank you, Jane. You may leave us."

Jane nodded then disappeared from the room in one fluid motion.

"What are your thoughts from last evening?" Lady Murray glanced up at Johnston, who took a seat in the chair opposite the desk from her.

"Setting aside the siege of Perth, those here are already wearied because of their exhaustion under the circumstance. They would not wish to continue to flee farther toward the highlands. This is advantageous for us." Johnston quirked her mouth, trying to find the right words. "A worst case scenario, the English army has scouts watching this castle." Johnston looked directly at Lady Murray. "I do not have any evidence to support this to be true." She paused for breath to physically relax before continuing, "You are the steward of this castle, of these people within these walls." Johnston remembered her history. Cromwell would be heading south about now in pursuit of his prey. "The question you need to ask is, do these people have the energy to continue running, or do you make a stand knowing that your fate ties with those seeking refuge within these walls?"

Alarm crossed Lady Murray's face as she sighed.

"You know these people better than any advice I can give you. Stay here or keep running?" *It would be best to stay here*, Johnston thought. The English forces would soon leave without coming this far north. They were safe; they just needed to hunker down and stay here.

Lady Murray closed her eyes, breathing deeply. "We cannot keep running." She looked into Johnston's eyes. "You stayed, being of the last to leave your home when it fell." She looked up, thinking a bit longer, and then stated, "We must stand. We are Scots. Those within these walls are exhausted. They are here for refuge, safety. If we leave before there is a true threat, before the enemy is at our gate, then we are cowards."

"I agree," Johnston continued. "What about posting additional guards on the towers to give as much advanced notice on any movement this direction from Perth?"

"Yes," Lady Murray said.

The rapping of a staff from the other side of the doorway interrupted the silent tension, though Johnston suspected the thought had reached its conclusion.

"My Lady Murray." The old man hobbled in, favoring his left side. The staff hit the ground in stride with his right foot. Injury did nothing to lower him; he would only lower himself slightly in the presence of Lady Murray, when he removed his hat and leaned into a deep bow. With his grayish white hair pulled back under the hat, he reminded Johnston of a man she once loved.

"William, what news do you bring?" Lady Murray returned the greeting with a nod.

William looked cautiously to Johnston, but with an approving nod from Lady Murray, he continued, "The English army is dispersing. They appear to be heading back south."

"What evidence of this do you have?" The relief in Lady Murray's voice was apparent, though tension remained in her shoulders.

"The soldiers have broken camp overnight. The majority of the men had moved out by the time I arrived at the overlook, but they were still packing the supplies into the wagons. The wagons that were packed were headed back south. I can only surmise the rest of the wagons with supplies shall follow suit."

"What is your feel on this? Do you think they might be planning to flank our position?"

"I do not believe so, my lady. They would flank to the southwest, where the supplies can be moved up the elevation. They are headed southeast."

"Do you agree, Lady Ogilvy?"

"Yes. King Charles is at Sterling. Or that is where his men were regrouping. Sterling is southwest, the same direction Cromwell's are departing." Johnston sighed. "King Charles's forces have had almost two weeks to regroup. They will either fortify in Sterling or make a move. Either way, the English army will not wish to delay longer by continuing their northern conquest. My main worry now is to the safety of King Charles and our men. The English army are heading for them."

Johnston walked over to the maps unrolled on the desk.

Nodding confirmation, Lady Murray looked from Johnston to William. "What are your thoughts on this matter?"

William looked flat at Lady Murray, not hiding his mistrust of the newcomer in the room. "Her conclusions and information are consistent with that I have heard and seen."

Lady Murray leaned back. "There is much about you, Lady Ogilvy, that is still a mystery to me, but I appreciate and trust your consultation." Lady Murray's focus changed, now looking to the rest of the people within her chambers. She continued with unquestionable authority ringing in her voice. "No one will leave the castle until we have conformation Cromwell's army has left Perth." She looked to William. "You will return to the overlook and report back when all troops are gone, or tomorrow morning. We must be sure the army has departed.

"We will not bring attention to our presence by obligatory arming and readying for battle. We do not have the supplies or the personnel to do so. Discretion is what we need. Be prepared for the worst. Fortify the castle to prepare. Our loyal force to defend us is not here. We must rely on our cunning."

Lady Murray returned her focus to the maps as everyone left the room, leaving Johnston alone with Lady Murray.

***

Johnston rubbed her forehead with her index finger and thumb, reminding how much her eyes did not like reading in the dim candlelight. She reached, her hand gliding over to the wine glass, picking it up from the stand next to her chair. She slowly sipped the wine, allowing her eyes to remain shut a few moments longer.

She opened her eyes, hoping her eyes would adjust in the darkness to read the status of the history. According to the history in the Px Dome, with comparison to the flux around her, the English army headed south to encounter the Scotch army under King Charles II. The overall timeline was unchanged. Johnston breathed a sigh of release. So far so good. The lines on the map parchment meandering across the countryside resembling knots of string tangled in a

Scotland-shaped design. The lines of trails she would need to remember if she would ride to Dunnottar.

"Did you hear me?" Lady Murray's voice came from the darkness from the room. "We just got word from Perth."

Johnston closed her journal and rubbed her temples, head throbbing as her eyes continued to remind her that she was no longer young enough to read script that long in such lighting. "I am sorry?"

Lady Murray shook her head. "We got confirmation. The English army is heading for Sterling. They say King Charles mobilized his army." The next question hung in the air before it was uttered. "Where do you think our men are heading?"

"It is hard to say." Johnston drew out her words. She knew the answer, but what would she say to Lady Murray? Based on the date, the royalist army would be marching south. The king had decided on a last offensive toward London after arguing with his generals. This last offense might be a surprise, and she didn't want to raise suspicion on herself. Her mind wandered through the possibilities. Then again, maybe it was obvious. "North toward Perth and the English army, or probably headed south to…England or London? There are not too many options."

Lady Murray's head turned in surprise. "London?"

Or maybe it wasn't so obvious. Johnston looked over to Lady Murray, her youth coming through the facade. "There are truly only two directions the king's army would go. North toward Perth or south. If they had headed north toward our location, I suspect the English army would have been less eager to move. They would stay and find an opportune location to dig in and fight. Given the army has left Perth heading south, it is reasonable to deduce that they are in pursuit of King Charles's forces to intercept them before they reach their destination. It makes sense they would hit Cromwell at the heart, London, Parliament." Johnston sighed, sipping her wine again.

Johnston could see Lady Murray studying her, looking back and forth from Johnston to the fire, then to the wine. Johnston could see the thoughts running through her mind until Lady Murray finally settled on a few words. "Lord Campbell must miss your strategic insight?"

Johnston's mind calculated the projected source of the questions then looked over. Lady Murray trusted her. Her eyes were relaxed. "I am sure he does." She smiled slightly then started to waver as thoughts of her own husband crept back into her mind like a weeping wound she thought had healed. "He…he taught me what I know." Johnston looked away from the fire, away from Lady Murray's eyes. "We would play chess for hours. That is how he won my heart and hand. He beat my father. Then much later, I finally beat him. I love how much I have learned from him. I only hope I can make him proud." Johnston blinked the glistening tear from her eye.

Lady Murray leaned in, smiling, her eyes watering a bit at the memory of her own beloved. "I…yes…" She smiled, taking a deep breath before continuing again. Looking into the crackling fire, she smiled. "I love my husband, but it was not that way when I met him. My father arranged the union." Her voice deepened a moment, imitating her father. "Mutually beneficial to the families." Her voice returned again to her own sweet soft tone. "I was so young. I missed my family, my sisters, and mother. I was so lonely with the obligations. The image he portrayed to maintain his position was…" Her voice trailed off, looking into the fire. A sigh escaped as she continued. The words came slowly as though they had never really been said before now. "My mother came to visit, worried. She said love was a luxury that our status could not afford. That I should look for those things we hold in common. I should hold faith that Father would not allow a marriage where I would not be able to find a common interest." A smile returned as her distant gaze turned back to the room. "Exploration of the area and meeting the people under our protectorate." She paused as she started to smile. "Once I started getting to know the people around me and how he has touched them all, they became family. I started learning about my husband through those he ruled. In a way, they are our extended family. Charles, Mathew, every person within these walls." She looked back to Johnston. "He did not strive to earn my love through chess, but in the end, I love him and could not imagine my life without him." She smiled, holding her new locket in her hand, wiping away tears with lace embroidered tissue.

Johnston understood how her gift of the locket was so important to Lady Murray; it reminded her how much her mother and grandmother still stood behind her. Johnston raised her eyes, and Lady Murray tried to talk, but Johnston continued before she could interrupt. "We…" She paused to inject carefully. "John and I…" She then slipped back into the memories. "I had my duties, my obligations even then." Johnston smiled with the relief of finally being able to talk after years. "He…" She looked back to Lady Murray. "Sometimes life interferes with what you want. We would be happy together right now if…" Johnston sighed, collecting herself after emotions got the better od her. Johnston choked back a few tears. "We…we will get through this. We are Scottish!"

Lady Murray smiled. Both women sat silently for a long moment, understanding each other in the deep pain brought by separation from loved ones and the worry of the unknown and scared of the worst, yet mentioning the worry might make the worst fear come to pass.

"What will you do next?" Lady Murray tried to regain her voice with a cough before continuing, "If the English army is indeed moving south, we have a reprieve even, if a temporary one." Lady Murray continued looking to the fire. "You are, of course, welcome to stay as long as you wish." A hint of longing for a friend, an equal to talk with in the difficult times and challenges ahead until normalcy, returned. It haunted her voice.

Johnston watched the fire crackle, desperately wanting to stay here with a newfound friend, in a place that she felt comfortable and helpful. She was really contributing and helping, but deep down she was afraid. She was afraid of leaving, fulfilling the words of Father Granger, protecting the Scottish Honours but getting killed in the process. "I'm happy here," she muttered quietly. "But I need to…"

Lady Murray smiled. "You are needed elsewhere. Your beloved may be there waiting by the time you get there. The same way mine will return to me."

"Yes." Johnston let her wishful thinking escape her thoughts. "I would like to return when this is all over. When life returns to normalcy." Her voice faded. She said this more for herself then added, "We will have much to catch up on."

"Our friendship in one forged in battle." Lady Murray smiled. "You will always be welcome here." She paused a moment longer. "In fact, I expect you to return when this is all behind us."

Johnston looked from the fire back to Lady Murray. "I fear there is another act in this play that is about to unfold tragically. You have brought me courage to continue the journey. Thank you."

Lady Murray leaned back in her chair, raising a glass. "I am glad to have helped you along your journey." She sipped from her glass. The night grew long as the two talked of old times and hoped for the future. Each reminisced of friends and stories from years long gone.

The stories and dreams continued until the fireplace grew dim with glowing seas of red between the icebergs of cooling coals. The only light remaining in the room danced in from the few candles.

For the first time in Johnston's visit, they embraced, not with the formalities of colleagues with similar titles but as friends. They spent a long moment wordlessly passing understanding and support through embrace, protestation from the unknown pain for a brief moment before facing life, standing with the observed wordless strength.

"I expect you to say farewell before you leave tomorrow." Lady Murray smiled as her eyes glistened with moisture.

"I will deeply miss you too," Johnston said. "With the good news that English army will no longer be an eminent threat, tomorrow morning, I do not need to leave first thing. Would you be interested in breakfast before I head out?"

"I would like that." Lady Murray smiled.

H ajjar ran into the alcove, providing protection around the door. He was trying unsuccessfully to dodge the rain drops bombarding the street.

The white clouds gathered through the day. By the early afternoon, they had massed into a large angry black blanket that reached across the entire sky, announcing its presence with flashes and thunder rolling through the river valley.

The two-story yellow building looked almost gray green in the pouring rain. Hajjar stepped under the overhang and into the alcove, letting his trench coat drip and shedding some of the water before opening the door and stepping in.

The warm lighting invited him. Again, bar signs spattered the walls, but this pub was more selective to the signs and their placement. Budweiser Clydesdales marched around a globe light hung above the beer pulls. Hajjar could almost hear the dripping of water from his coat echo though the room.

"Howdy." The chipper blond with her hair pulled into a braid welcomed him. "Sit where ya like. I'll be right there." Her accent was southeast, more Georgia peach than Texas twang.

He smiled at her, nodding then looking around the room. A row of booths lined the wall to his right. Leather seats with tall wooden walls between each booth all the way to the ceiling made each booth a cozy alcove looking onto the bar to his left. Tall wood and mirrors with glistening bottles of liquor lined the back of the bar. The British pub feel veered to the Americas with that Budweiser light glowing proudly over the bar top.

Hajjar scanned the empty booths then stepped closer to the bar. He looked up to the balcony above him, which overlooked the bar.

A smile of familiarity washed over Hajjar's face as he looked over to the bartender. He felt more at home in this pub. With dim lighting and wood surrounding him, it was just like the bar he learned to drink in at the academy.

He wandered to a booth in the front of the bar. Thursday proved to be a slow night. He expected more traffic from the waitress and bartender than people coming in from the entrance behind him. He slid into the cocoon-like booth. He scooted all the way back into the corner, into his wooden cave with the only opening to the world in front of him. He could open his field notebook and be able to use it to review his notes using the written setting that disabled the 3D projection from the screen and the keypad adaptation. He wanted to look like a person curled up in the back of the booth with a travel journal, while actually reviewing his notes on the assignment.

The waitress must have the second floor because the bartender walked up, asking what he would like to drink. Hajjar sat looking at the bartender, a man with his head shaved, yet he wore a mustache and goatee. His cheeks were as smooth and shiny as his head.

"What can I get you?" Shiny Top asked.

"What's your name?" Hajjar asked.

"Brian." He paused. "Our Thursday special is fifty-cent draft."

"Do you have Shiner?" Hajjar knew they would not have the Irish reds that he loved.

"Yeah, in the bottle."

"That's fine."

Brian returned to the bar, and moments later, Hajjar heard the *psst* and *clink* of a bottle opening and the cap falling atop a pile of collected caps. "What are you working on?" Brian sat the bottle in front of Hajjar.

He looked up, smiling slightly. "Notes."

"The semester is over. What notes?" His intrigue collected in the lines around his smile.

"Research doesn't stop for semester break, I'm afraid." Hajjar smiled with the annoyance of a person deep in contemplation. "I'm visiting schools looking onto postgrad options for law school. I'm reviewing the pros and cons of UT Law versus the other schools."

His look of slight irritation must have worked instead because Brian continued, "Sorry, it's just slow, and I am bored." Then he returned to the bar.

Hajjar watched him walk away then looked back to his field journal. A new message from his parents caught his eye on the bottom of the page. He smiled, pulling up the image of his parents now with gray starting to migrate from their temples to the rest of their head. The two stood proud. Tall fluted glasses rose, glittering in a toast. Behind them, through the observation shield, spun the rings of Saturn with the sunrise. It was a brilliant point of yellow light glittering through each colorful band, stretching out and curving around the sixth planet. They were on their thirtieth anniversary cruise through the outer planets.

Hajjar relaxed, settling into the booth with the table under his right arm and his legs propped up on the leather cushioned seat of the booth. He lifted the bottle to his lips and started to say something to Johnston out of habit before remembering that he was alone on this assignment. He looked back to the message from his parents.

He could not have rekindled his relationship with them if Johnston had not shown him how to balance the sensitivity of the assignments with the need to remain connected to those who cared about you.

He could almost hear Johnston's voice in his memories: "That one was particularly challenging, but you pulled it off." She stood with her hands in the front pockets of her slacks with a mentor's job well done, and then paused. "What do you do after a difficult case like this?"

They had just closed a bad case of stolen identity made worse by its impact to history, but they managed to track the clues to restore the Jewish nuclear physicist's honor and the timeline without being killed by the Germans during WWII. Hajjar remembered the thrill, terror, and wanting to talk to someone about it all, but the fellow cadets were all at least four years older than him and were outsharing their exploits over drinks.

"Going back to my dorm, sleeping," he lamely said.

"Come on," Johnston stated. "You are coming with me."

She made all the arrangements, and the next thing he knew, they were standing in the yard with the sun dipping below the tree-covered hills, casting early dark shadows in the foliage behind them. The dark shadows didn't matter; the warm lights of the library shone from the other side of the bay windows, beckoning them with words of knowledge and possible answers to the unknown questions.

"Come on. They are expecting us for dinner."

"Who?" Hajjar hastened his step on the crackling leaves to catch up.

"My parents." Johnston turned to look at him. "They are looking forward to meeting you."

"How?" Hajjar gasped, shock in his voice. "You can't talk about classified…stuff"—he looked around wildly—"with civilians!"

Johnston knocked on the door. "I know. I don't give details." She paused "Watch and learn." Then she turned to face the door, opening washing light over her and then onto Hajjar.

"Come in, Liz." Mrs. Johnston stepped out, wrapping her arms around her daughter.

"Mom, this is Agent Hajjar…umm." She looked over to Hajjar's expression of acceptance to the situation. "Ryan."

"Hello, Mrs. Johnston." He reached out a hand.

"Kathrine. No formality here." Johnston's mother pulled him into the house with the handshake.

Hajjar could see where his partner got her cheekbones and angled chin from. He sat in the booth, sipping a Shiner, remembering how Mrs. Johnston looked then much like Agent Elizabeth Johnston did now.

They continued into the kitchen, greeted by a man fully gray with an almost white beard. "TDI Hajjar." He leaned forward, grasping Hajjar's hand, shaking it with the firmness and making him feel like a man.

"Umm, not yet," Hajjar corrected him. "Just agent…" He looked at them exchanging glances. Then he added, "Call me Ryan."

"Agent…well, from what my daughter tells me, you will be a Time Detective Investigator soon." He looked at Johnston with a fatherly smile.

He looked over to Johnston, then back to Ryan. "From what Liz says, you will be soon enough." He smiled, leaning into Ryan's ear. "You want to join me for a drink? Let the two of them catch up."

"I remember when Liz first entered the academy," Mrs. Johnston said. "She was so young."

"I was fourteen, Mom." Johnston sighed.

Ryan remembered how impressed he was at the offer. He was not yet of drinking age. "I'm only nineteen."

"Legal drinking age in Germany is eighteen." Mr. Johnston shrugged.

"Go on." Johnston shook her head in amusement. "We are off the clock. You sure act old enough. You might as well relax a bit."

Hajjar chuckled at the memory of walking into the library, listening to one of the records from Mr. Johnston's vinyl collection. The collection was extensive, with original presses of Beatles, Led Zeppelin, Cream, Janis Joplin, Jimi Hendrix, CCR…the stack went on and on.

"I've been collecting them for years. My daughter helps add to the collection when she can."

"No matter how old I get, I'll always be his little girl." Johnston walked over to her dad, wrapping her arm around his waist as he pulled her shoulders close to him with his right arm.

"Dinner is almost ready." She turned to head back to the kitchen.

"That is our cue," Mr. Johnston said, handing Ryan a snifter of Cognac.

He took it like receiving the Holy Grail of blessed liquid, cupping the snifter in both hands before sipping it.

"You need to swirl it to let the nose, the aroma of the XO Cognac fill the glass. Then inhale the aroma while you sip. It enhances the taste," Mr. Johnston advised, holding the glass in his right hand. He lifted it and swirled it smoothly. "Then inhale and take a sip."

Hajjar swirled the liquid in the glass again and breathed in deeply before taking a drink. Wordlessly, he smiled, and then he followed Mr. Johnston into the kitchen, admiring and taking everything in.

"What have you been up to lately?" Mrs. Johnston, Kathrine, asked.

"You know, keeping the world safe." Johnston glanced over, catching Hajjar's eye.

"I hope it wasn't dangerous."

"Mom, we are agents. There is always a high level of danger with what we do."

"Well…you know I always worry."

"Yes, it was a case of stolen identity. The man, victim, was kidnapped by the person who stole his identity."

"Sounds stressful."

"Yes." She paused again. "But it is worth the endeavor." She gazed at each of her parents with a hint of love that Hajjar took a second glance to recognize. She leaned in, resting on her elbows, sipping her wine, looking into her mother's eyes.

Mrs. Johnston leaned back, pulling her lips into an uneasy smile. Changing the subject, she continued, "I just finished *Sense and Sensibility*." She sighed.

"Again?" Johnston smiled. "How many times have you read that book?"

"Well…a couple times. She is my favorite author."

Johnston breathed out a chuckle. "Romantic escape. What are we having this evening?"

"Lasagna." Mrs. Johnston looked at her daughter and Hajjar. "We need to open a new bottle." She blushed a bit. "We drank the last of that bottle. What would you like?" She looked at Liz.

"Whatever you have," Liz said.

"We have an amazing Cab that your sister picked up. A nineteenth-century wine. It is amazing."

"No…that sounds like an extra special bottle. She must have paid a lot of money on that vintage. I'd like to share that with you and Mary, not tonight."

Mrs. Johnston nodded, understanding the special importance of the bottle. "Yes, definitely." She smiled. "Do you know what she is doing lately?"

"Not really." Liz shook her head.

"High-end antique auction."

"Wow." Liz smiled, looking to Hajjar.

The plates were full of red meaty and layered Italian deliciousness. The dinner progressed with light talk of daily goings on. Hajjar sat quietly, watching the evening unfold.

Johnston's parents wanted to know but didn't ask. Why? Did they not want to know, or was it more intolerance was bliss? They wouldn't want the answer, or did they? Were they advised what not to ask? The dance between asking but not and answering but not completely continued through the night.

The evening flowed despite the limitations to conversational subjects. Hajjar injected a few words, comments to add conversation.

He couldn't shake the longing for his own parents. His mom's hummus and matchbous were comfort food. He remembered smelling the roast lamb with rice, the spices wafting through the hallways of the loft.

He closed his eyes, sitting in the pub, imagining the aroma as his stomach started to growl. He loved how his dad would get home from work just in time for dinner. His dad would greet him and his sister from the living room, scooping them up in a tight hug. He remembered the smell of his father's cologne from the tight hug. They kept in touch, but letters just weren't the same as visiting.

He sat watching the conversations blooming around the table between Johnston and her parents with hope welling in him for the possibility of visiting his parents.

"Why don't the two of you head into the library for a nightcap while I help your mother finish the dishes?" Mr. Johnston leaned over, picking up Hajjar's plate.

Johnston stood up, handing her plate to her mother.

"I've got this." Mrs. Johnston smiled, taking the plate from her daughter, then walked into the kitchen.

Hajjar walked slowly into the library with Johnston behind him. She paused to refill her glass of Merlot before entering the library. He heard her walk into the room behind him, but his attention immediately gravitated to the old record player and the stash of music in the case next to the phonograph. "I never thought Mr. Johnston was such a collector."

"They are his pride and joy." Johnston sat, sipping her wine.

Hajjar paused, thinking of his father collecting first prints of novels. He closed his eyes, remembering the smell of literature in his father's office. He would sneak in there, opening the books to look at the beautiful writing across the page. He breathed in. This library smelled more damp, musty, like the paper was more humid than his father's library in Dubai. "Can I ask you something?" Hajjar stood holding a Jimi Hendrix record in his hand.

"Sure." Johnston sat on the leather seat beside the deck, sipping her glass.

"How do you visit? How do you have these conversations without giving away sensitive details?"

Johnston sighed, smiling with the relaxation that comes with a good meal and glass of wine. "I told them that the line of work that I was called to is top secret and that I wouldn't be able to tell them everything that I was involved with."

Hajjar wrinkled his forehead and pursed his lips.

"I also made sure they understood that I need them."

"What do you mean?"

Johnston leaned forward, resting her elbows on her knees and holding her glass in both hands. "They ground me." She looked back up to Hajjar. "Why did you join the agency? Why do you risk your life doing this?" She separated her hands, gesturing to everything around her. Her look penetrated into him questioningly.

"To guard our existence against those who would try to rewrite history for their selfish gains." His eyes flared. Why would she invite him to her parents' house, only to be quizzed?

His anger and frustration were replaced by surprise and confusion as Johnston shook her head slowly, looking down into the glass with disappointment casting shadows across her face. He answered the question correctly. He could show her in chapter one of the field notebooks. She sighed, looking back up at him. "Why do *you* want to do this?"

Hajjar sat there for a long moment, remembering that question. Why was he there? The question sat heavy on his mind. He remembered Johnston smiling, looking at him as a mother to her son. "You need your family. Everyone does. Family can be your mom or dad. Or family can be the close friends that keep you grounded, focused when the rough gets unbearable."

Hajjar smiled again, looking up from his memories to the bartender standing at the end of the booth, just beyond his knees, pulling up in front of him.

"Another?"

Hajjar looked over to the empty bottle. "Yes, please."

The bartender slipped away, and a moment later, another full bottle appeared in the place of the empty one.

Why couldn't it be enough to save the world from those who might rewrite history for their own selfish means? Why couldn't it be enough to be the hero that saves time, and the youngest to do so?

The lessons from the academy were his life. From the age of ten, when he first got to the academy, he was the youngest and brightest. Why wasn't that enough for her?

He kept in contact with his parents. His mother wrote E-Time Tempral Letters every week at first. Then as he got into his teens, the ETTLs began to come every month or so, and he always wrote back. She would keep him updated on his friends and his sister.

He sighed, taking a drink of his beer. What kind of a big brother wasn't even there when his sister was beat up by a bully? But he was in school; they would not let him return home to visit his parents three years into school. He knew the rules, so he didn't even ask. But now he wondered about her, them. With all the ETLs, he was a part of their lives, but now he started feeling like he had really been watching his family through a window. Their lives were played out in front of him as if characters in a movie.

How would things be different if he weren't taken straight to the campus when he was ten? What would have happened if he had been a normal kid with his parents and friends until midteens like all the other students entering the academy after their first time jaunt?

Hajjar shook his head, wiping the thoughts from his mind. No what ifs; there was no point in dwelling on what could have been.

I am the youngest TDI. The thought brought a smile back to his face. *I am brilliant and will crack this case. My first solo case, and again I am the youngest to complete an assignment without a partner, and yet again I am the best, even better than Johnston.*

Johnston had now spent more time talking to her escort with flowing black hair and deep chestnut eyes than she ever expected. She found it interesting that her longest and deepest conversation in the last few days was with a horse. Maybe the time alone was starting to get to her, and she needed an empathetic ear that would not interrupt her or try to give her advice when she really did not want any. Maybe she was just happy knowing her Liam would not be a gossip.

The gray day added to her mood. The sky looked as though it was trying to rain but just couldn't. Instead, the mist and occasional drip of rain just irritated her. Indecisiveness even from Mother Nature tended to get on her nerves. Her thoughts paused. Hadn't she been indecisive lately? She stayed with Lady Murray longer than she had intended, trying to decide on how best to approach the next step in the journey, her mission.

Taking the identity of Elizabeth Ogilvy was planned. She had done her research to ensure her alias as kinsmen to Sir George Ogilvie, or at least she hoped. *There were always holes in documented history. The name might be the only way I can gain access to the castle without drawing unwanted attention. What if they think I am there to steal the Scottish Honours? Castle Campbell did turn allegiance to Cromwell, but that would not happen for another few months.*

"Maybe I can find another plan to infiltrate Castle Dunnottar that wouldn't result in my death." She was talking aloud, again, to her horse, and being indecisive at that. She sighed in frustration.

The tree line opened onto a plain, leading down to cliffs in the distance. The path led meandering to the cliffside, jetting up like a natural wall and obscuring the full view of the castle behind.

Johnston pulled back on the reins. She sat still atop Liam, looking at the beauty of the fortress castle perched atop the rocky outcrop, partially obscured by gray mist.

The grassy meadow stretched on across the rolling green hills to an abrupt edge. The jagged rock dropped off as if to hold the meadow aloft on a rocky pedestal. The crashing sound of waves beating upon the rocks came from the bottom of the cliff as an endless army of blue trying to push upon an unmovable fortress.

Johnston's eyes continued scanning the horizon for movement. She looked ahead to where the earth seemed to lift the land, and Dunnottar stood even higher still. The path to the castle led to what looked like a natural gateway in the cliff face with a stone building above the entrance to the fortification.

She repositioned herself, unhooking her knee from around the front of the saddle to sit more properly for her status. And then she adjusted her skirts and cloak. Johnston took a deep breath, setting her mind to the task ahead before uttering, "No turning back now." Liam started to trot toward the entrance. The gray sky darkened as droplets started pattering on Johnston's cowl, running as glistening liquid beads down her cloak.

The two galloped steadily across the meadow toward the outcropping. Johnston saw the arch within the outcropping.

Two dark figures stepped out toward them from the grayness. She felt Liam's muscles tense under her. Instinctively, she reached to pat his shoulder to calm him, though he continued prancing in place with eagerness to leave the vicinity of the two men with pointy objects that could hurt him.

"State your business." The tenor voice came from beneath the dark hood, muffled by the steady rain.

"I am Lady Ogilvy from Castle Campbell, seeking shelter." Johnston projected her voice with slight annoyance.

The two stepped close together, muttering a moment before beckoning her through the entrance. The path climbed up around through the rocks. It was almost like someone took their finger in clay, pushing the rocky outcrop up and creating a perfect defensible position against an enemy. Johnston admired the placement of the castle within this natural setting.

The paths continued through dark arched entrance leading to the second smaller meadow, green and worn with paths of traffic.

Johnston expected to be detained before or at the outer wall at the edge of the cliff castle. Instead, one of the two guards walked alongside her horse, leaving the other at the second entrance to keep watch.

The guard briskly walked alongside Liam, keeping pace with the horse while he walked to the next point. Johnston felt the tension build as four guards approached to greet them, stepping out from the stone entrance. Johnston leaned over again, patting Liam on the shoulder. *Easy now. Easy*, she thought more for her own benefit, but she felt his stance relax slightly as she waited. She understood the items within these walls and the importance to protect them. She again felt the weight of the heritage that would be lost if she failed her assignment, her quest. She sat higher in her saddle with these thoughts as Liam pranced in place.

A man walked out toward them from the castle. Johnston would call him a young man, maybe ten years younger than her with dark hair and blue eyes. Then she noticed his worry lines collecting at the corners of his eyes and the gray stress streaks at the temples interweaving in his hair. Based on how the guards parted for him, lowering their heads slightly, she knew he would make the decision of her passing. "Who are you?"

"Elizabeth Ogilvy." Johnston straightened in her saddle, pulling her hood back from her head and looking down over the cluster of men before resting upon the icy blue eyes of their officer. "From Castle Campbell. I bring news of the English army's movement."

The guards gathered, conversing among each other, then all looked over as their superior raised his fingers to his lips in contemplation. The long moments drew out as the water dripped down his face until, wordlessly, he turned to the gates, giving a gesture. Then, turning, he walked back into the walls of the castle.

Johnston returned her cowl to her head, annoyed with the water now finding its way down the back of her neck. The grinding, scraping sounds of gates slowly started to rise, added to the noise of daily activities from the other side of the walls. Johnston continued to sit patiently until the entrance was fully open before nudging Liam to continue in past the walls.

As she rode in, a lady entered the courtyard. All attention gravitated from the new visitor to the regal presence. Her reddish-brown hair was pulled neatly back and hidden, her gentle expression of curiosity peeking out from under the hood of the cloak. Her midnight blue dress with glints of silver weaved in the fabric peeked from under her cloak. Her intense gaze held the weight of a kingdom. She stood evaluating Johnston sitting in her saddle.

Johnston gracefully dismounted from her horse, taking a moment after the splash of her feet hit the ground to check her skirt and cloak. She looked over the young man hurrying toward her to take the reins. "He is arrogant, but if you whip him, I will whip you. He is trained to my specifications, and I will not tolerate action that negates my training." Johnston's steady gaze bore into the man until he looked away.

"Yes, my lady." The young man brushed his black hair from his eyes as he lifted his head. He looked around twenty-three, maybe twenty-four, muscular with years of physical work and the scars of going head-to-head with arrogant beasts until one of the two broke, then he would continue training the horse for what was needed.

Johnston gazed coldly at him a moment longer before handing him the reins. She turned to Liam, speaking softly and patting him on the shoulder. "He will not raise a hand to you. Go with him now. I will check in on you later."

Liam stepped forward, lowering his head to her formally before raising it again.

Johnston cracked a smile, trying not to laugh as she nodded. *You love the attention*, she thought as Liam shook his head up and down. She looked from her horse, dropping the smile to the amazed look on the man's face, and then turned toward the castle.

She and Liam had practiced that maneuver only once for amusement. She marveled at Liam's perceptiveness and the quickness to learn. She let the moment pass as she got closer to the lady of the castle. Johnston lowered her head slightly. "Lady Douglas."

Lady Douglas inclined her head in respect. "Lady Ogilvy, you are welcome. Let us get you out to the rain." She gestured to the door. Johnston took up stride alongside her. "How is Lord Ogilvy?"

"I would hope *your* husband is well. My lord Campbell," Johnston corrected her, "is fighting the English army. I do worry as I have not heard from him since the English broke through a few weeks ago."

Lady Douglas relaxed slightly with a sigh. "We cannot be too careful these days. Anyone may try to infiltrate these walls."

"I understand, my lady." Johnston relaxed in response with a nod. "After all, we only met briefly at your wedding. It seems like ages ago, especially in these times."

"I feel I have aged decades over the last few months." Lady Douglas sighed.

"The travel and treachery wear on me, but seeing you again raises my spirits."

"We will get caught up this evening. You must be exhausted from your journey." She started looking back to the courtyard.

"I did not bring much, only the necessities under the circumstances." Johnston paused. "I left Perth this morning and bring news on the movements of the English army to pass on to Sir Ogilvie."

A slight surprise washed over Lady Douglas's face. "Perth, that is a far ride. What news?" The intrigue fluttered away as Lady Douglas's attention was diverted to someone behind Johnston farther down the hall. "This way. We will get you settled in." Turning her gaze back to the young lady with tall and slender features, she continued, "Anne, Lady Ogilvy is visiting for a time."

The young lady gracefully lowered her head and body, pausing a long moment before rising.

"Miss Anne." Johnston in turn inclined her head in formality, greeting the lady and taking a quick read of her body language for future use. "It is a relief to see you remaining at your lady's side, especially in these dangerous times."

"She is here to see my husband." Lady Douglas turned to Anne Leslie. "We have room at the end of the hallway. Would you mind showing her the way?"

"Of course, my lady."

"I will have your things brought up."

"Thank you." Johnston inclined her head to Lady Douglas before turning to follow Anne Leslie down the hallway.

The two walked through the castle and up the spiral staircase in near silence with the sound of swishing fabric and the occasional falling water droplets onto stone. Johnston held back her grin, feeling like a kid running through the walls of the castles. The cool damp air inside the stone walls made her fight to hold back a shiver.

Lady Leslie continued through the labyrinth of halls to a wooden door. She pushed it open and stood back, letting Johnston continue through the room. Johnston stopped in the middle of the room, taking in the space as Lady Leslie continued in through the door behind Johnston, walking over to the window and peering out to the yard below.

"I am sure Sir Ogilvie will want to greet you himself."

"Thank you. Your hospitality is appreciated."

"We are stretched thin, but we do what we can." Miss Leslie turned to Johnston. "I will have one of the chambermaids check in on you. Dinner will be in an hour."

"Thank you." Johnston nodded thanks.

"Andrea shall be by shortly to see to any additional needs you may have." Miss Leslie's face relaxed into a slight smile. "Look forward to hearing all about Lord Campbell and your heroic journey at dinner."

Johnston stood with a somber expression. "I have hope, which is what keeps me going. It got me through this far." Johnston allowed a smile to slip to the corners of her mouth. "It is good to feel safe within these cliffs."

"I will see you at dinner. Rest a bit." Miss Leslie turned to the door then paused. "You are safe here."

Johnston smiled. She hoped to hear that from Sir Ogilvie, the man she needed to impersonate the cousin of in order for her plan to work. Then her mind wandered to the months to come, how safe, and for how long? The door swung close behind Miss Leslie as her skirts swished from the grasp of the door before it shut.

Johnston stood motionless, listening to the castle. The movements through the corridors and hallways were muffled by inches of stone. She breathed deeply, letting the moist cool air enter her nose, reminding her of the caves near her parents' house. Slowly, she opened her eyes, smiling, enjoying the visit to yet another of the castles she loved as a kid.

She walked to the vanity table across the room from the end of the bed and then started unloading the numerous knives and daggers she concealed upon herself to ensure her safety on the journey through potential Cromwellian battle areas.

The last dagger lay neatly alongside the other five. She picked it back up, looking at the detail on the hilt and kris blade. A smile crept across her lips as she looked at the crest with four stars at the base of the hilt.

This time and place felt so familiar, like she fit. This time the research came as enjoyment. Johnston remembered how much fun she had researching all the details of the area and the people. Then to finally meet them, she felt like an excited teenage fan finally meeting the celebrity she had pinned up in her bedroom.

Then a pang of guilt crossed her mind, wishing to return and visit her friend Lady Murray. She knew Lady Murray would be fine. At the end of the war, historic records stated this, but Johnston still found herself worrying. It was so hard to remain objective when history was being written around you. It was hard to remain detached from the people as they struggled for survival, not knowing how it would all turn out.

Slowly, she loosened the corset, reaching behind her back, untying, and then loosening the laces row by row until her bodice fell from her body. Standing, she lowered the dress to the floor, stepping out of it and trying not to catch and trip on her long chemise. Falling face first onto the stone floor from tripping over her dress was not the best way to make a good impression.

She lifted the ocean blue and teal dress in front of her, sighing. Sarah would kill her bringing the dress back in this condition. Her long journey was apparent in each dirty smudge and worn rip in the skirts. Taking the dress over to the window for light, she inspected the embroidery on the bodice; at least that was still intact.

Carefully, she laid the dress across the chest near the window. One of the ladies of the castle could attend to the dress. She turned her attention to the rest of the unpacking, hoping that Anne Leslie or Andrea would not come in while she was prancing around in late Elizabethan-style skivvies.

Johnston spent her time methodically unpacking the rest of her travel items.

Finally, Johnston laid her dinner dress on the bed, inspecting it to make sure it survived the travel. Relief escaped her lips as she exhaled a sigh. All the golden beads and ruby embroidery intricately winding its way across the bodice plate was still as beautiful as when she left Perth.

Standing back to appreciate the craftsmanship of the delicate artwork, Johnston admired the sunset orange fading into a deep rose at the ripples disappearing into the depths and shadows, all caught within the folds of the dress.

Johnston walked by the stand, lifting the brush as she passed. Her bare feet felt the cold of the stone floor as she continued to the chair next to the fire. Setting her brush on the stand near the chair, she reached up to her hair, feeling for the implements used to hold her hair in place. Piece by piece, she released each curl from captivity to fall down past her shoulders to her waist. As each curl fell, her mind wandered to memories long past. Decades past to when her hair was piled high into a sculpture with curls, BioCement and jewels in place, images and light projected form the bobby-pin-3D projection units the size of pearls, allowing the curls to remain perfect while projecting an aura or halo of color and nebula-ish beauty around her, replacing the traditional vale for her wedding.

Light glistened from the white streamers of hair flowing through the dark red and gray locks. Johnston sat closing her eyes, smiling, breathing in the damp moist air. She stretched her toes toward the fire, feeling the warmth radiate up her legs to her face. She looked from the fire to the window on the other side of the room, listening to rain continuing to patter and watching the firelight glisten on the panes of glass.

A soft knock on the door made Johnston jump, jolting her back from her memories. "Come," Johnston called as the door cracked open. A young woman barely entering her teens crept up to Johnston. Her tall lanky body was still awkward as a teenager added to a timid manner, making her look even younger as she came through the darkness toward Johnston. The girl's thin form made the dress fit loosely, bought expecting her to grow into the lanky figure. Her blond hair with red streaks was pulled up into a loose bun atop her head.

"What shall I call you?" Johnston asked.

The girl paused on her way to the side table. "Andrea," she whispered, then continued to pick up the brush next to Johnston and started to work. Abrasively, she worked at Johnston's hair, passing the brush into the knots and then pulling on them, willing them to yield. Her frustration built as the tangles refused to budge.

Johnston's scalp screamed until she could take no more. Gently, Johnston reached up, placing her fingers on the handle of the brush. "Hold on."

Andrea jumped, looking at Johnston through the hand mirror sitting on the stand. Her suppressed expression melted onto shame as she lifted her hand from the brush, leaving it in Johnston's hand.

"You are obviously distressed over something." Johnston started working on the tangles near the bottom of her hair. "Please, do not take your frustrations out on my hair." Johnston turned to look into the pain and shame welling in Andrea's eyes.

"I'm sorry." Andrea sighed. "I am worried…about…" She reached forward to retrieve the brush from Johnston. "My brother." Her voice trailed off.

Johnston studied her a bit before handing the brush back. "This fight has put many loved ones in danger." Her voice carried warmth, lifting the tension. Quietly, Andrea finished removing the last bit of the morning's journey from Johnston's hair.

"There," a whisper came from behind Johnston as the brush finally made a complete trip through the hair without catching. "What would you like me to do with your hair?"

Johnston pondered the idea. "I trust your judgment, but nothing too complicated."

Andrea's hands quickly parted the river of hair into three parts and then weaved the parts into a braid, tying the end with a ribbon. She stood back as Johnston stood and walked to the bed where her dress lay.

In no time, Johnston was synched into the dress.

"Dinner should be ready in a few minutes. I am sure Lady Douglas and Sir Ogilvie are already in the dining room." Andrea tied the ribbons at the base of the bodice.

"It will be good to see them." Johnston smiled. "Thank you."

Andrea silently left from the room, heading to another duty or obligation. Johnston felt the sound of the heavy door latch as it shut. She walked over to the fireplace, feeling the warmth press on the bits of skin with the chill damp fingers of the castle behind her. Johnston took a deep warm breath and headed to dinner.

The closing door echoed through the room, announcing Johnston's entrance. A long hearth almost as long as the heavy wooden table lined the wall of the room. Beautiful tapestries hung on each side and opposite of the fireplace. She glided in past the long table in the center of the room filled with lit candles.

"Elizabeth," a deep gentle voice rumbled through the room as all eyes fell on her. The voice came from the man whose presence added to his stature. Probably the only person within the room who was near Johnston's own age, his graying hair and lines of wisdom that had collected at the corners of his eyes telling of worry and heavy burden of the castle and property.

"Sir Ogilvie." She stepped forward, clasping his outreached hands as she inclined her head with a low curtsy. Then she rose smiling, meeting his warm eyes.

"Anyone who has the cunning, not to mention the courage, to beat me at chess will always call me George." He patted her hand then picked up her glass. His deep brown eyes held warmth and optimism, and maybe the lines around his eyes were also jovial lines as they gathered with his smile.

"George, it is good to see you again. I wish it were under better circumstances."

"You remember my wife."

"How could I forget? We share the same name." Johnston turned to Lady Douglas, inclining her head. "Elizabeth, as beautiful as the day you wed."

Lady Douglas nodded with a smile. Her midnight blue dress from earlier looked different in the dimmer light of the fire. It looked near black as the midnight sky with flecks of silver glistening as the stars within the bodice. She smiled, gesturing to the woman beside her near the window. "This is Anne Leslie, my dear friend."

Miss Leslie stood quietly in a modest sky-blue dress with white wisps of clouds on a clear day stitched into delicate designs across her bodice and down into her skirt. Her youthful face looked a bit younger than Lady Douglas's, where the wariness of life had yet to touch it and leave lasting marks.

Johnston turned to the man on George's right, recognizing the icy blue eyes of the person who allowed her entry at the gate, though his icy stature melted a bit in the warmth of the firelight with these comrades. "Lord Keith?"

Keith's eyes iced slightly as he contemplated how she would know his name. He hadn't greeted her at the gate; none of his men uttered his name on approach. She saw the resolution that he would have to find this out later and then reached for her hand. "Lady Elizabeth." He lowered his head to her. "I hear you had a rather interesting journey to get to us. What news do you have?"

Always the strategist, Johnston thought. "No good news, I'm afraid." Johnston's expression sobered, but before she should continue, a young woman stepped forward, handing Johnston a glass. Then she filled it with dark red liquid, pouring smoothly from a dark green bottle. Johnston nodded thanks then took a sip.

"Shall we sit for dinner?" George gestured to the table with one hand while holding his wine with the other.

Each of them slowly walked to a seat at the table. Johnston took her seat across from Keith and Miss Leslie as George and Elizabeth each at opposite ends of the long table.

When they were all settled, a procession of servants filed in holding plates of food. A small pile of meat was pulled from the bone next to sliced fruit and piled atop a pewter plate.

Johnston waited for the head of the table to start eating before she started munching on the fruit. She continued to watch the others at the table. Looking to Lady Douglas, watching her admire George still melted into his looks and gestures. She turned her attention across the table to Keith and Anne. Anne caressed Keith's arm gently while looking over to Elizabeth, hiding her gesture of affection. Keith quickly looked at Anne and then shifted his attention to George. Johnston, too, looked to George, meeting his eyes. She met his gaze with a slight smile, wondering how long he had been studying her.

"Dear cousin, what are you pondering?"

Johnston could feel all the eyes at the table shifting to her. She did not like being the center of attention. She nodded. "I am still contemplating everything within the last few days, and the journey was long. Studying all of the pieces on the board."

"Yes, do tell us what news you have from the English army." Keith looked to her.

Johnston's gaze shifted from Keith back to George. "Lord Campbell was with our ranks when the English army crossed the firth or fourth the end of July. The English army invaded my home within a few days after the news of the crossing reached me. We held out as long as we could, but it was only a matter of time before the fall of the castle was inevitable." Johnston paused briefly. "The choice was hard. Go down with my home or escape to fight another day."

"You chose to leave your home under siege?" Keith glanced to George with a look of disdain. "I thought you would stay. That is not the *Elizabeth* Sir Ogilvie described to me. Why did you flee?" He paused. "Un-Scottish," he muttered.

"Please let me remind you, sir, of two things. Number one, it is hard to defend a home when not the legal owner, just the wife. And second, it is hard to defend a castle when everyone is away defending the land." She looked daggers at Keith. "What was the name of the castle? Remind me who actually owned the castle?" Johnston sent her icy glare on Keith. "I, unlike Lady Wandesford, could not stand off the siege with legal claims for a castle that I did not own, because I became steward of Castle Campbell through marriage. They claimed that John was dead, and the only way I could hold the castle was to fight or pledge allegiance to Cromwell. Only my chambermaids and a few women and their children remained to defend the castle. All of the men left days earlier, called to battle." Johnston leaned forward, glaring at Keith. "Lord Campbell and our men left the castle to fight Cromwell. I made a hard decision to sacrifice pride rather than the people close to me if there was *no* fighting chance, not legally or physically." Johnston leaned back in her chair, glaring now at the ceiling bitterly at the situation. Then she returned her gaze to the table. "I would ask you why you are here instead of helping the king in his final assault."

Silence fell on them all as Keith leaned back, sipping his wine before opening his mouth as if to speak.

"We are all fulfilling our duties," George spoke before Keith could reply.

Keith continued studying Johnston as he seethed at the implied insult.

Johnston shifted the emotion, turning her attention back to George as he said, "Tell us more of your plight."

Johnston relaxed her temper, reminding herself that she was still only playing a roll. She settled back into her chair, nodding to her cousin and taking a piece of pulled meat in her fingers, eating it slowly before continuing. "Our forces were south, engaging the English army after they crossed the fifth. The English army broke the line and soon surrounded the castle." She shook her head. "I fled north. I made it to Castle Huntingtower to find out the English army was in close pursuit. They took Perth five days ago and then left quickly, headed back toward Sterling. I can only guess that the English army is headed to meet or chase King Charles."

"How could you possibly know that?" Keith shook his head.

George leaned back, watching the entertainment at the table.

Johnston felt her face flush with frustration and anger to a young know-it-all. Then she swallowed the annoyance as she decided to continue after taking a calming breath. "The English army regard women with little respect. They seem to only value us for *breeding stock*." The words tasted bad as they came out. She looked over to George and continued, "There is a benefit to being overlooked and dressed below your status. The soldiers around my home talked as though my presence did not matter. Little did they know that I have a good memory."

"Clever," George muttered.

"King Charles's army was broken more severely than I have originally feared. The English army had punched through the center, dividing our forces. We lost the advantage of both cohesion and position." She shook her head. "I had not lost hope of John returning to me, but the news of the battle's outcome left me with little hope."

"Why do you think the English army turned south to Sterling after making it so far north?" George spoke softly, rubbing his gray beard with his fingers.

"I was not hiding within their ranks at that point, but I speculate that King Charles is maneuvering the forces for something brazen, with the speed the encampment at Perth was taken down and moved out. If the king's army were merely planning to fortify in Sterling Castle, then Cromwell's forces would not be in such a hurry to confront them. It would be wiser to continue their march north and pull our forces out of Sterling, giving up an advantage. However, if our forces were planning to confront Cromwell's men and march on Perth, then why would Cromwell move his troops toward Sterling? It would make more sense to dig in and gain the advantage by staying in Perth and holding the higher ground, anticipating the attack. Most likely King Charles has started a brazen campaign south into England to pull Cromwell's men into action."

"That would make sense," Keith muttered before looking at George. "With the entire army of Cromwell north in Scotland, there are no troops between King Charles and the throne in London."

"That is quite a distance to cover, and with larger forces that have proven their mobility in pursuit, I will be interested in how this plays out," Elizabeth calmly stated.

"I will not start the celebration yet," George stated. "We will continue to guard our home here."

Johnston listened contentedly, picking the strings of meat and eating slowly. She smiled, wanting to get out of the focus of the table. Conversations continued around the table through the evening until the late night, making Johnston's eyelids heavy with sleep and wine. She returned to her room, falling into her bed and huddling under the blankets. Her long chemise felt soft and smooth against her skin. The dreams drifted her into slumber.

***

One day blurred into the next as Johnston fell into a routine. The first few mornings after the dinner, she was hoping for news from the front, status, location, anything that would confirm passing days to the tick marks in her diary. But each day brought the same routine: exercise, breakfast, morning duties, lunch, training in the meadow with Liam, dinner, bed.

She desperately wanted to start practicing her maneuvers with a real sword but feared it might bring too much attention to her if she started practicing with the soldiers within the castle walls, and even worse if she smuggled a sword into her bedchamber and it was discovered. She even contemplated jaunting back to the agency to practice there, but the idea of a person entering her room as she was phasing out or back in would be horrifying to them, and it would end her stay in the castle one way or another. After pondering this for many days, she opted to continue her exercise in secret to avoid disrupting the balance in the castle.

Unfortunately, this only contributed to her feeling of confinement in the walls of the castle. She dreaded the day when the castle would be under siege and she would not be able to take Liam out onto the meadow. This was the part of her day she loved the most, and she looked forward to teaching him new things. He, too, loved escaping the confinement of the stable.

As the days drew on, Johnston started wondering if she was remembering to record the passage of time in her journal. In desperation, she decided this morning to take the journal up to the wall overlooking the meadow, anything to break the routine.

Johnston leaned on the wall surrounding the top of the castle; her gaze on the page in her field notebook kept drifting up to the view of the meadow. The day should be September 6. Could she have been off, counted a day twice by accident? She thought she was keeping an accurate account of the days as they trudged by. The Battle of Worchester should have been three days ago. How long did it take for news to reach this castle? Frustrated, she flipped through the pages of her journal, trying to figure out where she might have made an entry error.

She closed her eyes, rubbing her forehead with her fingers. Only one month, she had been within these walls for only a month. There were five more to go. She could feel the tension in the castle building, growing tight as a rubber band about to snap. The last word on the war was received weeks ago when confirmation came that King Charles had in fact taken the Scottish troops on a final offensive to take London. Johnston knew the push would be long, but there were at least three major confrontations between August 3 and now. Yet no word, nothing. She hated being in the dark.

She closed the Field Notebook in frustration. The Field Notebook only displayed the timeline from the agency within the Px-Shield. It did not have the capability to project the multiple, maybe infant, variations currently playing out with manipulation coming from those wanting to steal the Honours, or even the effects that she was having on the timeline with her presence there. It would be nice for the field notebook to document and project the effects that she was currently having on this specific timeline. She sighed.

Her attention suddenly focused on an echo of the sound of hooves that reached her ears from the distance. She opened her eyes to see a rider galloping in as fast as his brown steed could manage.

The young man rode in with one purpose on his mind. The brown horse glistened with sweat and white froth collecting at the corners of her mouth. No pause of formality, he galloped through the cliffs, entering the meadow outside the castle walls and yelling something to the guards as he halted his horse, flinging his leg over the saddle and jumping to the ground in the sprint. He ran into the small door next to the gate.

Johnston turned around on the wall, walking to the inner edge and looking down. The young man ran through to the inner courtyard.

Excitement ran through her, quickly followed by extreme anxiety. At the same time, she could not wait to sit in on dinner this evening and hear news. She felt the anxiety knowing the details that might reach George. *If the tension was already at a breaking point within the castle now,* she thought, *just imagine when George hears the outcome from the Battle of Worchester.* She ran the profiles of each of the dinner companions through her head. She thought about what each of them would say regarding the situation. Holding the book in her hand, she played her knowledge of history through her head. Lady Ogilvy and her relationship with her cousin, distant, but still her cousin nonetheless. Family was family. The clans were as tight as any family. She thought about her role in the days to come then decided not to dwell as her thought shifted to Lord Campbell. Would news of his turning ally to Cromwell reach George's ears? What about the real Lady Ogilvy, laying low in the castle and waiting for her husband? She shuddered at the thought; she hadn't fully prepared for this inevitable moment. She was in neck-deep. She might as well take a breath and go under.

The hum of the castle changed into a symphony reminiscent of the flight of the bumblebee, though the time seemed to crawl by as her anticipation built to find out the news. The energy and chatter of gossip around the castle increased as speculation built while no one truly knew the information the rider brought. Everyone was eager to tell what they heard from someone who knew someone who had an ear against the wall or door.

Finally, as the sun descended in the sky, she headed in the side door of the castle. The hallways and stairs leading to her room became almost too familiar to her over the last month.

The door to Johnston's room blocked most of the noise from the castle, but the hum seemed to reverberate through the stone. She forced herself to slow down as she got ready for dinner, taking down her hair. Andrea entered the room, finding Johnston brushing her own hair with nearly all the tangles gone. Johnston quickly removed the two remaining tangles before handing the brush over to Andrea.

"My lady, have you heard?" Andrea's excitement brought the words before she could fully realize that she had spoken them. "Of course, you have heard. What have *you* heard?"

Johnston closed her eyes a second, recounting the last blur of sentences. Andrea's energy revealed her deeper accent, thick with vowels. Johnston turned, placing her hand on Andrea's, hoping she translated English to English accurately. "I have not heard directly, but I believe I will learn what news was brought this evening at dinner. We may hope for the best." Johnston tried to force calm optimism into her voice.

Andrea smiled. "Oh, I hope so." She continued to brush Johnston's hair as each of them turned to face the fire. "My Duncan will return to me sooner, my dear brother."

"Braiding my hair will be perfect tonight." Johnston held her impatience out of her voice. The anticipation started getting to her. Andrea said nothing as her hands smoothly worked the weave into a rope then tied the loose hairs at the base of Johnston's neck. The eternity of ten minutes passed as Andrea finished tightening the corset and skirts of her evening dress. "Thank you." Johnston turned to her.

The hallway stretched as she walked. Anticipation pressed her patience, and it took all of her self-control not to run down the hallway into the dining room. The excitement of experiencing the stories of history went like electricity down Johnston's spine.

She held her hand on the handle of the slightly ajar door, pausing a moment before knocking. The familiar voices came from the room, replacing the excited electricity with a cold chill of fear.

"I don't trust her." Johnston could identify the suspicious voice of Keith through the slightly opened door.

"You don't trust anyone." The calming feminine voice was Elizabeth.

"I trust everyone within *this* room, but I am not even sure that she is Lady Ogilvy. You even said yourself she was not the cousin you remembered. She could be a spy to flush out our defenses."

"I admit there are differences. She is much older than I imagined she would be, and her chess strategies have changed. I hardly think that is enough to accuse her of being an impostor or a spy." The deep resonating voice of George brought finality to the accusation.

"I think we should—"

"Should what?" Johnston stepped into the room, shutting the door behind her. "Banish me from these walls?" She met the eyes of everyone in the room. Keith's mouth remained open as in midsentence. "You are all talking loud enough. Almost everyone in the hall could hear you. Not too subtle for a strategy meeting on the news of the defeat."

"Where did you get that information?" Keith looked over to George. "Sir, the security of the castle?"

"Keith." Johnston tilted her head, looking upon him with tired irritation. "Do you think I am an addle-brained child? The news must be disheartening, or you would not be questioning the loyalty of people within the castle walls. These accusations are rarely made during military success." She sat in a chair, finding her hands on the table in front of her as if to fortify herself in her position, looking up at each to them. "As for looking older." She looked over to George. "I feel older, unfortunately. Life and all of its obstacles, especially a war, will do that." She glanced around the room with tired resolution, deciding to get it all out in the open. "If you would prefer, I will take my dinner to my room while you four discuss the details of the war, the status of the King, and what will become of the Royal Jewels. Then—"

"How?" Keith slammed his fist on the table. "That is not common knowledge."

Johnston glared. "First, I am not common." Then she turned her gaze to George. "Oh, don't tell me they are still within these walls? I knew they were not returned to Edinburgh, or we would have heard of their destruction last year, but I was rather hoping they might be hidden somewhere discreetly between here and there. Maybe buried in a crypt of a cathedral where even Cromwell wouldn't defile the dead."

Johnston looked to George's face to read the truth in the royal jewels' location. She only lowered her head, shaking it slowly.

George walked toward Johnston, placing a hand on her shoulder. "These are dangerous times, and I do not deny I may question your loyalty again in the future, but as for now, I may need your insight and strategy more than I need worry of treachery." He smiled impatiently at her. "And so long as you remain within these walls, I can monitor your correspondence."

"As I am sure you already have, Sir Ogilvie." She looked up at him with a smile of a game well played.

"How will we know you can be trusted?" Keith injected.

"I believe"—Johnston looked to George—"we have established that I am not yet be trusted, but I am sure George is more than competent to make his decisions accordingly."

Anne slowly walked over to Johnston with a glass of wine held out to her. Johnston took it, nodding thanks.

George looked to the door to confirm that it was shut solid before continuing, "The battle was lost." George's words felt like a heavy boulder crushing whispers of hope from across the room. "King Charles's army pushed to Worchester. The push was long with many encounters with the English army along the way." He sipped on his glass, walking around the table. "The battle was hard-fought, but in the end our forces were broken."

Johnston closed her eyes, remembering only two, maybe three, encounters before the final battle at Worchester. She opened her eyes, smiling at Sir Ogilvie's flair, already embellishing the Scottish side of the story.

"What of the king?" Elizabeth stepped up to the table.

George looked to her, regaining a smile to his eyes. "He escaped the battle uninjured and not captured."

"He is alive. That is good." Keith sighed with relief.

"Yes, but for how long?" George looked around the group. "He is either separated from his troops or in a small group. How well will he avoid capture like that?"

Keith's face turned from a shade of light green to gray with his little optimism draining quickly.

"He will elude capture," Johnston whispered with her eyes closed.

"How can you possibly know that?" George and Keith said in near unison, facing Johnston.

Johnston's attention shifted from her distant thoughts back to the room, reprimanding herself for losing focus on the now. She searched for a plausible explanation other than "read it in a history book."

"Faith." She sipped on her wine. "Charles has support even in England from those who supported his father and the crown. Though they may not be openly advertising their support, afraid of the consequences, but they are out there. They may not rise up to join the fight, but they will secretly hide him on his attempt to flee the country."

"How can you be sure?" George leveled his gaze on her.

"Again, I do not know for sure, but I have faith and hope." Johnston relaxed, meeting his gaze with her own. "If we have no hope, we might as well walk out of this castle, giving the crown to Cromwell. I don't want that." The relaxed expression changed as her gaze shifted to George. "Do you?"

"No, of course not," George stated.

"Good." Johnston's smile returned. "Then you share the same hope that King Charles will live to regain his crown another day." She acknowledged Keith for the first time since the beginning of the whole conversation. "You might want to hold on to that anger that I call hope, and it will carry us through the difficult times to come. Things will get worse before they get better."

The fire within George's eyes refocused in his eyes, gathering the wrinkles at the corners. "You"—he sighed—"are right."

"It seems that we have migrated to the dining table." Johnston remained sitting at the table, opening her hands in front of her, looking to each of them in turn now standing around the table. "What shall we do, Sir George?"

George stood at the head of the table, expressionless, accessing the situation. "We shall eat." He sat at the head of table.

The dinner plates were presented, but no additional word was said. Each of them sat eating in near silence, and the room filled thick with tension and anxiety for the future. Johnston could feel the fear of an unknown outcome and dread of what was inevitable.

The evening ended silently as they all headed to their rooms. Elizabeth and Anne bid a good evening and returned to their own rooms.

Johnston quickly decided to retire for the evening as well. As the door to the dining room shut, a wave of relief washed over her, and she walked through the halls to her room. She did not want to put on the persona of Elizabeth Ogilvy through the rest of this evening. She wanted to ponder what was next to come in solitude with her notebook.

Her room flickered warmly with the fire as she closed the door behind her. Reaching for her back, she found the laces holding her tightly. Practice over the month made untying the laces easier, and they fell loose down her back. Within moments, the dress was off and draped in its usual place. And with her notebook in hand, Johnston padded over to the chair near the fire.

Leaving the notebook on the stand, she continued to the fire. She bent, extending a small wooden wick into the fire and lighting it. And then she carried it, cupping the flame in her hand, to light the candle near her chair. Light filled the area near her chair as the flame hopped to the wick of the candle. She settled in, pulling her feet beneath her on the chair.

Her thoughts weighed heavy. She was resolved to her fate on this mission but still wanted to run from it. She could ride out on Liam to the Northern Islands, marry, and live past the end of the year.

Thoughts of how to ensure her survival started rushing through her mind. She knew her practices of sword stances would have to remain in secret, and without a sword. She worried that though she would know the maneuvers, knowledge was not enough. Maybe her death would come from a slight second not anticipating the slight weight of the sword. Her strength and stamina would not hold out without the proper training with the actual weight of the sword.

At moments, the time seemed to fly too fast to catch a glimpse or stop for breath before the moments were lost to memory, and at other times the hours did not pass quickly enough. Almost six weeks had passed as she fell again into the rhythms of the day, but she still had another six or so weeks before she would be trapped in the castle under siege. With each passing day, her resignation to her fate solidified.

Looking deep into the fire, mesmerized by the dancing flames, she sat, deep in thought. A checklist started solidifying out of the flickering of her mind, a to-do list to stay alive and accomplish her assignment.

The time spent left remnants of exhaustion as the morning light invaded her room. Memories of stumbling to her bed blurred, but the list remained in focus.

With the morning's light, the list of the things remained clear in her head, and she started on them with focus. After the morning passed, Johnston was relieved to be allowed to go on her afternoon ride, alone with her thoughts.

She wondered for a moment if Liam was also relieved, as he was free to just run.

Johnston let Liam run his worries and frustrations out until he slowed panting. She empathized with Liam, feeling trapped, playing a role in a story and wanting to just run until exhaustion caught up with her instead of pushing the story in a way she knew she couldn't.

She directed Liam over to a tree that looked familiar with its low hanging red apples glistening like jewels. Dismounting, she led him over to the tree.

"I don't know what to do." She found herself talking aloud to Liam. There was no one else around. "I am neck-deep in these events. History is weaving around me, and I can't change them without risking a change in the events. But just being here has changed events. If I do nothing, pretend to be a bug on the wall, then they will not trust me and think I am a spy taking note. They might even exile me before the Honours leave the castle. On the other hand, if I interact and try to play the role of the persona I adopted, I might alter history or events now as they unfold." She reached up to the tree, grabbing an apple for her, inspecting for any spots to avoid when eating it. "I'm not making any sense to you," she muttered to herself. "I don't know if I'm making sense myself." She bit into the apple. "I just want to make things better, but I can't. I want to live through this. But I don't know how without potentially changing things that maybe I shouldn't change." She took another bite. "I wish saving me didn't mean abandoning you here."

She felt a nose under her arm. She turned to meet the deep brown eyes filled with confusion and worry.

Johnston smiled. "I brought your over here for an apple. Don't worry about me. Have a couple."

She looked up to see that the last apple within easy reach had been plucked. Liam strained, reaching for one of the lowest hanging apples, unable to reach it. He huffed in frustration.

"Hold on a moment." Johnston handed him the rest of her apple then rubbed his neck. "Sorry about that, my big puppy." Walking around to the saddle, she climbed back, throwing her skirt over the back along with her leg onto the back of her impromptu therapist. Placing both feet in the stirrups, with the skirts puffed up around her, she stood on the saddle, reaching up into the tree and plucking three more apples. Slowly, she lowered herself down and onto the ground. Liam turned in anticipation to be greeted with the red gems handed to him in her palm. Johnston held back the apples a moment to remove his bit, and then she watched him devour the juicy treats.

One by one, he took each apple and scarfed it down. Johnston sat on the ground, looking up at the large black horse with his white star and snip. He was still searching the area for the possibility that more apples fell, and he just needed to find them.

"The worst part is either if I survive this or get killed in the process, I will still abandon you." She sat looking down at her hands, holding one last apple. She held the apple out to him, trying to smile through the pain reality had presented to her. Her smile flickered as her eyes watered up.

Johnston stood, holding out the apple to the large jock with big brown eyes. He stepped forward to nuzzle under her lowered hand, looking for scratching, then looked to the apple with his nose.

"We'll get through this." She smiled. "Maybe I can come back and retire here..."

Liam shook his head.

"No, you are probably right." She gave Liam the last apple and then wiped the slobber on the grass. "Shall we head back?"

Liam bobbed his head.

Johnston returned the bit to his mouth and climbed back onto the saddle. The entire ride back to the confines of the castle was cluttered with thoughts pushing their way back into her focus. Would she be approached about her ride, questioned about leaving the castle? All struggled for their place of importance in explanation to her cousin. She chuckled. *Her cousin*, she spoke her thoughts. *Am I going native?*

***

The early nip of cold bit her nose as she walked from the castle into the yard. Johnston was readying herself for the morning's practice. Johnston wondered if Keith had actually started warming to the idea of sparring with her or looked on it as an obligation. Within the first few days, she had determined despite her extensive training at the academy, it was far different from sparring with the men who developed the fighting styles with these swords.

It was clear that George knew by now that she had started sparring with Keith, but he said nothing. At the same time that Johnston felt more a member of the castle, she also felt more alone, isolated within the walls as she walked from the castle. This morning, she felt a change.

The excitement in the early hours surprised her while she walked toward the forge. All the men stood in the tight cluster around Keith, focused on his words.

"The enemy is upon us." His voice reached through the silent crowd to Johnston, standing a short distance behind them. "We have secured all entrances to the castle. Guards, stand watch over the walls in all directions. They will not get in."

George's voice came from beside Keith's. Johnston stepped to the right to see George through the sea of heads. "We received word late in the night that King Charles has escaped to France." A cheer rose from the men around. The cheer was silenced by the strong solid voice. "He is our king. The English army is nearly upon us. They wish to break us and destroy the crown. We will not let them. We will not let them take our history or our pride. They will not take our home."

A cheer of agreement rose from the men standing, clinging to every word.

"The English army will be here within a day. We must prepare for a long siege. Collect all the animals and food we can to overstock the pantries. We will send Kevin, Dunkin, and Scott to scout for their position and movement. Ryan, Charles, and Robert, man the tower. We may need to lower the gate at the first sign of the enemy." Keith's voice continued from behind the cluster of heads. "You have your tasks. Now go!"

At that, the cluster of men each set to their tasks, separating like a droplet of oil on the surface of water. Within moments, none stood between Johnston and the two men still standing after giving the order. A moment of silence passed before Johnston stepped forward. "I can take it that there will no longer be afternoon rides into the meadows."

"You presume correctly, Lady Ogilvy. Though I would not consider them ended, merely postponed." Keith lowered his head to her and then set to his tasks.

"I am also guessing that postponement refers to your sword training?" George looked sternly at Johnston.

She continued holding her insecurity tight within her racing heart. "I fear there may be a day when I need the skills, and on that day, I will need them tuned, sharpened, and ready."

"I pray that day does not come." George looked from Johnston to the people working around the castle in the early dawn light. "But I fear that day may be closer than I ever wanted."

"The king is safe then?" Johnston looked into George's expression, reading his eyes. "But you worry the battle is already lost."

Johnston could see the firmness setting in Sir George's jaw. She continued before he could say anything.

"We will prevail." There was resolved confidence in her voice. "We stand firm so the crown does not fall. The king will return."

Johnston started to walk away then stopped, turning back him. "You are the steward of the crown. This is bigger than you or me. Take faith in Luke 12:42 to 47." She turned toward the entrance to the castle she came from.

Johnston heard steps catching up to her, and then George's deep voice softly caught her. "How do you know King Charles will return?"

Johnston turned to George, stepping close and speaking in a low voice "Cromwell cannot live forever. His hold will falter when he is gone. At that time, King Charles or one of his successors will return to lead the kingdom forward. As long as the Honours stay safe, there will be a king." Johnston stood a moment longer, looking to George. No smile or fear, only resolve settled on her face. She lowered her head to him, then she turned again to continue her path to the castle.

Johnston walked slowly, silently into the castle through the side entrance, up through the stairs and into the damp hallway. She solemnly returned to her room, retrieving her notebook. Sitting in her chair, she opened the notebook, writing, "And so it begins."

Grabbing the handle of the door, Hajjar stepped forward, resting his forearm on the wood a second before stepping back and opening the door. This was the night, and he didn't have any suspects. He would have to watch the pint-sized waitress to see who she handed the device to at the end of the concert.

The dark bar beckoned him in. Three steps in the door, he paused to let his eyes adjust to the dimness, and then he continued to the corner of the bar where he made notes. As he walked, he scanned the crowd; the place was more crowded than two days ago. Hajjar weaved through the cluster of people to the corner near the serving well, hoping to have a better view of the little girl from there. He pulled up a stool, dreading the possibility of failure on his first solo assignment.

"You're back," Bridget greeted him. "What can I get you?"

"Maker's on the rocks." Hajjar settled in.

"Harder than last time." She grabbed the square-shaped bottle with red wax on the top and started to pour.

"I have a bad feeling about tonight. Might as well start it off on a good note."

"Bad news from your visit to UT?"

"Sort of," Hajjar lied.

Bridget handed an amber glass to Hajjar who picked up the glass, smelling the smoky undertones. He sighed as he took a sip, savoring the smooth and slight oaky burn down his throat.

"Wow, that is bad news." She sighed. "I'm sorry."

"We'll see." Hajjar watched the young woman with a guitar take the stage. She sat for a few minutes, fiddling with the microphone and the tuning pegs at the end of the guitar neck. "At least I have legendary entertainment." Hajjar watched the little waitress run up to the stage, a glint of silver as she left something near the back side of the speaker.

"Legendary? Janis is good, but legendary?" Bridget walked to the other end of the bar.

Hajjar could have kicked himself. He was so focused on dulling his nerves that he missed the start. He missed when she got the device.

He looked around the place. None of the people from Wednesday night were in the building. He continued to look around the room and scanned the crowd, trying to determine groups of people and facial expressions for relaxing enjoyment versus focus on something else.

He wished he could sit and enjoy the music as his focus drifted to the stage, watching Janis play her guitar lovingly then looking up, singing to the crowd and opening her inner feelings raw for all to hear. The microphone just happened to catch it and project it all the way to those who stood along the back wall.

The back wall...

Hajjar refocused on the people standing on the back wall, watching who was talking to each other, the groups. A group of three seemed very enthusiastic in their conversation between the next songs. He continued studying them as one of the young women in the group came up to the bar. He leaned in, listening to her order intensely.

"I'd like to order for my new friends."

His hopes dropped like a rock. He continued to scan the crowd but glanced back to the group, hoping for something.

Anything.

Three of the small groups remained. He started trying to study them one by one. He was looking for the profile of the girl with the dark hair and a guy with size 9...maybe...9, flip flops.

His attention drifted from the crowd to the music.

Three groups of three, guys and girls, but they were groups of dates. The groups that Hajjar was looking for...

The music distracted him as he continued to watch for suspicious groups of people. He scanned the back side of the bar for the girls who once stood to head to the bar or restroom, each couple or small group in the bar one by one. His eyes continued to dart around the crowd.

"Another?" Bridget's voice invaded his mental calculations.

"Yeah, Maker's." He didn't turn to face her as he was intensely scanning the crowd.

"Bourbon on the rocks, sure." She walked off, annoyed, and returned a moment later, placing the glass next to him.

He continued looking around the crowd, listening, waiting. He desperately wanted to find the person or people before the end of the concert. He closed his eyes to listen. He had already heard this entire evening once before. He just needed to focus. "Juneteenth..." He remembered this. He remembered in a lightning bolt that his ordering of the bourbon was already on the recording. *He* was on the recording. He just didn't realize it. He sighed with frustration. No one recognizes their own voice on a recording.

Moments later, he heard Bridget's voice say, "Cosmo right up." Again, just like the recording. Maybe he had not done enough research before coming here. He would not be able to come back, for fear of two of him in one place would cause a paradox.

Hajjar desperately scanned the crowd as the concert came to an end. The crowd stood clapping. Hajjar stood to look over the heads, looking for someone who met the profile of the teenage girl he saw in the pawnshop.

"That was amazing!" The voice caught Hajjar's attention as he looked down at the little girl. She stood bouncing with excitement. Any minute now... "I love it here!" The little girl continued to bounce.

"I'm glad you are happy." Bridget leaned over to kiss her on the forehead.

The exchange was about to take place. Hajjar watched as the little girl sighed happily and ran up to the stage through the crowd, picking up the device and stashing it in her pocket. Bouncing, she ran back to Bridget, hugging her.

"Um, sweetie?" Hajjar frowned, looking at the girl.

"Um, Bethy," Bridget corrected him angrily, leaning toward him and glaring daggers of a mother bear protecting her cub.

He looked at Bridget, having a knot in his stomach climb up into his throat. "Um…Bethy, what is that, and what are you planning on doing with that recording of Janis Joplin?" Hajjar's voice quivered as the knot settled in his throat. He continued to stare at Bridget as she started to bristle.

Bethy fidgeted a bit, looking down at the ground. "I wanted the recording for my dad. I broke his album." She looked up at Hajjar with glistening wet eyes, fighting back tears.

Hajjar paused as the shock sunk in. How could he not see this before? He reached over, lifting her chin to look into her eyes, the familiarity setting in. Only these eyes were not looking at him as the critiquing teacher. Her eyes had not yet seen the academy or the agency. "Bethy?"

"Yes?" Her eyes continued to water.

"Elizabeth…Katy…Johnston?" Hajjar held his breath, hoping he was not correct.

"That's what my mom calls me when I'm getting in trouble." She shrunk back, waiting for bad news. "Am I getting in trouble?"

The knot in his thought tightened, cutting off his breath. Hajjar smacked his forehead with the palm of his hand, turning to the bar and looking to Bridget with pleading eyes. "Another…"

"Sure, right up." Bridget frowned, ushering Bethy behind her cautiously.

Hajjar held his forehead in his hand. "Oh…crap!"

***

Hajjar sat at the bar with his head buried in his hands. The blur of the last three days swarmed through his head.

Three days. *Three days!* How? Why hadn't he recognized the pint-sized bartender in three days? Who was the girl that sold the device to Redwing? Elinor Dashwood was clearly a false name. How did Elinor get the device from Bethy?

Hajjar chuckled for a moment, thinking of his mentor and senior officer as Bethy.

Was the girl Elinor, Bethy? Or did the device change hands one more time?

Clearly Bethy time jaunted, so she should be taken to the academy, but that would change history. Johnston, Bethy was six, but according to historic records within the PX shield, Hajjar was the youngest to time jaunt and was ten years old when he jaunted.

What about the woman or man? he thought quickly, with the sandals that met up with Elinor in the alley. *Who is she or he, and what role do they play in this?*

A hand on Hajjar's shoulder made him jump, bringing him back to the bar. The house lights blinded him as he lifted his head from his hands. The empty silence was almost shocking compared to the crowded joint with loud music, bustling crowds, and smoky house setting over the bar.

"Where…where is everyone?" Hajjar looked around in surprise. How much time had passed? His head turned frantically, desperately hoping he hadn't missed or…maybe…somewhat hoping he had missed something like the hand off, which would make the decision he knew lurked in the back of his thoughts easier.

"We closed an hour ago." The light and flirty personality had left with the crowds. Hajjar looked around again, noticing the chairs on top of the tables and stools upside down on top of the bar around him. Only one stool remained on the floor, currently held down by him. Bridget stood leaning on the mop in the bucket with her last patience draining with each passing moment that he prevented her from finishing up and going to bed. "Do I need to get you a ride?"

"Where is Bethy?" Hajjar stood looking around, regaining his excitement.

"*She is in bed. It is late.*" Bridget emphasized each syllable as a mother trying to make the simplest thing clear to an obstinate child. "Go back to your hotel and get some sleep!"

Hajjar stood, taking a deep breath with his whole investigation starting to slip between his fingers. His first solo investigation was slipping into failure. He breathed deep, swallowing the knot in his throat back down.

He felt the squeeze of the hand still on his shoulder grounding him as he looked back into Bridget's exhausted eyes. "We will still be here tomorrow. *Work it out* and come back then" She sighed, guiding him off the remaining stool then picking it up, putting it on the bar and mopping the last two square feet of the bar floor. "Go. You have a lot on your mind. Figure it out before you come back." Her soothing, reassuring look iced over as she finished, "I *am* Bethy's guardian here. Whatever *it* is, you will take it up with *me* before dragging her back into it."

Hajjar walked out the door, looking up and down the dark deserted street. The tantalizing symphony of lights and cornucopia of sounds luring people into the clubs and bars were silent, and the crowds of people had gone home.

Hajjar walked, kicking the occasional can as the swirls of ideas tried to organize then solidify in his brain. His feet kept moving along to power the cogs in his mind to keep turning or walk himself to exhaustion in search of the dream to calm of sleep.

Something kept bothering him about the encounter at RedWing. How did the dark-haired girl with emerald eyes get the device? And who was the person in the alley wearing sandals who met up with her?

Another turn took Hajjar down another street of thought. How had Johnston been in the agency long enough to be a veteran, and yet *he* still stood as the youngest person to time jaunt in historic record? He jaunted when he was ten years old, fourth grade. He remembered it all. Bethy was five maybe six now, in Austin of 1963. She had to jaunt here. Hajjar had met her parents when she was thirty something. She had to have jaunted here and said nothing. How was she not the youngest on record?

Hajjar found himself sitting on red granite steps. His feet were killing him as he kicked the sandals off his feet to keep pondering.

The twinkling stars started to hide in the deep purple sky as the dark red wisps of feathers reached across the sky and slowly turned shades of fire red and pink, and finally gold as the remaining stars fell asleep for the day. The purples drifted to blue then lightened more.

Hajjar sat in awe. An unpolluted sunrise was a thing to be savored. He sighed. "Might as well head back to the motel." He leaned forward to get his sandals to start the walk when the treads caught his eye. The sandal's soles were made from rubber that looked like tire tread. Reaching out, he picked up the sandal to look at the bottom of it closer. The zigzag designs though the center of the bottom was unmistakably a tire.

It was *his* sandal. It was his sandal that made the print in the alley. He was intercepting the girl.

All the pieces started fitting into place.

He was the person intercepting the girl in the alley. She was Johnston when she was at fourteen. He remembered the dinner with her parents. She told him that she entered the academy at fourteen, the same age as the girl at RedWing.

The memory of the dinner with Mr. and Mrs. Johnston suddenly took a new perspective. When he walked into the front room, Mr. Johnston greeted him warmly. "TDI Hajjar…I figure you will be soon enough?" The sudden glance he made to Liz was lost on him at the time, but now. What if they had already met him, but this was the first time he met them? What if they already knew him, but from when? Had he broken the rules taking her home instead of taking her to the academy? This way, he would keep his status of youngest time jaunted on record.

What if she requested him as her partner to make sure she gave him the clues he would need to guide the choices he was making now. How could he take her home to her parents if he had never been there, so she requested to be his senior officer mentor to be able to take him there?

All the recent and past events came into focus. Excited with the plan coming clear, he ran back to the club. The warm morning sun brought beads of sweat as he turned the corner on Sixth Street to continue his jog up to the thick green door. He leaned on the door, lowering his head to glance over to the window a moment. "Open."

They must have been open for lunch already. He lowered his head a moment longer to slow his breathing.

His hand wrapped around the handle, and he leaned back to pull the heavy door open.

"Bridget! I know what to do!" Hajjar smiled with a wild and excited grin.

"Okay?" Her tired voice drew out the question. "And what is that?"

"I need to take her home."

"Home, where else would you take her?" Bridget's glare turned dark, protective and thinking of all the horrible other places he might take her. "Where else would you have taken her to?"

"The academy." Hajjar stepped back, insulted at the implication. "A school to teach her to…she is…special…"

"But instead you are taking her home?"

"What if I don't want to go home?" Bethy's voice cut in.

Hajjar and Bridget looked over at the little girl standing, fists clenched and emerald eyes blazing. "What if I don't want to go home?" She stomped.

"No one is sending you home. No one is making you do anything." Bridget smiled at Bethy and then looked at Hajjar, dropping her warm and comforting smile for an icy glare of challenge.

Hajjar pursed his lips and then turned to face Bethy at the end of the bar. He squatted, looking her in the eye. "Why didn't you want to go home?"

She stepped back, looking down at her feet, trying to twist a hole through the floor. "My mom and dad hate me." She looked up through the tears in her eyes. "They'll kill me."

Bridget bent forward. "You don't have to go home. You are safe here."

Hajjar shook his head. "I've met your parents, and they love you dearly. Why would they kill you?"

"I broke my daddy's favorite record." Bethy started to weep. "I didn't mean to."

Bridget frowned. "A record?" she whispered. "Over a record." She stepped closer to Bethy, giving her a hug. "What record?"

"Janis Joplin record. It is over three hundred years old. It's priceless, and I broke it."

Hajjar bit his lip, holding back a snicker. "You know, Bethy, we are in 1963 right now. You just saw Janis play music. I'm sure there is a record store around here." Hajjar smiled "We can get a replacement LP for the one that broke."

"Really!" Bethy hopped up.

"Just one moment." Bridget stood, looking at Hajjar. "What did she mean three hundred years old? Where are you from?"

Hajjar slowly shook his head. "We are not from around here."

"Well, no shit!" Bridget crossed her arms in front of her. "*Don't* insult me!"

"We are from England, Greenwich," he said, letting his accent drop in. "Only a couple hundred years in the future. Only we are not supposed to interfere with the past."

"It's a little late for that now. What do you think you are doing right now? More important, what about Bethy? I doubt she came here intentionally."

"I'm supposed to take her to the academy to learn to control her abilities."

"Buuut." Bridget drew out the statement into a question. "You're not?"

Hajjar looked over at Bethy and slightly frowned, not fully understanding himself. "That's not what is best for her." He looked up into Bridget's eyes. "That is not how it happened."

"How do you know what is best for her? Wait a second. This already happened?" Bridget lifted an eyebrow.

"This has already happened for Agent Johnston, the Bethy I already knew. She trained me in the agency when I met her five years ago. But not yet for her, now." He pointed at the girl in front of him.

"Maybe this is not the same Bethy that you know." Bridget frowned. "What if she doesn't want to go home?"

"*She* is standing right here." Bethy placed her fists on her hips, pursing her lips and scowling fiercely at the two. Once she looked into Bridget's worried eyes, she melted. "Bridget, I love you. You took me in when I was lost and scared, but I want to go home. I will come and visit." She looked up at Agent Hajjar.

Bridget sniffed back tears. "I know. I knew you were passing through, but you...you will always be my little pint-sized waitress."

Hajjar knelt down, placing his hands on Bethy's shoulders. "Do you want to stay here while I head out to get Janis Joplin's album before we take you home?" His eyes slid from Bethy's watery eyes to Bridget's eyes, filling with tears.

"Yes." Bridget choked back her watery voice to be strong for her little one.

Hajjar headed out, looking back over his shoulder and smiling. The warmth of doing the right thing brought a smile to his face as he looked over his shoulder at the two embracing with their arms wrapped around each other, hoping to never let go. They sobbed at the knowledge that the hug might be the end, and they would part forever. The sadness of splitting the foster mother from her child suddenly weighed on Hajjar. He paused, pushing the door half open before wiping a tear. Then he headed to the record store he saw three doors down.

Weeks passed. Old routines never really returned while new routines set in. Guards changed every few hours to avoid exhaustion or fatigue in the cold. The castle's servants prepared the day's food and performed chores. Johnston, too, returned to a routine of sparring in the early morning. Some mornings were harder than others. Her bones, joints, and muscles reminded her that her almost forty-year-old body just wasn't as agile as it used to be.

This morning, she opened her eyes to the darkness and the chill on her nose. Her muscles protested as she coaxed them into movement. The blankets were warm, and she was comfortable, but eventually the morning routine and Johnston's desire to survive this ordeal won out as she gasped, placing her feet onto the cold stone floor.

She was greeted in the courtyard by the first dusting of snow, a thin layer of white glistening dust hiding in the lower recesses where the melted water collected and refroze, but the grass sparkled in the light of the setting moon. She stopped to marvel at the image before the daily routine left the muddy footprints in the snow.

The fire of the forge warmed the training area, which was nice for the first few minutes until the warmth of exercise set in and Johnston just wanted to be in the cool outdoors again.

Catching her breath as a bead of sweat rolled down the side of her cheek, she wished to be out in the snow.

"We will have to cut this session short today." Keith breathed heavily, wiping the sweat from his forehead with his sleeve.

"Training with your men?" Johnston asked, lowering her sparring sword.

"No, we are negotiating the entrance of Father Granger."

"Oh." Johnston felt the optimism in her voice and continued to catch her breath before lunging in for another exchange of maneuvers. She paused a moment. "It has been a while since we have had a proper mass."

"Yes, that is the goal." Keith swung his sword, starting another sparring maneuver. "And it will be nice to get word from outside the walls."

"I pray it is good news." Johnston breathed.

"Well…" Keith sighed. "It will tell us how dire the situation is."

"I am typically the realist, grounding the optimism." Johnston walked to the rack, returning her practice blade.

Keith smiled. "I guess we have switched places." He walked over, returning his blade. "Who would have expected this?" A sigh of weariness left his lips.

"Tomorrow then?" Johnston finally started breathing normally.

"Yes, hopefully we will have good news to discuss this evening at dinner."

Johnston wrapped her cloak around her shoulders, pulling her hood over her head. "To good news." Johnston tipped her hood.

Her time with Liam was cherished. Sneaking him treats got harder and harder with each passing day of the siege. She would take an apple from the kitchens, eating some of it on the way to the stable, leaving most of the apples for her confidant. He would snub the leftovers each time, and then after she held her forehead next to his, thinking what she wanted to say aloud, reassuring him of the troubles, she went to get him this treat.

Half the time, he would take the rest of the apple, savoring the crunchy sweetness. Other times, he would gesture to give the apple to someone else. She pulled her small dagger, slicing the apple in half, giving each half to a different horse who enjoyed the treat.

She wished she could have more time to train Liam, but she didn't want to draw attention to herself by training him in the courtyard. She still looked forward to sitting with him and talking. He was such a good listener. Johnston found herself more and more often in the stall, feeding slices of apples to Liam and talking her way through the situations.

Again, the day passed feeling like an eternity. And again, Johnston was getting prepared for dinner. She found herself in a situation where she knew the end of the story but couldn't give anything away to the character.

"You are more quiet than usual this evening." Andrea's voice intruded Johnston's thoughts. "Lady Ogilvy?"

"Sorry. My thoughts have me somewhere else." Johnston trailed back into her worries.

"You are nearly ready." Andrea's fingers tied up Johnston's hair, then she stepped back, eyeing her work. "There," she said with finality in her voice.

Johnston picked up her hand mirror. "Beautiful as always. Thank you."

Johnston lowered her head in thanks to Andrea as she left the room to dinner. The added layers under her dress weighed heavy but was well worth the extra insulation.

The stiffness in the dress reduced Johnston's movement. She noticed that for future reference and opened the door to the dining room.

"Will Father Granger be joining us for Sunday dinner?" Elizabeth's soothing voice carried through the opened door to Johnston as she entered the room.

Again, all eyes turned to her as she tried to avoid the loud creaking of the door, with no luck.

"Lady Ogilvy, we have good news this evening." Anne greeted Johnston as the door made its final protesting groan then latched shut. "Father Granger will be giving mass this week."

"This is great news!" Johnston continued to the table. "It will be quite a refreshing change to have Father Granger here in these walls. Will his wife be able to join him when he comes?"

"No, only the father shall join us this Sunday," George said with hints of tension lifting if even for a moment.

"I am looking forward to his guidance through scripture." Anne closed her eyes with a smile.

Johnston's thoughts escaped. *A link to the outside that will give us an outlet for...*

"What was that?" George lowered his eyebrows in question to Johnston.

Johnston wondered how he could have heard her. "A link to the outside," she stated, looking around. "Hopefully, good news or possibly encouragement to the men through the Father's words." She had her expectation to the answer. "He is an ally to the cause?" Her answer came with a shocked look from George's face at such an accusation. "This is the same Father I remember having heard about from...well...everyone here?"

George's expression relaxed a bit. "Yes, this is Father Granger and his wife. They are friends to us, to the cause."

"I look forward to meeting him. His reputation precedes him." Johnston nodded.

"We all look forward to his visit," Anne continued. "How long will he be able to visit?"

George looked over to her, drinking from his glass. Then he looked toward the window with disappointment. "Only Sunday mass. It took much negotiation to even get Father Granger in for mass." His eyes seemed to focus on something far in the distance. "We are in a war," he muttered.

"Well, at least we do not have to be heathens without spiritual guidance." Elizabeth walked over, placing her hand on George's shoulder. He reached across, placing his hand atop hers, and then turned to face her and the rest in the room. Slowly, he walked to the dining table. "This trial will test us."

***

The bright cloudless sky greeted Sunday morning with a bustling castle alive with anticipation of the guest. Johnston wandered through the dry patches between the puddles of melted snow.

Her mind raced, wondering what words of encouragement the father might pass to build hope within the walls.

The father was not expected for another three hours; however, the people scurried around as though he were already within the walls. The dry patches of courtyard led her to the chapel.

Wanting to see if there was anything that she could help with, she slipped in the door. The room was small enough to be personal but large enough for voices to echo in the vast vaulted ceiling when it was empty. This morning, the sanctuary was filled to the brim. Johnston felt like she was weaving through the tight crowds of a packed nightclub without flashing lights, loud music, or crowd surfing.

Two hours before Sunday mass, and people gathered, filling the aisle and overflowing into the back and side aisles, standing because of the limited seating. "Lady Ogilvy!" A loud voice carried over the intimate crowd.

Johnston looked around for the familiar face to match the voice. A face lightened as her eyes fell upon Keith standing along the side aisle. His hand beckoned her to his position. Weaving through the crowd along the side aisle, she couldn't believe how many people were still in the castle and how many were already standing in the back of the chapel hours before Father Granger was due to arrive.

The first row of the pews sat vacant, awaiting Sir George, Elizabeth, Anne, Keith, and possibly her. She then followed Keith into the side chamber. "When is Father Granger expected?" Johnston looked around the empty chamber, smiling. "Is there anything I can do to help in the preparation?"

"You seem as excited as Anne and Elizabeth." Keith passed the side door, looking back. "When he arrives, we will lead him in here to gather his thoughts before the service."

"Umm…" Johnston's expression flattened, trying to ask her question without offending Keith. She had worked so hard to keep what little trust he granted her, and they were starting to get along, or at least he did not seem to mistrust her as much as he did when she first arrived. "Well…" The thought came to her. "Do you think we might get a preview of the sermon topic?" She brought excitement back to her voice.

Keith studied her a moment flatly. "Make sure his Sunday sermon will not be influenced by the English army sitting right outside our walls?" He shook his head. "You are cynical. Do you trust anybody?"

The excitement left Johnston's voice as she answered, "No, I learned that as a hard lesson early in my life."

Keith stood near the window, looking out over the courtyard. Looking back over his shoulder at Johnston, he asked, "And family, do you trust them?"

That remains to be seen, Johnston thought. She looked over to Keith without saying a word.

He looked back out the window with a slight smirk. "The topic will be previewed by George, but not in great detail. Father Granger is an ally, earning the trust of Sir Ogilvie and continuing to reaffirm loyalty over the recent years. But yes, to your question, Sir Ogilvie must have learned that same lesson early, as did we all. In these times, we leave nothing to chance."

"This is a relief, though not enough to allow my vigilance to relax."

Keith moved his head, catching glimpse of something on the other side of the more translucent panes of glass. Johnston's watchful eye followed Keith's attention as moments later, the light from the window, golden with hues of blue, were shadowed by three figures passing by toward the door.

Seconds passed in eons as a series of three raps came muffled by inches of wood. Keith knocked on the door twice, followed by a silent whisper, "One...two ..." Then one more knock. He closed his eyes, pulling his sword out of the sheath an inch and counting, "One...two...three." A single knock followed, paused, and a second knock on the wooden door.

Johnston watched the sword fall back into its sheath as the tension released from Keith's shoulders and he unbolted the door swinging it open. Three cloaked figures swept into the room, shedding their layers.

Father Granger's leathery face and piercing green eyes emerged from the second cloak. The white hair remaining on his head made a halo of glistening fluff that stuck with static to the hood of the cloak. He quickly set to work, flattening his hair. Johnston remembered him only a few months ago. She recognized the look of resignation and acceptance to the less favored path but the one that must be taken. Under the resignation, she could also see a spark of rebellion in his eye, still looking for a way to defy and find a path not yet revealed, a better one.

Johnston sat studying Father Granger's expressions as he greeted Keith, grasping his hand with both of his own and leaning in to add emphasis.

Rising slowly, he turned to Lady Douglas. His leathery face gathered wrinkles at the corners of his eyes as his lips rose into a smile. He stepped forward, grasping her hands. "My lady." He glowed, radiating warmth.

"Sir Ogilvie will join us shortly." Keith gestured the father to the desk near the window. "How was your journey?"

Father Granger's gaze swept the room, falling on Johnston sitting in a chair to the side of Lady Douglas. "I do not believe I have had the privilege of meeting you…Lady?"

Johnston gently smiled, slowly rising from the chair. "Lady Ogilvy." She stepped forward, reaching for Father Granger's hands, lowering her head in a respectful bow. "My cousin—"

"Is Sir Ogilvie." He smiled, masking his guarded glance to Lady Douglas.

"Her home, Castle Campbell, fell to Cromwell's advancement months ago," Lady Douglas noted. "She is staying with us for now."

Johnston watched Father Granger's gaze swing back to Keith.

The moment of truth, Johnston thought as the seconds passed in slow motion.

A slight nod from Keith relaxed Father Granger's shoulders. "You have a lot of soldiers surrounding this castle."

"I know." Sir Ogilvie walked into the room. "Is Cromwell among them?"

"Not from what I have heard." The father smiled. "Though he may be joining later. They seem to be stalling."

Sir Ogilvie cringed. "Bringing reinforcements."

"Most likely. They did not get my sermon. I had my notes safely stowed." He pulled them from the lining of his Bible.

Sir Ogilvie reached out, taking the extended papers. Skimming over them, he started chuckling. "Good selection, Father. This passage has been on my mind as of late." He looked over to Johnston with a nod. "I look forward to your guidance." He folded the parchment, handing the pages back to the father.

Sir Ogilvie stood, reaching out for Lady Douglas's hand. Gracefully, she stood, gliding over to him and placing her arm and hand atop the back of his arm. Together, they glided into the sanctuary.

"Shall we?" Keith extended his arm to Anne Leslie. She rose, leaving the cloche draped across the back of the chair, and then joined him on his right side. As with Lady Douglas, she placed her left arm atop Keith's arm. Both turned to the now opened door.

Johnston stood, slowly taking a deep breath to collect her thoughts, and then followed the group.

"You are not quite as I remember you, Elizabeth." Father Granger's voice sounded like he was whispering, but Johnston could hear him clearly, the voice of stone standing against the howling wind and storm.

Johnston turned to him, speaking softly. "I wish I had more time to tell you my journey of getting here and seeking your counsel on the current events that fill my dreams with such images." She turned back to the door. "Hopefully, you will visit again, and we will have more time to lay some of your concerns to rest."

"I look forward to that day." The soft steady voice followed Johnston to the door.

Johnston paused, turning again to Father Granger. "Thank you for coming. Everyone is looking forward to your words of guidance. Bless you for making the journey." She inclined her head to him and then turned to enter the sanctuary, finding a place on the first pew. Sir Ogilvie and Lady Douglas sat regally alongside the podium.

The room prickled with electricity, alive and buzzing with excited patrons. A hush fell over the crowd as Father Granger entered the room.

"I am blessed today to be here. In these times, we are fighting a feud. Not a feud of clan or kin but a battle of faith."

Father looked around, glancing at the faces in the crowd, and then continued, "We look to the book of Luke, chapter 12. And the Lord said, 'Who then in the faithful and wise steward, whom his master will set over his household, to give them their portion of food at the proper time? Blessed in that servant whom his master when he comes will find so doing. Truly, I say to you, he will set him over all his possessions. But if that servant says to himself, 'My master is delayed in coming,' and begins to beat the manservant and the maid servants, and to eat and drink, the master of the servant will come a day when he does not expect him and at an hour he does not know, and will punish him and out him with the unfaithful."

The father looked again to the crowd, sweeping his gauze and resting on Sir Ogilvie for a moment, and then looked forward to the crowd. "These words of Luke remind us that we must maintain our faith in our purpose. We must not lose sight of that which we were given in trust to maintain and protect in the absence of our master and king. He shall return. We must hold strong."

Johnston paid less attention to the remainder of the sermon. She sat attentive in posture, but her mind wandered. She started contemplating the scenarios, the dangers. Father Granger and his wife were…well, were key in the safe extraction of the Honours. A fear washed over her a moment as she thought how fast news traveled. History said the stewards of Castle Campbell handed the castle over to Cromwell's men. Some historic references named them as traitors to the crown.

As the Sunday mass closed, she brought her thoughts back to the present.

Father Granger headed into the side chamber, catching Sir Ogilvie's eye, passing words in a glance and followed the father into the room.

Johnston stepped out from the side door into the brief sunlight peeking between the clouds that had decided to move in. Movement in the corner of her eye caught her attention as Sir Ogilvie escorted Father Granger to the gates. They grasped arms then parted ways as the father lifted his hood over his head, leaving through the door next to the gate.

Johnston lifted her head against the sun, letting the warm rays wash away her many worries of the father and George's discussions. She was warm for the moment.

She meandered through the kitchens to retrieve contraband in the form of a bright red apple, and then she thought better of it. She was wearing her dress that had captured the hues of sunset within its folds. She wore this to dinner, and it had better not smell of the stable, like her other dress. She missed the rides in the countryside, being able to freely verbalize her thoughts while the wind filled her ears with beautiful nothingness.

She placed the apple back into the basket in the pantry. *Spring will be here sooner than we expect*, she thought. She sighed and started walking through the halls, trying to clear her head of thoughts. Soon she came face-to-face with the door to the dining room before remembering that dinner this evening would be in the great hall. She shook her head in disgust at her own absentmindedness then headed back down the hallway that she came in.

By now she would probably be fashionably late. Johnston doubted that Sir Ogilvie would appreciate the fashionably late grand entrance. She paused with her hand on the side door, smiling, letting her mind wonder to an amusing image of herself, white-streaked hair, wrinkles, and all in a white dress, singing "Happy Birthday, Mr. President." She couldn't even pull that look off when she was a teenager.

She took a deep breath to bring back her focus to the present. The last thing Johnston needed at that point was a return trip to the 1960s. She exhaled slowly, pushing the door open and slipping in. With the ruckus of the dining room, she walked up the long side of the hall along the wall.

Two long tables ran the length of the room. The gigantic room that once echoed with emptiness now seemed claustrophobic with all the people laughing, talking, and enjoying the rare relief from the tension. She wanted to ask Keith who remained on watch, worried that in the evening's relaxation…then she thought otherwise.

The energy within the room lifted her spirits as she continued along the wall beside the long table to the corner of the room behind the head table at the end of the room.

Five places were set at the head table. Sir Ogilvie stood in the center of the table, glass held high. Lady Douglas sat to his left with her glass held high. Keith and Anne sat to George's right with Anne at the end of the table. As Johnston stood along the back left side of the room, Lady Douglas caught her eye, gesturing to sit next to her. Johnston nodded to her then gestured to the crowd along the long tables with their glasses held high, hanging on Sir Ogilvie's words, indicating she did not want to interrupt by taking her seat just yet.

Johnston took in the room. Her nose decided to ignore the musk of the people crowded in the room and instead focused on the aromas of roasted meats and vegetables being carried out on trays. The room erupted in a huzzah of cheering as Sir Ogilvie's glass was lowered to take a sip. The relaxed jovial feeling of those in the room was a stark contrast to the tightly wound ball of stress around the castle of late. This evening was much needed by all. Slowly, Johnston took her seat next to Elizabeth.

"You are late," Elizabeth leaned over, whispering in her ear.

"I found myself in the private dining room." Johnston smiled sheepishly. "I must be getting senile."

Elizabeth snorted, shaking her head with held back laughter.

The celebrations lasted well past the time when Johnston decided to retire for the evening. She slipped from the great hall after saying good evening to her hosts, then headed to bed.

The sounds of the evening's celebrations carried through the walls of the castle until predawn. After that night, the dinners were less frequent, training with Keith continued, but Johnston could feel the castle hunkering down to last the long months ahead, surrounded by the enemy.

***

A breath of spring scared away the winter chill, at least for a day or two. Her journal made it mid-March, and the bipolar temperatures supported that assessment, but Johnston really didn't know for sure. The days were all blurring together by now. Some mornings, she wondered if she could remember how to get home.

The cool breeze lifted her spirits as it desperately tried to unravel her hair from the tight braid on the back of her head. The air felt good against her flush face. A small bead of sweat threatened to forge a path all the way into her eye.

Excitement swelled in her chest, looking forward to Father Granger's return visit. She felt herself succumbing to the excitement and energy around her. She slowly walked through the courtyard, looking at the walls around her.

The tall stone walls housed the castle's people and work areas. The doors looking out onto the green area each hid quarters and trade work area with a tall wall overlooking the meadow and cliff dropping off behind them. The walls and dwellings gave a sense of life within the protective shell. Over the last few months, the protective wall grew to feel more like a prison with the guards pacing along the top. Even the guards atop the wall seemed to move more and more like captive cats, pacing and itching to get free to show those on the outside watching the true predator, the true warrior within.

"Lady Ogilvy." The deep voice pulled her vision from the tip of the walls back to the courtyard. "Lady Ogilvy." George walked with purpose, an agenda to the day's duties.

She could feel their relationship drifting apart over the previous month. Johnston hoped that this was her paranoia and that he was merely distracted with the duties of a castle whose enemies camped on the other side of the walls.

"Father Granger and Christian are here. He has asked to see you."

"Oh, thank you." Johnston looked around the courtyard to the conservatory on the side of the chapel. "In the chapel?"

"Yes. Follow me." George paused for her to step up beside him as he turned to start toward the chapel behind her.

The two walked a few steps before Johnston broke the silence. "It is good to have Father Granger and his wife come for Sunday mass. Everyone is encouraged by his visit."

Sir Ogilvie or George? Johnston wondered if she had lost the privilege of familiarity with him as they continued to walk in stride without a word.

Johnston sighed silently, breathing slowly as she walked across the grass and stones to the side door of the chapel. The familiar series of knocks struck Johnston as slightly silly from this side. They were already on the interior of the castle; an intruder would have no trouble coming in another door on the interior of the chapel that did not have a lock. She repressed a smile as the door opened.

She stepped in, pausing a long moment for her eyes to adjust to the dim colors streaming in from the stained glass. The group sitting around the room slowly came into focus. A clutter of items sitting on the desk in front of Father Granger created an odd pool of shadows at the bases of each of the item. Her eyes moved to the longer pools of shadow and then to the people attached.

Silence remained as she scanned the solemn faces looking at her from around the room. Keith stood eerily still with his hand resting near his hip. Johnston looked to Anne sitting in front of him with her lips pursed in a line of concern.

Lady Douglas, Elizabeth…had Johnston lost the privilege of familiarity with her too? Lady Douglas stood in the corner, the trickle of a tear glistening as she wiped her cheek where webs of red spread from her eyes down to meet her passing hand. Father Granger stepped forward, reaching to Johnston's arm and gesturing her to a chair nearby.

Johnston's eyes scanned each person for a clue, calmly taking a seat with the grace and dignity of a lady to her stature.

"We have some news." Even in giving what Johnston could tell was going to be bad or shocking news, Father Granger's soft-spoken voice was reassuring as a stone that would remain by your side through the storm. "This may not be easy."

Johnston could pick up on undertones of his voice that made the hairs on the back of her neck start to prickle. *Calculation now, Johnston*, she thought. She allowed her emotion of worry to flicker across her face, the kind of worry for a loved one. She was careful not to show any hint of it tinged with fear and blow her cover.

"We have word of your husband."

"John? Is he…" Johnston's voice trailed off as she looked around then whispered, "Is he okay?"

Father Granger's look over to Sir Ogilvie spoke volumes.

"Is he…dead?" Johnston croaked. She guessed where this might be going. If she hadn't altered events at this point, Castle Campbell might have aligned with Cromwell, but Elizabeth Ogilvy's husband could never be a traitor to the crown.

Again, Father Granger looked to Sir Ogilvie, this time a question in the father's face on what to do. Sir Ogilvie walked to Johnston's chair, placing a comforting hand on her shoulder. "We are family…" His voice trailed off.

Johnston sniffed. "At least he died defending the crown." Her lower lip quivered a bit as she looked to an empty spot on the distant wall. *Here it comes*, she thought.

"Not quite," Sir Ogilvie continued before any interruptions. He took a deep breath and pushed on, trying to rip the Band-Aid off quickly. "He joined Cromwell's forces."

Johnston sat a long moment, allowing the emotions to visibly wash over her. The stunned look sat on her face with her mouth ajar, and shocked open eyes and a dash of denial. "No, he knows I am here, with you, defending the crown." She looked from the spot on the wall to Sir Ogilvie. "Our family clan Ogilvie supported King Charles even in death. How could he?"

"I am not sure how he could turn so…*easily*." Father Granger emphasized the last word.

Johnston allowed a few more emotions of grief to wash visible across her face and body. Denial in her eyes, believing that he would never betray her, washed away. Her eyes widened, darting around face to face before looking down to their hands clasped in her lap. She brought a tear to her eyes; the abandonment of her loved one, clearly separated from her… "He knows I'm here with you." She looked up at Sir George and then returned her gaze back to her lap. "He…" Then the solemn resolve a moment before her eyes squinted, focusing on the beam of furious rage. "He abandoned me," she hissed, "and…" The anger in her eyes fled as her eyes widened with fear. "The crown." Her eyes widened with fear. "You don't think…I have been…oh god! You…you don't think I'm a spy for the enemy, for Cromwell." She looked around to Keith. "You said yourself that I might be here as a spy." Johnston closed her eyes and took a deep breath, bringing her emotions back into check. She opened her eyes and looked back to her hands in her lap, ashamed for her emotional outburst. But before she completely bottled her emotions again, she whispered, "He will pay for this betrayal." She hoped she was not pushing it too far. She regained her composure, straightening her back and wiping her emotions from her face except for the narrowing of her eyes, looking again to the empty space on the opposite side of the room.

Johnston tried to gather the reactions of all around her without sweeping the room with her eyes. George's hand closed again on her shoulder then released as he walked around to the desk where Father Granger sat. "We have more pressing matters at hand." George's resolve settled the dust storm of emotions in the room like a rainstorm with ominous thunder. "Father Granger tells me that Cromwell is staying in London."

"This is good news." Elizabeth Douglas perked up. "Maybe we are no longer…" Her voice trailed off.

Johnston looked up, seeing the expression on George's face that drove her to silence. She knew the news, the reason for the grim look of a man who had accepted the diagnosis from the doctor that his days were numbered.

George swallowed hard, rewetting his dry mouth, continuing, "He will not let our defiance stand. The king is in exile, and we are now the only castle in the area remaining true to the arms of King Charles II. The flag on the spire declares our defiance."

"What do they plan to do?" Anne's voice came, barely audible, as she looked over to Lady Douglas with shock that her words were spoken before she thought to remain silent.

Lady Douglas's expression to Anne was part relief and part exasperation. She was relieved it was not her voice that chipped the tension of silence, asking the question everyone was afraid to ask, yet knowing she would hear of her personal friend's indiscretions.

The silence stretched, pulling the tension out like a string fit to snap. Not even George could bring himself to utter the news, as if saying it meant that it was inevitable. Even though he did not set this upon them all, he knew that all among them here in the room shared in the finality.

Johnston remembered how history played out. *They are sending the cannons to assault and possibly breach the walls, aren't they?* Johnston thought to herself.

A gasp escaped from Lady Douglas as she whimpered softly. "Are they bringing reinforcements?"

"We need to get the papers out of the castle." George sighed. "As well as the crown jewels."

"Why?" Anne leaned in to ask Keith, who shushed her.

Johnston nodded slowly, remembering how nervous she was. In the matter of politics and war, it was sometimes better to be blissfully ignorant of the information to make the hard decision.

"Who is guarding the castle?" George asked, looking to Father Granger.

The father smiled. "Cromwell loyalists from England."

Johnston let a concerned smile lift her lips as she recognized this scenario play out.

George looked over to her, lifting an eyebrow. "Why the amused look?"

"You look as though you are forming an idea." Johnston smiled. remembering her first night describing her assessment of the English siege of her own castle.

Lady Douglas's face slowly transformed from confusion to recognition and finally to the chess setup for a stalemate. The rook may fall, but the king and crown are still intact. Her body sank a moment before she stiffened her back, inhaling, lifting her chin, and blinking slowly. "I see."

"We should start a slow evaluation of the women and children." George brought all eyes in the room to him. "Anne." He looked over to her. "We will need you to go with them to guide them out of the castle."

Her eyes widened. "I will not leave Keith. If he is staying, I shall stand next to him." Anne looked over to Keith.

"You should lead them out to sanctuary." Keith looked from Anne to George. "What will you have her carry out?"

Anne shifted from defiance to realization and finally fear. Her mouth opened a little to protest, plea, anything. Nothing but a squeak escaped her lips before she closed her mouth again, sitting still.

"What will you have her smuggle out?" Lady Douglas's soft voice broke the long moment of silence.

"The papers," George stated as fact.

Keith smiled as he looked confidently at Anne. "King Charles's papers are critical, and they are the most easy to smuggle out. Most importantly, this will test the strategy of smuggling items out of the castle."

"What happens if they find the papers?" Anne's face blanched as the thought became real in her mind.

They won't, Johnston thought to herself, smiling. She realized as George looked over at her.

"They won't. They won't search her undergarments." Lady Douglas looked into Anne's eyes with a confident smile. "We sew them into her undergarments. The soldiers would not dare defile her or compromise her dignity by searching there. Especially knowing her stature within this household." She paused a moment before continuing softly.

"The English soldiers will not question or think that we women of the castle would play a critical role in the misdirection of this plan," Sir George stated.

Anne looked around the room with a sigh. "We will gather a handful of staff that will not want to remain through the final assault. I should not leave alone. It might arouse suspicion if I am the only person in the castle abandoning my friends and duties to Lady Douglas."

"I agree," Keith added.

"Then it is settled," George stated with firmness and resolve.

Father Granger smiled warmly. "Will we be able to organize this by the time I leave this afternoon? They will receive safe passage if I travel with them."

"We will be ready." George looked to his wife. "Have your chambermaids sew the papers into the lining of Miss Leslie's riding clothes while Father Granger gives Sunday mass."

"Of course." Elizabeth stood to leave the room and then turned back to Father Granger. "I apologize if I miss your sermon. I was looking forward to it."

Anne stood to follow Elizabeth from the room. "I should go too, and I will need to make sure the alterations to the garment do not affect the fit."

"I should go too," Johnston continued. "I may be of some help in the sewing." Her voice trailed off, wanting to retreat without drawing additional attention to herself.

"Will you stay?" George demanded more than asked. "I value your tactical input, Lady Ogilvy, and wish for your addition to the counsel." His seriousness caught a glance from Anne. Pity or worry, Johnston could not fully read the look.

"Yes, sir." Johnston sat back down calmly. "As you see best."

The women retreated from the room, leaving Johnston with the men. Father Granger clearly did not trust her. She wondered if Keith and George trusted her loyalty. Johnston sat straight astute to listen. She took a deep breath to refocus.

"As you know," George started slowly, "we are up against a losing battle. The siege will not last forever, and we are now on our own. We will not win this."

"We can make sure that the crown is not found by Cromwell. Either we find a way to get it out of the castle or we hide it such that it cannot be found when the castle is inevitably ransacked." Keith walked to the window.

"How can we hide a four-and-a-half foot sword on a person?" Father Granger asked.

"The women from the nearby town gather moss and seaweed at the bottom of the cliffs below. We could arrange to lower the sword, scepter, and crown over the wall when they are gathering the moss for bedding," Keith suggested.

"That could be arranged." Father Granger furrowed his brow.

"I don't know…" Johnston contemplated the situation, letting the words slip into the room.

"Go on." George leaned forward, placing his elbows on his knees.

"Cromwell is fortified, embedded around the castle. Do you think that we could lower a large parcel over the wall without detection by one of his men? If we do get the items down to the beach without detection, how do we know the townswomen are loyal to the cause or that they might divulge the information to Cromwell's army out of fear? The more people we involve, the more complex the plan gets. Then the more likely Cromwell will find out and thwart the plan." Johnston looked directly to George.

A brief smile washed over George's face, reminding Johnston of the maneuver she pulled in chess, taking his knights. Then as quickly, it was gone, replaced with the worry and resolve returning to the lines around his eyes. "We shall see what obstruction Cromwell's men pose to Anne as she departs. I agree. If we can smuggle the Honours out ourselves, then we should."

"I have a place near the corner of the rectory that we can hide them." Father Granger smiled. "We have been working on a crypt in the floor for a dearly departed member of our congregation. It will work well to hide the Honours. Not even Cromwell would disturb the departed." Looking to the door of the sanctuary, Father Granger rose. "I believe it is time I give the Sunday mass."

"What words of scripture do you have to inspire us this Sunday?" Johnston smiled briefly at Father Granger.

"Luke 4:28 to 30. The Lord shall watch over us and grant us safe passage."

George stood, grasping Father Granger's arm, shaking it and smiling. "That will give hope to those leaving with Miss Leslie."

"Father?" Johnston looked up.

The father turned to her. "Yes? Lady Ogilvy?"

Johnston paused, looking down, then back to his eyes. "I know your time is precious. I wish there was time that I could seek your counsel on the betrayal and pain I am feeling on the news on my… Lord Campbell." She squeezed a smile from her lips. "Emotions are a luxury we cannot afford at the moment. They will interfere with strategy."

Father Granger turned to her. "Yes, we can make time. Maybe during my next visit." He paused a moment longer before leaving the room.

"You and my Elizabeth should retire one of these evenings after dinner." George turned to Johnston. "She will need a confidant with Miss Leslie leaving. I trust your counsel."

"Thank you, Sir…George."

"I do not deny I had my doubt, but you have proven your loyalty today, both in your strategy counsel as well as remaining when it could be easier to leave and return to your lord."

"How could I turn my back on family?"

George smiled. "I still wonder why you have been spending so much time honing your fighting techniques with the sword and training your steed."

"As I told Keith, I want to be prepared for the worst. I hope I will not need the skills." Johnston paused before adding, "We will need to get the Honours out somehow. As I said, the fewer who know the plan, the better our probability of success. I want to be able to defend if it comes to that. Any armed guards will raise suspicion, so they will not be able to accompany us."

"Have you have been preparing for this from the day you arrived?" George questioned her.

"No, I have been preparing from the day I learned the Honours were still within these walls." Johnston sighed. "I did not know the Honours would still here when I came…but yes, my focus is on the Honours. Cromwell destroyed the royal jewels of Britain and made quite a spectacle of it." She looked to George with defiance. "They will not do the same to the Honours of Scotland if I can help it."

George sat with his age collecting in the corners of his eyes, adding years to his appearance. The siege was clearly taking a toll on him. "My focus has been on the castle and the people who live here." He turned his gaze to Johnston.

Before he could complete his thought, she interjected, "As well, it should be. I only hope my preoccupation with your added burden might relieve you in some minuscule way." She knew she was grasping and hoped at that moment that she did not push too far.

George sat still. A flick of a smile crossed his face, wrinkling the corners of his eyes. "I guess only history will tell." He stood and turned to the door.

Johnston sat still, watching him leave. The door shut with a loud heavy echo through the room. The silence settled as Johnston sat a few long moments before deciding not to interrupt mass. Instead, she would head up to Elizabeth's room to help with the conspiratorial tailoring. Slowly she stood, feeling every minute of her thirty-seven years in her muscles, or maybe it was just the hard workout. She walked out through the courtyard, pausing at the door into the castle.

The moments grew longer as she paused thinking with her hand on the door handle, looking at the dark grain running through the wood. The iron hinge and door latch shone from the constant flow of people touching it as they passed through the door. She didn't know why she hesitated. Maybe keeping up the persona was getting to her, and maybe she was just tired, dreading the approach of her final day. Maybe…

She shook off the thoughts, looking up from the door handle, and entered the castle.

A hush of tension filled Lady Douglas's room as each of the ladies worked securing the papers into the lining of Anne's dress. Anne looked to the door where Johnston had just stepped through, meeting Johnston's worry-filled eyes with her own. The pressure of what was about to happen weighed heavily on her. The atmosphere of the room reminded Johnston of the preparations for a wedding—the kind of wedding that secured an alliance between countries, the kind of wedding where the daughter of the house was expected to fulfill her duties to her family and lord by leaving her friends and family for the unknown.

The ladies Anne considered her closest friends and family worked tirelessly to make sure the dress was perfect. Lady Douglas walked around Anne, eyeing the blue riding dress and looking for bulges or folds that might seem out of place. "Can you move freely?" Lady Douglas asked while walking the full circle around the dress.

The ladies tucked and pinned, stitched and tied. The dress and fitting must be perfect without catching or tearing the papers. "Hush!" Lady Douglas raised her hands, silencing the room. "Now move for me," she stated. "I need to listen for sounds of rustling papers when you move."

Anne moved around gracefully, going through the movements she expected to use leaving. The room fell to silence. They closely listened for sounds that might give away the cleverly concealed documents.

"I think we are ready," Lady Douglas stated, stepping back to take one last look as worry crept into her smile. "You will be fine."

"I will miss you, Elizabeth." Anne looked around the room. "Andrea, Jane." She turned to give each a small hug of farewell. "Lady Ogilvy." She turned to Johnston. "We have not known each other as long as I would like, but I will miss you as well."

Johnston walked over to Anne, trying to hold back a tear. "Friendship forged in adversity is the truest. I wish safe passage for you and that we will not be long behind to reunite again outside these walls."

With tearful farewells, the mournful procession headed down to the courtyard and out near the stables where Father Granger and Keith had gathered the handful of people who would wish to depart with them on this journey. A long moment passed as they gathered themselves to face the enemy encamped around the outside of the castle.

"You will be fine." Lady Douglas walked to the side of the horse where Anne sat tall. "You will be fine." Then she stepped back to George, who put an arm around her.

With a clatter of hooves and squeaking of cartwheels, they were gone.

Hajjar sat on the stool at the bar and checked his Field Notebook. Bethy, Agent Johnston...he shook his head, still wrapping his head around the consent. She overshot the spot by a few years. Agent Hajjar chuckled a bit. Not bad for a first time, and especially at the age of six. He smiled with the confidence that he hit his target, granted he was ten, but with age comes wisdom. Agent Hajjar stood looking at Bridget and then bent down, facing his senior partner thirty-one years before now. "I'll be right back."

Hoping the shop would still be there in one year and the city layout would not change in one year, he ducked down a nearby alley.

A moment later...

He walked out of the same alley a couple years later. Then he turned the corner to walk in the record store. Rows of twelve-inch LPs lined the walls and the center aisle.

"Can I help you, sir?" The pretentious attitude of the clerk almost dripped from his lips.

"I'm looking for *Cheap Thrills*. It should be out by now. Do you have it?"

The clerk quirked his head. "Good choice. She is..."

"Local, yes. I saw Janis a couple of years ago here. Do you have it or not?" Hajjar could feel his patience draining from him as he stood there, looking at the kid who had experienced less in life than he had in travels alone.

"Oh." The clerk stood tall. "Yes, we have it." He strutted to the rack, pulling a thin twelve inch by twelve inch album, then strutted back. "I have it. It is hard to come by as her first album, but I have it. Here you go." His smug face radiated with pride of his rare gem.

"Great. She was amazing in concert." Hajjar pulled out his wallet. "About a year and a half ago. Two doors down."

"Oh yeah, I've been there." The kid's smugness drained a bit. "That must have been something to see." He opened the drawer, pulling out the change.

"There is a lot of good talent around here." Hajjar put the bills in his wallet then the change in his pants pocket before turning to leave.

He walked back into the side alley of 1968 and walked into the sunlight of 1963.

His steps slowed as the pub loomed closer. Was he really doing the right thing, or was he trying to preserve his status as youngest to time jaunt? The rules stated that all who jaunted through time must be brought to the academy to be trained.

Hajjar slowly opened the door, trying not to intrude on the goodbyes. The attempt only produced a long screech as the door announced his return. Bridget looked over her shoulder with a resolve settling over her face and body.

He walked back to the bar, sitting on the stool a few feet from them and putting the record on the bar top. Then he picked it up to read the back of the record. After reading the song titles for a few minutes and then few minutes more, he started at the third song on the list. He gave up on pretending to read.

Bridget chuckled then sniffed back a few tears. "You come visit. Any time!"

"I'll try."

"I don't think…" Hajjar's voice trailed off. He decided not to dash this moment with the reality of the regulatory agency and academy, like his was. He remembered not being allowed to say goodbye to his parents when they took him to the agency. A slight bitterness settled on his stomach with the memory of missing his parents.

"You will always be welcome here." Bridget pulled the little girl tight to her chest, holding on and unmoving except for occasional sobs. Slowly, Bridget lowered her arms and got up from the floor. In that moment, she looked as much like a little girl losing her best friend as a protecting mother bear.

"I'm going to miss you, Bridget. You are like the big sister I wish…my protector."

"Are you ready?" Hajjar tightly held the album, looking back and forth between the two girls.

"I think so." Bethy's eyes looked up, red and glimmering with tears.

"Do you have the device?"

Bethy pulled it out from her pouch.

"Now I want you to imagine your parents' house. Hold my hands tightly. I want you to remember the living room with the big window looking out onto the woods."

Bethy nodded. Hajjar knelt in front of her, holding her hands and looking into her eyes.

"Close your eyes and relax. Breathe in, feel the cold air on your cheeks from the spring breeze brought in from the open window looking out over…"

Hajjar's voice started lulling her into a dream. She could almost feel the breeze through the house on Saturday when the windows were open. She could hear the rustling of leaves in the woods out back and the birds chattering. Bethy could smell the lilac growing near the house with subtle hints of grass and fresh rain. She smiled at the tantalizing wafts of Saturday morning muffins. This morning must be blueberry.

Hajjar started to see the image that she was imagining envelop him. He could see the same images and hear the leaves.

Mom always brings them out on a plate before anyone gets up to lure us out of bed. She smiled, wanting some fresh warm muffins.

Crash.

"Bethy! Bethy! Is that you?" There was a loud frantic shriek from the other side of the room through the house. "Who are you and where did you take my daughter!"

Suddenly, the house erupted into frenzy. Doors opened and slammed; herds of footsteps pounded above on the stairs.

"Thank you, sir, for returning our little girl." A gentleman with slender cheekbones and an angled chin stepped forward with his hands stretched out.

"Oh!" Mrs. Johnston exclaimed as she ran to Bethy, dropping to her knees and pulling her little girl into her arms, smothering her. Bethy's mom stood back up, straightening her sundress. "You look like you were stolen by Gypsies." She pulled Bethy back to her chest again. "I'm so glad to have you home."

"Yes, Gypsies." Mr. Johnston stroked the graying stubble on his chin. "Gypsies from the 1960s or 1970s?" He paused, looking up at Hajjar as he stepped closer to shake his hand. "Where did you find our daughter?"

"We need to talk." Hajjar placed a hand on Bethy's shoulder. "It's important."

Mr. Johnston stood looking Hajjar in the eye, squinting and trying to get a read on him. "This way." He gestured to the side room. "It'll be okay, Kathrine. Take care of Bethy."

Hajjar caught a flinch from Bethy at the use of the full first name of her mother.

Mr. Johnston led Hajjar into the side room. The dark wood bookshelves on all sides were filled with hardbound books. He remembered this room, a quiet sanctuary surrounded by lavish knowledge. The hardbound books were long since obsolete and difficult to find, and here stood a roomful of them. Hajjar smiled, noticing the row of windows overlooking the woods, open and letting a light breeze through. It was the only place Kathrine allowed her husband to smoke inside.

"Can I offer you a cigar?" Mr. Johnston turned to Hajjar. "A drink?" He lifted a crystal decanter, pouring himself a glass.

"No, thank you, sir."

"Very well. Now business. What do you want?" Mr. Johnston's expression darkened. "You are clearly dressed like *her*. My only thought is that you kidnapped her and are now bringing her back for the reward." Mr. Johnston puffed visibly. "I don't know what you are playing at, *sir*, but you won't get away with it!"

Hajjar started chuckling that crescendo-ed into a rolling laugh.

"Well, I'm glad *you* are amused, because I am not. Not one bit."

"*No*, no, sir." Hajjar chuckled a little bit more. "Not only am I not asking for a reward, I came bearing gifts." After a few more chuckles and a sigh, he watched the anger on Mr. Johnston's face turn to confusion. "Your daughter went missing on the same day your Janis Joplin album was broken."

Mr. Johnston's face scowled back into anger. "How would you know that if you were not here taking her?"

"Here to replace your loss." Hajjar pulled the LP out from under his arm, handing Mr. Johnston the record purchased in Austin moments earlier. "Your daughter told me she broke your album when I found her. She told me why you were going to sell her to the ice mines at Antarctica when I found her and brought her home to you."

Mr. Johnston looked down in shock, holding the album. He looked back up. "I would have never hurt her." He looked down at the twelve-inch LP album in his hand. "I would never..."

"Sir. I'm with the agency." Hajjar pulled out his badge, flipping it open. "We need to talk."

"About?" Mr. Johnston looked up at Hajjar.

"You are aware of jaunting?" Hajjar asked, standing aside the leather sofa in the room.

"Well, yes, we all jaunt. Bethy even jaunted before she could walk. We would take her on family trips when Kathrine carried her."

Hajjar squinted his eyes. "Carried her?"

Mr. Johnston lowered his eyebrows in concentration. "Carried her, while pregnant. Then jaunting with her before she could walk, before she could jaunt on her own." As if it was the most normal thing in the world.

"How is that possible? She didn't leave Bethy behind or lose hold of her midjaunt?"

"No, we never had that issue with any of our children."

"Hmmmm." Hajjar frowned. "Back to the point. She jaunted back to 1963 when I found her."

"Jaunted back in time? I've only read of such a thing. She did that?"

"Yes, and the album is additional proof."

Mr. Johnston again looked at the record in his hand, flipping it over and over in amazement.

"The rules say I should take her straight to the academy for training." Hajjar paused.

"Then what are you doing here?"

"I think she needs to be older before I take her into academy...otherwise...well, I think she needs her parents to guard her and influence her now. Grow into the...Liz I know."

"I see...?"

"The next time she jaunts, I will take her in. She will leave for a long time. Make sure she jaunts only when she is ready to join the academy. Make sure she jaunts with this." Hajjar handed Mr. Johnston the small recording device. "Tell her to sell it, and I will find her. To take her in."

"How do we prevent her from time jaunting before heading to join the academy?" Kathrine's voice came from the door behind him.

"That is up to her." Hajjar walked over to Bethy, kneeling to look her in the eye. "You need to remain calm and grounded. If you ever find yourself away from home, remember how we got here today to get back home."

"I understand." Bethy smiled shyly, showing her dimples.

Hajjar stood. "I hope I'm doing the right thing," he whispered under his breath, but loud enough for Mr. Johnston to hear.

"Thank you for bringing our daughter back to us." Kathrine clasped her hands around him. "Thank you."

Hajjar stepped back and placed his hands on her shoulders. "Take care of her. There are greater things ahead for her." Hajjar turned to the large wooden doors of Mr. Johnston's library. "I will take my leave." He bowed his head to them.

H turned to leave as Mr. Johnston stepped over to wrap his arm around Kathrine and his other hand on Bethy's shoulder. The doors opened to the outer foyer. The ornate Art Nouveau chandelier hung over the granite entrance and stairs. It wrapped around the wall to the second floor, where two kids peered down. A sandy haired big brother, maybe fourteen, had his hand on the redhaired girl, a bit younger than her brother. Both looked at Hajjar with wide, inquisitive eyes. At the moment, he paused, looking at them. They scurried behind the corner. Hajjar smiled, hoping to meet them later.

Mr. Johnston walked out to the foyer. "It was interesting meeting you." He gestured to the door.

"Thank you." Hajjar grasped the door handles and opened the door to the sunny afternoon. He walked to the base of the stairs in front of the porch, hearing the door shut behind him.

He let his mind drift to the alley two buildings down from the Redwing Pawnshop, the brick of the building within arm's length of each side of him, and the summer heat blocked by the brick buildings on either side of him. He had arrived. He envisioned the date he was there as Bethy fled the pawnshop, briskly walking to where he now stood.

Slowly, he reached out, feeling the brick texture of the alley wall an arm's length away. He filled his lungs with the dry air and opened his eyes, hearing the patter of footsteps heading his way.

The girl in a black T-shirt stopped at the corner of the alley, looking back at the entrance of the pawnshop. Her blue Murphy Moo ball cap swung around as she took a few steps toward the point where the reality she saw in front of her caught up with her feet.

"Bethy."

"I was just running from you. How…" Her voice quivered, taking a few steps toward him.

"I took the long way, through 1963." He smiled. "Are you ready to go to the agency?"

"Not really, but does that really matter?"

"You are more ready now than when you were litt…" Hajjar stepped forward, grabbing her wrist. "I need you to clear your mind." He pulled out two silver disks that he placed on her temples. "Relax, Bethy. This will give you the image of the destination."

"Oh, I've been there before," she muttered.

Hajjar pulled her close to him, wrapping one arm around her back, placing the other hand on the back side of her head. "Come with me."

Fog rolled in, masking the dawn and covering the castle in a dense blanket of gray that decided to remain like an unwanted houseguest. Even in the late morning, the soupy mist hung around, adding to the apprehension hovering in the air. Ominous sounds echoed off the stone walls surrounding the courtyard. The screeching wheels of something large that did not want to be moved combined with clanging of weapons and men shouting danced around them without specific direction; they were not from within the castle. Dunnottar had been all but evacuated for at least three weeks. George whittled the castle occupants down to only the essentials for the remaining months. It would only be weeks now before the cannons were within range. Only sixty-nine men would remain within the walls—blacksmiths, cooks, and soldiers, all of them willing to maintain the castle and ready to fight to the death for the flag that hung high above the castle.

Johnston stood in the courtyard with the final group to leave. She and the other three were going through the preparations before leaving the castle for the final time. She stroked Liam's head, trying to instill him with more courage and calm than she currently felt. Today was the day. It was the day she had been dreading for the past nine months.

George walked up to the side of Lady Douglas's horse, placing his hand on his wife's knee and looking deeply into her eyes. "You will be fine," he said reassuringly, trying to convince himself as much as her. He stepped back, walking slowly around the horse and evaluating. He slowly made a full circuit around the still horse and rider. He started on the second trip. This time, when he reached the right side, he crouched down, keeping a hand on Ivey's side and taking care not to alarm her and get kicked. He looked under the horse at the draped skirts from the back side. "Amazing. Even looking for the crown I cannot see where it is hidden." George stood back, sharing an approving glance with Keith.

Lady Douglas looked over her shoulder to her husband, smiling to hide her worry. "We sewed a pouch in the lining on the skirt so that it is nestled where you expect my foot to be."

"The layers of the skirts with the cloak on top of it all…" George shook his head in astonishment. "You will be more than fine."

"It is not for me that I am worried. What will—"

"You are right," George interrupted Elizabeth. "Keith, inspect Miss Fletcher, though I suspect the scepter will be much easier to conceal than the crown or sword." He walked over to Father Granger, clasping arms. "It is a pleasure to see your wife again." He looked up to the stout woman, speaking the words more to her than her husband. "Her visit has brought sunshine to this dismal gray day."

"You are a flatterer." Christian Fletcher glowed with the fullness of life. Her dark brown hair was covered with only her bangs peeking out. Her skirts were modest but elegant with the attention to detail in finishing and reinforcing the construction for durability in her daily work. Lady Fletcher was accustomed to work but looked as though it brought her satisfaction and pride in the accomplishment. The toils of daily life did not show in her face; the rounded features gave a cheerful yet tranquil aura about her, that she was a mother to a congregation.

George looked back to Father Granger as Keith scrutinized Miss Fletcher atop her horse; he searched for anything within the folds of her skirts that looked out of place. Like Elizabeth, Christian sat with her skirts draped over the side of the horse. Her relaxed gaze followed the two men as they walked the full circle around the horse, twice scrutinizing each fold and bulge in the fabric.

"I do not see any indication of a concealed scepter." Keith looked back at the two men before joining them. Satisfied, they stood nodding and then turned to Johnston. "Lady Ogilvy." Father Granger inclined his head to her. "I am afraid that you will be forced to abandon yet another home."

"I will manage," Johnston stated, looking over to Christian and Elizabeth. Then she leaned forward to scratch the neck of her steed, Liam. She walked with George and the father to the makeshift cart harnessed to the gray mare.

"I wish we had a better way to conceal the sword," Father Granger stated. "This seems somewhat distasteful." He walked over to the elderly man lying on the cart, arms crossed in front of him, stiff with rigor mortis.

"John died defending his home and the crown, and now he is concealing the royal sword." George looked over to Johnston. "I think it is rather cunning."

"I doubt that they would defile the corpse by fully searching him. Removing his body from the cart is the only way they might find the sword." Johnston leaned back to look at the gray mare, Lilly.

"Cunning." George looked back at the thick gray beard and deep wrinkles around the eyes of John. Somehow, the peace of death made him look younger. "He would want to continue the fight to protect the crown, and now he will be able to." His gaze shifted to Father Granger. "How else would you recommend smuggling it out of the castle without breaking it? A sword of that size does not fit as neatly under a woman's skirt."

Father Granger looked as though he wanted to protest but decided against it.

Keith took the reins of the gray mare while Johnston climbed atop her steed. Keith then handed the reins to Johnston to lead the gray mare out of the castle. In a low voice, he looked up into her eyes. "I am sorry that I doubted you when you first arrived. I hope our sparring will not be necessary on this journey, but I am somewhat set at ease knowing your capabilities."

"Thank you, sir. I hope I will not need..." she trailed off and just nodded.

"Please tell Anne that I miss her more with each day that we are apart, and that I look forward to reuniting with her when this is finished." Keith looked to Elizabeth as he walked back to George and Father Granger.

"We will hold them as long as we can." He looked from Father Granger over to his beloved. "I know this is a battle we cannot win, but we can distract them long enough to get the Scottish crown to safety to await the return of the king."

The father nodded agreement.

George returned to Elizabeth's side, and in a low voice, inaudible to nearly everyone, he spoke truly. "You should not worry for me, my love. I do not intend to die here. I and Dunnottar shall weather this as we have weathered much before and remained standing." He looked up into her glistening eyes filled with worried tears of farewell. "We shall unite once again when this is all behind us."

Her lips could not speak the words her breath would not make audible. "I love you."

George nodded then turned to rejoin his men before the moisture in his eyes could form a tear. His strength would give her strength to lead them all, strength in their exodus from the stone fortress to their safety.

Father Granger nudged his horse into movement, and once alongside Christian, she spurred her horse to join him. Soon the five horses were slowly walking out from the inner castle walls to the meadow headed to the stony entrance overlooking the English army, and the first trial.

The meadow felt so much bigger than when Johnston had ridden up to the castle seven months ago. She looked over to the outcrop standing high above the sea where she and Liam sat many an afternoon exercising their minds and muscles to prevent destructive boredom and despair; she wondered then if that was more for her than for him. She looked over to Gray, who was keeping up with the procession without tugging on the reins.

On the other side of the rocky entrance, they emerged from the shadows to be surrounded by a crowd of men with swords and spears. Gray pranced uneasily, and Liam's muscles tensed.

"We are passing from this siege." Father Granger spoke calmly. "Lord Barrington is aware that we would be passing though."

"Let them come over here." A tall man holding an extremely dangerous looking sword stepped through the parting crowd. "We are aware of your exodus from the castle. Just because you negotiated safe passage does not mean we will not search you."

The crowd reluctantly parted. Yearning for a spectacle, they clustered in as hungry children pushing and shoving for a morsel of sugary violence. A man walked calmly, yet flaunting undermined his power over the situation and the group. He led the horses out into the meadow where Johnston could see the dire situation. The English army had moved in with hundreds of tents. The peaceful meadow where Johnston had spent many days escaping the castle had become a muddy armed town. The soldiers moved between the dimly lit tents as maggots swimming among muddy bones, picking the last of the loyalists from the countryside.

"I am Lord Stafford," the man announced as the soldiers closed in to grab the reins, preventing any of them from making an escape. "As I was saying, we will allow you safe passage, but we must make sure that you are not smuggling any valuables from the castle."

"Very well." Father Granger gestured with his hand to the rest of the group behind him. "We have nothing to hide."

A handful of men started looking over Elizabeth as she sat aloof above them. One of the men lifted the side of her cloak, revealing layers of skirt underneath. She watched him carefully, silently, until his hand reached for the bottom of her skirt, starting to lift it. "Do you mind, sir? My husband is the only person with the privilege of peering there. You, sir, are not him." Her expression morphed from placid tolerance to utter disdain for their lack of common courtesy.

Johnston sat patiently as a few men broke from the crowd, coming toward her. Two of them seemed to pull rank and walked over to her, leaving the other three to inspect the dead body on the cart. The grizzled older man walked to Johnston, lowering his head a bit. "I apologize for the intrusion, my lady." Johnston inclined her head, not uttering a word and splitting her attention between herself and the cart. As the grizzled man walked around them, he looked up to Johnston briefly. "This is quite a fine steed."

She could feel Liam start to get antsy and looked over to a redhaired pimply boy looking under his belly to the back side of her skirts. "I wouldn't touch him there. Horses are generally quite sensitive of being groped and might kick." She calmly turned her attention to Lord Stafford with slight intolerance for making a child perform duties where his ignorance could get him killed. "I would hate for any of your men to get injured due to their unfamiliarity with horses." The young pimply boy looked wide-eyed up at her and crawled out from underneath Liam.

The three men had started to prod John's stiff body. They lifted the cloth covering his face, looking at the serenity in the closed eyes. One of the men stepped back, turning his head, while a second man started to lift one side of the body as to look under. "Do you mind?" Johnston's scolding voice cracked through the muttering crowd, hushing everyone to silence and making the three men freeze for a moment. "That is *my husband* you are defiling." The arrogance of the man melted into fear as he met her glare. "Would you wish to be treated with so little respect when you die?"

"Sorry, my lady," he muttered as he started to back away.

Lord Stafford stepped forward. "They must search."

"I understand that," Johnston stated, "but they do not need to defile my husband's remains in the process by moving it about in such a disrespectful manner." Johnston almost saw a glimmer of entertainment across the somber face of Father Granger with the claim of John being her husband.

The arduous task of searching the travelers was complete. The crowd seemed disappointed in not finding anything of value. The crowd parted, letting the five of them pass through.

"Look." Lady Douglas gasped, pointing to the left. A line of large cannons were being hauled to the edge of the cliff. The cannons pointed into the gray fog with water crashing yards below. Lady Douglas could imagine the other side of the rocky outcrop jutting out into the ocean and Dunnottar concealed in the gray blanket. She bit her lower lip as worry for her husband started to penetrate through her mask of defiance.

"Come now, Lady Douglas," Christian said, drawing her attention back to the path that lay ahead of them, leading away from the regiment surrounding the castle.

The horses walked to the edge of the trees. Lady Douglas paused a moment, looking back across the meadow swallowed by fog and troops, hoping they would all go away and leave Dunnottar in peace. She let her guard down now that she was no longer under scrutiny by the enemy and started to weep softly.

Johnston stopped Liam alongside Lady Douglas, wishing to take some of the pain away, knowing full well that would not be possible. Lady Douglas forced a small smile to her lips as they traded glances; they looked to Father Granger and Christian forging ahead toward the chapel. Lady Douglas called to them before they disappeared into the mist.

The trees closed in around them as they left the meadow. The branches with nubs of sprouting leaves reached through the fog, trying to snag them. The shadows and darkness moved slowly just beyond the gray vale passing them. Sounds reached through the gray trees to them as they continued, intensely listening for the silence of any unwanted visitors.

The horse hooves and dripping wood hitting hard ground added tension with an occasional snapping of a twig that was unfortunate enough to find itself under hoof as they passed. The light grays of the outer woods gradually transitioned to a deeper gray as the sunlight was almost fully blocked through the canopy, creating an ambiance and planting a seed of apprehension in Johnston's stomach.

Clop…

Clop…

Snap…

Johnston twitched, placing her hand on the small throwing spike sticking out of her bun on one side. Taking a deep breath, she lowered her hand.

Elizabeth looked wide-eyed to Johnston, then to Father Granger. "How much farther to the chapel?" Elizabeth's voice was high, tense with fear.

"We are nearly there. Just another mile or so. There is a clearing ahead, then another stand of trees that we will traverse. That is all." Christian soothed the tension as she continued calmly, "We have not seen any soldiers this far from the castle. I believe we and our parcels are safe."

"I will believe that once we are all in the chapel." Johnston scanned the shadows. Johnston's uneasiness knotted in her throat at the mention of the parcels, plural. She did not want any keen ears to hear verification of the Honor's locations. But she did not point this out to Christian as it would only confirm the items' presence to any prying ears.

The limbs of the trees opened as the deep blue gray mist lifted along with a bit of the tension into a light gray haze. The tree line cleared into a meadow. Johnston breathed deeply, feeling less claustrophobic, if even for a moment.

Too soon they had plunged back into the darkness of the trees. Johnston steadied herself as she continued to breathe deeply, calming her nerves. The silence from the trees worked to keep her unsettled; even the birds were scared to sing. She focused on the sound of the hooves on the earth.

Clop…

Clop…

Clop…

Slap…

"Pardon me, ladies…and gent…um…Father."

Johnston's heart sunk, and the knot in her stomach crawled up into her throat as the first figure stepped through the gray vale, pointing a crossbow up at Lady Douglas.

Then two more men stepped through the fog. One of them partially pulled a sword from his scabbard on his hip and then decided to return its sheath. The sword was not from the area, not even from this island. The blade was shorter than the claymores that she had been sparring with, and the handle was only long enough to fit one hand with little room for a second hand on the hilt.

The rogue-ish man with the crossbow walked over a few feet from Lady Douglas's horse with a slight limp, favoring his left leg as he walked. Limper, Johnston named him. Limper's blond hair with gray streaks was pulled back into a tail. He looked over to a taller and leaner man for direction once he had set himself into position with the arrow trained on his target.

The suspected leader stepped forward, holding a blade. He had a scar across his eye that stretched down to his cheekbone. The scar was a remnant of past battles. Scar stood hawkishly, assessing the group, just as Johnston was sizing him up.

The third man slowly emerged from the fog near Johnston, who brought up the rear of the group. This man also looked to be battle hardened; his torn shirt revealed a few scars of his own. Johnston spotted the sword at his side and then looked back to the first man, seeing that all three carried their swords for backup if the crossbow was insufficient to do the job.

Scar stepped forward, eyeing Lady Douglas. He wore a flat expression as he walked around her horse. Her breathing became shallow as he continued around. He walked closer as his lips curled into a wolfish grin as he reached up her skirt.

Lady Douglas swung her leg forward, trying to clip his jaw, but her movement was slow and restrained because she did not want to fall from her mount.

He stepped back gracefully, in no real danger. Then he spoke to his men in a language that Johnston could not translate, but it sounded familiar. Nordic, Danish, maybe? They nodded to him, and then he continued, "Where is the sword?" He looked to Christian, nodding. Limper stepped closer to Christian, training his bow on her, smiling maliciously.

"We will not betray our duty, you heathen." Lady Douglas hissed at Scar, disdain dripping with each word.

Christian looked at Lady Douglas wide-eyed, shifting her glance back to the point of the arrow bolt, then back to Lady Douglas. She shifted in her saddle as she looked to the skiff and then to her husband, hoping for direction.

"That will do." Scar nodded to the cart where John lay rigidly on guard.

The man beside Johnston stalked over to the cart. Not wanting to set his crossbow down, he prodded around the corpse, finding only the obvious preparations of the dead. Exasperated, he set the crossbow down and heaved the body. John's corpse reluctantly toppled with his upper body drooping over the side of the cart. He stepped back with a toothy grin stretching across his face. "It's here." He leaned over, sliding the sword out from under the slumped body. With a look of a fox that had just successfully opened the door to the hen house, he retrieved his crossbow and trained it on Johnston.

Scar and Limper turned their gaze to Father Granger and Elizabeth. Scar looked hungrily at Lady Douglas. "I will have fun taking what I came for." He curled his lips, undressing her with his eyes. "And then some."

Limper turned his crossbow on Christian, stepping away from Father Granger.

Johnston tapped Liam on the haunches, turning him slightly, while she continued to watch Scar as he assessed the situation.

Scar looked to over to Limper. "Kill them."

Before the second word escaped his mouth, Johnston reached to her head pulling two of the spikes from her hair. She quickly extended her arm, finishing with a precise flick of her wrist, sending them sliding silently through the twenty feet, embedding them in Limper's head and chest. Surprise washed over his face as he dropped the crossbow and fell to his knees.

"Run!" Johnston called to her traveling companions.

Scar turned to Johnston, amazement morphing to fury as he pulled his sword.

The stunned expression on the third man's face did not last long as he stepped forward, raising his crossbow and aiming at Johnston.

She hoped Liam remembered all his training despite their inability to practice as often as she hoped. Johnston crossed her fingers and uttered the command, "Capriole." Liam laid his ears back and lurched. Then he jumped high into the air, kicking out with his rear hooves into the man standing behind them.

Johnston slid from the back of her steed, landing with a wild grin of satisfaction in gaining the upper hand. "Good boy, Liam!" she called, patting his shoulder. Then she headed back to the third man who was lying out cold in the mud. She picked up the crossbow, tossing it away from him in case he came to, and then she picked up the claymore from the dirt.

Soft silent footsteps rushed in from beside her, followed at the last by a guttural scream. She raised the Sword of State just in time as Scar slammed his sword down at her head. She looked to see the tail of Lady Douglas's horse pause at the edge of the fog. *The crown and scepter are safe*, she thought briefly before returning her thoughts to surviving.

She looked back to Scar, who glared at her through the crossed blades. He was heavier and stronger than her and currently pushing down as she knelt. She shifted her weight, pulling out from under the attack, and rolled to the side clumsily as her skirts tangled around her.

Scar attacked again. His blade was smaller and lighter, more agile. He came in swinging from the side; she dodged at the last minute, hoping that his momentum would carry him off balance.

He stepped forward, catching himself before he was vulnerable from overreaching. Johnston used the opportunity to swing the Sword of State at his back. He twisted, catching her attack. Then he pushed the sword away from him, stepping back from her. Sneering at her, he stepped in for another attack, this time low from the side.

Johnston jumped back out of the reach of his sword, mostly. The tip of the sword grazed her arm, and she felt a warm trickle. Looking at the wound would only give him the opportunity to strike a more critical blow.

Scar glanced down at her left arm and then back to her eyes. He smiled wickedly as she started to feel the sting and the warm trickle down her arm.

He stepped in for another strike, swinging the blade over his shoulder down toward her, this time holding the sword. She was not quick enough to dodge out of the way, so she raised her sword to meet his slicing blow. The two swords met this time with a sickening snap as part of Johnston's blade fell to the ground at her feet. She looked stunned at the hilt and part of the blade remaining in her hands as his sword came in again directly for her stomach.

How interesting I can read the blade, Johnston's thoughts started to fragment with the searing pain as it pulled from her stomach, and she crumbled forward to the ground.

"Elizabeth, *no!*" The scream penetrated the fog. Johnston looked to the silhouette at the edge of the fog as they turned to flee.

Scar looked over to the figure disappearing in the fog and then turned back to Johnston. Slowly savoring the spoils of victory, he picked up the blade then walked over to Johnston. She held tightly to the hilt of the broken sword. The piercing pain of a boot to the stomach made her vision start to darken, and she lost her grip.

Rolling on her back, the searing flash of pain pressed on her as she fought to breathe. A familiar presence lay next to her as she groped in the darkness for her companion and confident. At least she would not be alone in these final hours.

She could hear footsteps before her memories continued to fragment.

...

"You broke it!" A shrill arrogant voice pierced through the darkness.

...

Running.

...

A soft voice entered Johnston's thoughts. "Take him to the stables."

"We need to get her some help," a gentle fatherly voice continued. "It looks like a sword?"

...

The voices faded into the dreams from which they came.

"How long has she been here?" The sweet voice of Jen replaced the dark silence.

"I'm not sure." Concern made TDCI Stewart's voice more fatherly.

Confident that she was not about to be run through again, Johnston relaxed. The blanket radiated warmth, penetrating deep into her muscles. Suddenly, she became aware of the searing heat on her arm and at the base of her ribs. She breathed slowly, deeply. The damage to her lungs must be mending.

Confident that she was not hallucinating on the path next to Liam or dead, she dared to open her eyes. The darkness was invading by piercing sterile light; she winced at the onslaught to her pupils.

"She is stirring. I think she'll be okay." Relief washed over the chief's face as he smiled.

"That is under debate," Johnston croaked. "Sir." A searing sensation at the base of her rips made Johnston breathe in sharply. Wincing, she pulled up her light blue hospital gown to look at the spot above her stomach. The wound stung with heat, glowing with a pale yellow illumination. She lowered her head back onto the pillow.

"You are lucky. They got you here in time," Jen said softly.

Johnston looked up at the ceiling, feeling her organs fusing back together and her shin growing back with the nano-surgeons repairing the damage to her. She felt the heat of the tiny metal things probing her muscles, cauterizing and weaving new muscle fibers, then moving to the skin cells. It had been awhile since she needed this intensive reconstructive surgery. The nano-surgical technology was expensive and contained a level of danger in its own right. The programming of the tech was expected to rebuild tissue specific to the damaged area using the viable cells near the wound to make repairs.

The nano-surgeons would enter the cell using the same method that a virus invades a cell, then rewrite the RNA and proteins of the cell, tricking it into thinking it is a stem cell in the beginning of life, building anew and replacing the damaged or destroyed cells in the area, replicating at the same rate they did when they were embryonic of growth verging on cancerous rage. For the most part, the bugs in the technology had been worked out, but Johnston still remembered the stories from when they were still developing the technology. Storied where recoding of cell DNA went awry, convincing the new cells to start creating the wrong organs as a deep slice through the muscles in a man's leg started to mend, and then he noticed fingers start to protrude for the gaping wound as the nanotech initiated cellular regeneration. The rate of cellular regeneration was not stopped once the wound had been healed for one person, and they had to be quickly transferred into the cancer ward as the cell growth continued out of control. Johnston swallowed hard, watching her intravenous line for the silvery cloud to emerge from her arm and return to the cylindrical glass vial that they came from, indicating the repairs were complete and successful.

She pushed herself up onto the pillow, wincing at the nano-surgeons reminding that they were not done with the mending, but she could see TDCI Stewart and Jen better.

"Are they safe?" Johnston added, "How long have I been gone?"

"You have been away for a week." Stewart handed the update to the case file. "The crown and scepter arrived safely to the chapel, but the sword did not." Concern collected in the corners of his eyes. "What happened?"

"We have historic record of someone joining the group with the Honours. I assume that was you. Then there are reports of an ambush, which is how you got here. But do you know who ambushed you?" Jen leaned in with worry.

Johnston closed her eyes, recalling the language spoken and the swords. "What did it say?" She reached over to her field book sitting next to her bed. How did she bring it back with her? She opened it to the back page with her finger. On the slick surface, she wrote the letters on the sword as she remembered them sliding from her stomach. "+VLFBERHT+" She opened her eyes, looking down at her pad and wincing, remembering the pain. "A Viking-style sword? In Scotland?" she asked herself, and then answered her own question. "That makes sense, sort of." She looked to Jen then to TDCI Stewart. "The man that spoke had an accent and spoke to his men in, I think, Nordic. They must have taken the sword from me."

TDCI Stewart sighed. "It sounds like you have more questions than answers right now. You have the updated file." He stood. "I am glad you are on the mend. Come to see me when you are well." He leaned over, squeezing his shoulder, about to say something.

"One more thing. Hajjar..." Johnston looked up to TDCI Stewart. "How is he doing on his current assignment?"

TDCI Stewart chuckled softly. "He completed the assignment successfully. You should..." He smiled and headed to the door. "One last thing. Go visit your parents. They are worried."

The memories of the voices—*We need to get her some help*—came back to her like whispers of smoke through the darkness.

Once he was gone, Jen leaned in. "That does not make any sense. Why would Vikings be in Scotland to steal the Honours, using a type of sword that was centuries old at that time?"

"I am not sure." She opened her field notebook, adding the updates from the case file. She looked over the updates. "Oh, this is good. The lab completed the analysis of the evidence I brought back from that little trip I took to Warsaw."

"Oh." Jen scooted forward on her chair. "What does it say?"

Johnston watched the upload indicator line reach completion and then slowly closed her notebook without looking at the file. "I will look at it later." She took a deep breath, setting the notebook on the small desk next to her bed. "I'll have plenty of time to look at that when I am out of here."

Jen restrained her excitement a little before asking, "What was it like in Scotland? How long were you there?"

Johnston grinned. "I wish I could have visited without an agenda." She started recalling her time spent in the lowlands, the friends she made, and the adventures, deciding to leave out the details on how she got her injuries.

By the time she finished her account of the events over the last nine months, the medical nanotech physician stood next to her. The young man looked part doctor—clean cut, shaved, and lab coat—and part engineer with his spiky blue hair with green tips. Data stream spectacles hovered in front of his eyes, displaying reflecting light from the room, and streamed information in the glass.

He pressed a few buttons on the side of the bed. The sheet covering her glowed a pale blue for a moment before an image of her body appeared hovering in the air directly above the bed. With a flick of his fingers, the skin shifted from a solid to a translucent outline, revealing the muscles underneath. The physician moved the hovering body, inspecting the area just below the ribs, then flipped the image over to look closely at the muscles in her back. "Very good," he accessed.

He flicked his fingers again as the image of muscle structure slowly shifted from a solid red-and-white striated strips hovering above her into a transparent outline, revealing the major organs underneath. He looked closely at her stomach, diaphragm, and lungs. Another flick and he was inspecting her bones for proper healing. Finally, with a tap of his finger, the entire body was translucent with a cluster of five yellow small crowds of light migrating back to her arm, joining the others nanites in the glass vial. Once the few remaining nanites joined the rest in the bottle, they all changed from a yellow shade to an intense green. "Excellent," he muttered, removing the nanite storage vessel from the IV drip line. Then with a gesture, he removed the hovering body from the air. He turned to Johnston, smiling as he started to physically take her vital signs. "The nano-medics did their job and are completely out of your system. Tell me if this hurts." He pressed on Johnston's stomach, just below her ribs on her left side. "The blade went in here, just above your stomach, but pierced your diaphragm and left lung. The sword emerged out your back between the bottom two ribs. You were lucky that it missed your heart."

"I don't feel any pain." She shook her head. "Not now."

"Can you lean forward for me?"

She did as he touched her lower ribs, pressing lightly. Again, she did not feel any tenderness.

"Okay," he stated. "I think you are ready to be released and go home."

***

The dim lights in the pub created deep shadows that swallowed corners, and sometimes the whole table, when the light above the booth was out. The rich dark wood filled the lit areas with warm reds and browns.

Johnston walked over to one of the tables in the back corner. A table was filled with drinks and young agents doing their best to relax in the back corner. They turned their heads. She felt like a teacher intruding on the secret spot where all the students kicked back, or worse, the boss everyone vented about suddenly deciding to join with the group for drinks.

She liked a good pub but usually avoided this one. Despite the fact that she didn't smoke, she felt there was something inherently wrong with a pub that didn't have a thick haze, preventing a clear view across the room. Truthfully, she felt more at home in a different pub, a bit more dingy, smoky, with neon bar signs lining the walls.

Scooting into the booth far back in the corner of the pub, she caught the eye of the waiter and soon had a short glass filled with smooth twenty-year-old bourbon. This started the waiting game; fortunately, she brought something to read.

She pulled out her field tablet, opening it slowly. Her fingers started shaking as she looked at the data package from the case file summarizing her trip to Scotland. She closed her eyes, remembering the feeling of a sword sliding into her ribs, then flicked past the data summary. Maybe later.

Her fingers flicked onto the results from her Warsaw trip. At the traces from the footprint, her eyes drifted to the summary, reading, "Horse manure mixed with limestone." She continued reading as her right eyebrow rose into a bewildered expression.

The mud was actually horse manure with small flecks of limestone. The limestone was identified as Greenbrier Limestone, unique to the Appalachian Mountains. She closed her eyes, starting to imagine who this person could be. An image of a hillbilly moonshiner came to mind. Some people chose to live in the recesses of the Appalachian Mountains. The terrain with dense woods and the caves like tendrils burrowing for miles through the hills and valleys made it difficult for law enforcement to penetrate.

She opened her eyes and read on. The horse manure contained microbes with genetic markers that were predominate during the 2550s, give or take twenty-five years. Again, she closed her eyes, continuing to narrow down the person and places based on the profile she had on hand. They had to live on the western side of the Appalachian Mountains. All the cities on the east coast had sprawled like tendrils of a glowing life until they all fused into each other, creating a solid stretch of city from Quebec to the Florida Keys, then west halfway through the Appalachian Mountains to the Eastern Divide. Horses were outlawed within the cities, along with most other animals. The person had to be in Kentucky, Tennessee, maybe the western sliver of Virginia or West Virginia. Those areas were still considered horse country when she was a kid.

The caves that ran through that area would be the perfect place to hide or hoard valuable items. The cave systems stretched for miles through the Appalachian Mountains. Even now, it was thought that only a small percentage of the cave systems had been explored. She remembered hiding her special items in one of the caves near her home growing up and remembered how the moisture destroyed the paper and electronics over time.

The surface of her notebook flickered with more information. The hair in the muddy track was a black horsehair. *That is not too far of a stretch*, she thought. The hair had an insect egg attached it. The egg was from the genus and species of louse known as *Haematopinus asini*. The morphologies of this sample resembled a species resurgent in the western portion of Virginia in the year AD 2556 and were quickly brought under control; the species was originally documented in Britain and Scotland during the seventeenth century. The seventeenth century was where she had just spent the last nine months.

Johnston closed her eyes again, remembering her childhood on the border between Virginia and Kentucky. She fondly recalled saddling Chestnut and riding her south a few miles through the forest into Tennessee as a teenager before joining the agency. She loved to explore the caves behind their house with the limestone stalactites and stalagmites. Could that be the limestone she found in Warsaw?

There were two places this species of lice had been documented in: seventeenth-century England, AD 2556 Virginia, and now muddy footprint in the house in Warsaw.

Johnston's heart started racing as she remembered being a teenager, and how it might all have been different if she was taken to the academy instead of back home. Had the truth caught up with her? Her tutor said history was a fragile thing. She tried to remember some of her exciting trips as a teen, but still nothing, no more than the following morning. Could diverging timelines create a doppelganger within the Para-Dome? Could the person she was chasing in the picture of Warsaw be her, but a doppelganger formed from an alternate timeline where the two timelines split here within the Para-Dome. The very Para-Dome that was designed to prevent this sort of thing.

"Johnston?" The tired voice jerked her back.

"Hajjar." She breathed deeply. She could get to the bottom of this. Hajjar would know what happened. "How was your first solo? I assume you didn't need my help," she added in jest.

His eyes narrowed. "Funny." His sarcastic tone held more annoyance and irritation than jest. He continued, lowering his voice, "I went from upholding the laws of time travel, upholding the laws of the agency, to blatantly breaking them in my very first solo assignment."

"So you did take me…um, Bethy back to her parents so she could join the agency when she was mature enough to leave home." Johnston looked up at Hajjar with a smile. "As history was written."

"Yes, I returned *you* to your parents." He hissed. "I'm not even completely sure why. Maybe it was because I was afraid to rewrite the timeline."

"Maybe it was because you like being famous, the youngest." Johnston's voice trailed off as they looked over to the group of green agents the waitress pointed to as she set the drink in front of Hajjar. "Like I was saying."

His expression chilled a few degrees. "Is that all you wanted? To make fun of my traumatic solo assignment?"

"No." Johnston sighed, realizing he was no longer a junior agent. "You rose to the challenge and handled it fine. I was waiting to pick your brain on my assignment. I have hit a step that baffles me, and maybe I am just too close to the case to see the details."

Johnston asking assistance from Hajjar, this was a rarity. He leaned in, his face lightening under the overhead lamp.

"I wanted to confirm that your assignment went as I remember it because I seem to be chasing a doppelganger. I was worried that if there was an alteration in the events of my history, it might split onto an alternate reality within the Para-Dome." She slid her field notebook to the center of the table, flicking her fingers and pulling up the image of the square in Warsaw. The image was of the woman who looked all too familiar.

"Let me see that." Hajjar shifted the image, studying it, long and ponderous. "Wow, she looks just like you. She could be your sister."

The words echoed in Johnston's head, rushing in along with the memories, bringing a phantom pain below her ribs. *You broke it!* The voice played through her head again; it was familiar, too familiar. "Oh crap!" she lowered her head, shaking it in disbelief.

"I recognize that strike of brilliant stupidity." He laughed. "Those were my words exactly when I finally recognized you, Bethy." He leaned forward with a smirk. "Tell me."

Johnston held her forehead in her hands. Lifting her head and looking at him through her fingers, she muttered, "She could be my sister." She started to laugh, wheezing with phantom pain. "When I was facing the men." She paused, correcting herself. "People that were trying to steal the Honours of Scotland, and I was stabbed with a sword."

"Wow, you were run through with a sword? What did it feel like? Is there a scar?" Hajjar gasped with awe and horror.

Johnston sighed. "Like a giant piece of metal was shoved through my lung and out through my ribs." She emphasized each word.

Hajjar was left speechless for a moment. "Nope." He lifted his eyebrows, holding up his hands in submission. "You had the worst assignment, and I thought mine was bad because I was conflicted on my motivations." He muttered, "Sword for stabilizing the win."

"You know this was never a competition." She looked into his eyes, annoyed with the distraction. "You are exactly what I remember myself being at that age. After meeting you, I knew you were the only one clever enough to put it all together exactly like I remembered from my childhood." She sighed again, holding back her exasperation. "Besides, I need to figure out if my parents are involved in the thefts. I don't think they can time jaunt, but then again, I didn't think my sister could time jaunt, and I am clearly wrong."

"I guess it is time to go explore the caves behind your family house."

"I could use a little backup, if you don't have another assignments." Johnston shuddered at the idea of confronting her big sister. She wondered which scenario would be worse: if her parents were oblivious to what Mary had been doing or that they knew and encouraged it. "I think I might need help on this trip." A sly smile crept across her face. "I can bribe you. I'll get you a drink at my favorite bar, employee discount."

"That one in Austin?" Hajjar started to wonder how many times she might have returned after he brought her home to her parents.

Johnston nodded. "Oh, the memories."

Hajjar followed Johnston, or Bethy. He smiled at the image of his mentor as a cute little girl with pigtails. A small chuckle erupted from within him. A stern look from Bethy, Johnston, brought his focus back to the house that stood in front of them. He remembered the last time he came here; it was last night for him and roughly thirty years ago in the timeline of the house.

He looked around to the flowers and shrubs decorating the front of the house. Mrs. Johnston decided on the color scheme of gold, copper, and red mums matching the leaves blanketing the lawn; the other flowers were starting to wilt from the morning frost that hung in the air, still glistening on the leaves from the night before and sending a chill, making him wish for a heavier jacket.

"Are you coming?" Johnston asked from the porch, holding the glass storm door open with one hand, her other hand poised to rap the door with her knuckles.

"Yeah, just enjoying the colors." He hurried to the front, hearing the rhythmic knock on the door, shave-and-a-hair-cut-two-bits, as he scaled the five stairs leading to the door in two bounds.

A long moment passed. Hajjar had never seen his partner get tense before, but he could clearly see the muscles in her shoulders and jaw tightening up.

The door started to open slowly, the shadows behind not giving away the identity of the person. "Bethy!" The door flew open as her mother grabbed her daughter, holding her tight. "Oh, my dear, I was so worried! I thought you might have died." She pulled back, looking at her baby girl of thirty-seven or thirty-eight. Hajjar was not quite sure.

Johnston liberated her arms from her mother's embrace in order to return the hug. "I'm okay. The hospital at the agency fixed me up. I got there in time." The words came slightly muffled by the embrace. "Hajjar is here."

"Oh." She straightened, regaining her composure after seeing Hajjar over her daughter's shoulder. "Come in."

The aroma of baked muffins invited them into the kitchen. Hajjar could almost taste the spices in the paper cup. "Do you want one? I just pulled them from the oven." She leaned over, pushing a warm spiced muffin to Hajjar as if to read his mind. She whispered, "She always seems to know when I'm baking muffins." Worry returned to her face again as she looked back to her daughter.

"Did I hear someone at the door?" Hajjar would recognize Mr. Johnston's voice in any time.

"She is in here," Kathrine called back to the study.

"Oh! Elizabeth!" One moment of seeing his daughter standing in the kitchen transformed Mr. Johnston from the scholarly image of a professor into Bethy's dad, holding her tightly and wanting to never let go of his little girl. "What happened?"

Johnston held her dad for a while before stepping back and taking a tall chair at the island in the kitchen. Hajjar picked up his muffin, stepping back, leaning on the counter near the stove. He wanted to remain behind them to watch the interactions and expressions of her parents through the conversations. He started to peel the paper from around the base of the muffin slowly, wanting to give the illusion that he was not observing them.

"I kind of wanted to ask you. What happened? All I know is that I woke up in the hospital wing of the agency. I vaguely remember voices. I think they were your voices, but those moments are like grasping in the darkness for images and sounds that may be nothing more than illusions."

"Well." Kathrine exchanged glances with her husband then continued, "We heard a commotion outside and hurried out to see what was going on."

"What caused the commotion?" Hajjar stuffed a piece of muffin into his mouth, meeting Johnston's questioning look. He continued while chewing, "What? Given the condition you were in when you got to the hospital, there was no way you could have caused a commotion." Hajjar read the raising of her eyebrows as gratitude for his observant question.

"Stop talking with your mouth full." Kathrine frowned. "Youth these days."

"Yes, Mrs. Johnston." Hajjar glanced over to Johnston, who was trying to hide her laughter.

"Your horse made the commotion." Kathrine looked to her husband, hoping she did not say something she shouldn't have. "He was so defensive."

"Defensive? I didn't think I still had a horse here. After Lilly, I have not had a horse here in quite a few years." The words stopped. "Wait, he?" Elizabeth stated, shooting a quick "that's not possible" look at Hajjar.

Hajjar broke off another piece of the muffin, studying the interaction in front of him. Could they be implying the horse…jaunted… with Johnston? That *was* impossible, wasn't it?

"No, Lilly is buried under the pear tree. I don't know where *this* boy came from. Black with four white socks and a beautiful blaze and star, and an attitude. He is very protective of you."

Mr. Johnston shook his head slowly. "He brought one bad case of lice that we are still fighting off."

A long silent moment passed between them as Johnston sat speechless.

"So when you found her…" Hajjar started making the connections for himself as he walked up beside Johnston, reaching for another muffin. "These are amazing, Mrs. Johnston. They are what I imagine my own mom baking, if she knew how to bake."

She smiled. "Oh, you are quite welcome."

"Once we got the horse settled, we called the number the agency provided if there was any emergency," Mr. Johnston said. "You know, the one we were given when you first went to the academy to call in case of an emergency."

"This *was* an emergency," Kathrine stated.

Hajjar wanted to continue the questioning about the horse, but he saw Johnston take a deep breath, refocusing, and didn't want to interrupt.

"Whatever happened with that cave Mary and I used to play in as children?"

"Do you mean the cave behind the house in the hills? The one where Mary had the horrifying accident and broke her arm," Kathrine stated.

"When did this happen?" Johnston asked, concern gathering in her eyebrows.

"About twenty or so years ago. It was six months after." Johnston's mom looked to her husband for confirmation. "Six months, maybe a year at most, after you headed to the academy. She was exploring the caves and fell into one of the ravines, breaking her radius and ulna."

Johnston cringed, knowing how bad that would hurt and how long it would take to heal without the nano-surgeons to reassemble the bone. "You are sure no one has been in those caves after they were sealed?"

"Why would we go there?" Mr. Johnston stated.

"I ride my horse by there occasionally when I am in the area and noticed the seal starting to decay a bit, but that looks like age, not someone trying to trespass." Kathrine's concern and confusion crossed her face and entered her voice.

"Do you mind if we ride out there to look for ourselves?"

"Sure." Kathrine paused, dying for an answer that she was afraid to ask. The question poised on her tongue until the expression on her face clearly stated why not. "Where did you get that dress? And the weapons you came back with?"

Johnston contemplated her response. Looking to her father, she said, "You remember teaching about Cromwell's invasion of Scotland? The Honours of Scotland?"

"Yes, that was quite heroic. Lady Elizabeth Douglas, Christian Fletcher, and arguably a cousin of Sir Ogilvy smuggled the Honours out of the castle to the chapel. They were ambushed, and the Scottish Sword of State was taken by Cromwell's men and destroyed, lost."

Johnston's father smiled as if he loved this story, the heroics of someone underappreciated by their enemy but prevailing.

"Why? Does that story matter?" Kathrine asked.

Hajjar watched Johnston's face suddenly change from that of a child waiting for her father's heroic bedtime story to that of a sad daughter acknowledging confirmation of a parent facing Alzheimer's, not knowing the memories they have lost. She stood slowly from the stool, anger building in her closed fists. "We are going to fix that." She closed her eyes.

Johnston's mother and father exchanged glances of worry as Johnston opened her eyes again with her emotions back in check.

"Can we borrow some tack and a coup…a horse." She looked over to Hajjar. "You still ride? The cave is about two miles from here."

"Yes, of course."

The two walked in silence out the back door through the carpet of crunchy leaves to the stable. Johnston looked hopeful, walking briskly to the rear stall, tall and solid. It was the only stall built to keep in raging hormones. She paused long enough to press the open command, unlocking the latch on the solid wooden stall. She held her breath. The door opened. Her breath did not return for a long moment as the shock wore off from after seeing who was behind the stall door. Her breath came back, and her eyes filled with tears as she stepped into the stall, reunited with her guardian.

The sound of delight that came at that moment from both within the stall and Johnston simultaneously filled the stable. Hajjar had never thought he would ever hear a horse sound so joyfully excited, but that was the only thing that came to his mind to describe these sounds. Johnston melted into a child reuniting with a best friend, running and wrapping her arms around Liam, muttering tearfully into his neck, "I don't know how."

Hajjar stepped back along the stall doors, waiting for one of the mares to peek out and greet him. He remembered Johnston saying to let the horse pick you. It was what made for a more enjoyable ride.

In no time, the two were riding through the dramatically rolling hills covered with fiery reds, yellows, and oranges falling like rain from the trees when a strong gust of wind rustled through the canopy.

The leaf-crunching silence lasted longer than he felt comfortable. "So what was all that about?"

"What?" Johnston asked.

"The history lesson your dad was telling." Hajjar tried to avoid the other glaring question.

"My father is a history professor at the University of London."

"Nice commute."

"He manages to jaunt in and out of his office. He..." She sighed. "His first PhD thesis was on history of the Cromwell crusade. He knows the history of the Honours of Scotland. I was raised on these stories. Only, in the story I was raised on, all three pieces made it to the chapel, and Elizabeth Ogilvie, the cousin, was not in the story."

"Does he know what you do?"

"No." Johnston paused. "I hate that his reality is slipping from the stories we grew up with, and though I can fix the outcome getting the sword back, the story will permanently be changed." They continued crushing the crispy leaves, not speaking a while before she added, "It galls me that someone could do this. Change the childhood I shared with my parents, and for what? Greed."

They fell back into silence until Hajjar could no longer hold his burning question. "So what is with the horse?"

"This is Liam. He was Lady Murray Rose's at Castle Huntingtower before he joined my"—she decided on the word—"quest."

"You mean he did come back with you?" Hajjar was stunned. "How? Why would you?" His curiosity brought him back to "How?"

Johnston breathed deeply, calming her nerves. "If I had planned this, don't you think I might have quarantined him to prevent apparent parasitic infestation of lice that would take six months to get under control?" She sighed. "I don't know how. Frankly, I am afraid to report this to the agency. I'd rather not find out what happens when Liam and I become a test subject as they try to understand all this. You know how many people died when they were trying to understand the specifics of jaunting, and then again with time jaunting. I literally had to be put into a situation where jaunting was life or death, and my"—Johnston refrained from calling him a pet—"companion wanted to join me, or protect me so desperately, that he joined me. Even more, how did he know where to go? I was tested. I'm only type 3 telepath. How could I project my images of the destination into his head?"

Hajjar could hear frustration building in her voice and decided to let it lie.

The remaining quarter mile passed in more leaf-crunching silence.

They pulled their horses up to the portion of the rolling hill that dropped to a house-sized cliff. The base of a cliff where the jagged white limestone seemed to be held together by a horse-sized ball of cement shoved into the base of the cliff and smoothed off.

Hajjar lowered himself from the saddle, stepping lightly onto the rocky ground. Looking over to Johnston, he noticed her grinning. "Watch this." She looked at Hajjar. "Down," she sternly commanded.

Hajjar watched in amazement as Liam knelt, lowering his body so Johnston did not need to use her stirrups to get off his back. She grinned at Hajjar then turned to Liam, stroking his neck while he stood back up. She continued stroking his neck, muttering, "You like the western saddle, don't you? It's more comfortable."

"You treat him like a pet dog."

"He is a giant puppy dog," she said, stroking his neck then touching her forehead to his star. The focus returned to her face as she looked around. Hajjar watched her walk up to the cement slug, starting to inspect it closely. What was she looking for? He had started scrutinizing her movements even more after his last mission; even now he looked for hidden motivation and things that he was missing.

Again, he felt like a novice. She started touching the cement surface with her fingers while looking closely. Suddenly, the surface started to glisten, and she pulled her fingers away from them. She pulled them out of her mouth, looking at the slight scorch marks on them. "I knew it."

"Holographic projection with a security grid." Hajjar stepped forward, pulling out his specs from his back pocket. He touched the knob on the side to harmonize the resonance of his glasses to the shield to inspect the door himself. He pulled a glove out of his pocket and slid it on his right hand and over his wrist up to his elbow, and then he started touching the cement-looking grid. The ultrahigh frequency of light beams pulsed over his glove, setting the polarization frequency of his specs, and the illusion of the cement pixilated in his vision.

"What is there?" Johnston asked.

"Wow, this is some nice security tech," Hajjar replied. Once he could see through the wall, the keypad was easy to spot. "What would your sister's pass code be?"

"Pass code?"

"Never mind." Hajjar pulled out a small device from his pocket. He aimed the beam into the center of the security platform, just above the touch pad. "I recognize this model. This is where it is vulnerable. Come on, sweetie. Open." Almost as if it was an obedient pet, the door clicked and opened. "That's my girl." Hajjar stepped back, removing his glove and specs, making sure the holographic grid was gone. His smugness bubbled to the surface as he made a grandiose courtly bow, gesturing for Johnston to proceed. "After you, my lady." He spoke with a very bad British accent, heavily laced with his own Middle Eastern spice.

Johnston sighed and then pulled her flashlight from her pocket, proceeding into the cave. Hajjar returned his specs to his head, flicking the frequency to night vision before following her. Deciding to keep his distance, he let Johnston take the lead with the flashlight while he slid through the shadows behind her. It was not that he did not trust her, but he thought he'd rather keep the element of surprise, if he could.

The loose gravel of the cave floor shifted slightly with each step. Hajjar took great care to tread slowly enough to be silent. His eyes darted around with each step. He could see the low hanging rocks and stalactites but wanted to be cautious. The moment you become too comfortable was the moment you become negligent and dead. Oh shit, he had been with Johnston far too long. He could almost hear her voice in his head.

The narrow corridor twisted around a corner as Johnston's light went dark, swallowed by a brighter light from inside a room on the other side of the natural doorway. Hajjar watched her stand at the edge of the shadow, trying to look into the room without stepping into the beam of light cutting into the safe darkness. She poked her head in and pulled it back suddenly.

Hajjar stepped up beside her, leaning in as close as he could so his whispers would not be louder than the dripping of water around them. "What do you see?"

She flicked a worried look at Hajjar, whispering, "Stay here." She took a jittery deep breath, grabbing her field notebook in her pouch, and stepped into the light. "I thought this cave was closed up, or that is what Mom and Dad said."

"Mmmm, my dear sister Bethy. How *are* you?" The arrogance and pretension made her sound like a cross between a politician and a gold digger. Hajjar shivered at the slimy sound to her voice.

"Well, my stomach stopped bleeding. That is a plus."

Hajjar heard the voices from around the corner but dared not peak in until Johnston's voice was farther from the door, or he, too, would be spotted.

"Well, you know what I always say. You can't let a little thing like a sword to the gut get you down." Again, the voice slithered its way to Hajjar's ears.

"It seems that we have a lot of catching up to do, like when did you start time jaunting?"

"Oh, it had been awhile. Before you went to the academy. And you can invite your little stooge in. I'm sure he is there. You certainly couldn't figure out my security. Old dogs, you know."

"You know I hate you sometimes."

Hajjar stepped into the light, watching Johnston hold back her raging emotions. He continued to watch Mary press Johnston's buttons.

He slowly walked around the room. The gravel ended at the beam of light turning into a glistening marble floor. The lights were aimed in all directions, spotlighting paintings, sculptures, carvings, jewelry that glistened. It sent a spray of light dancing across the stalactites hanging like ancient chandeliers and spotlights, illuminating places yearning to be filled with priceless items each with its own

Stolen Honours

story. Or worse. Had they been filled and recently vacated? Johnston continued forward. Hajjar walked by a pedestal with a red velvet lined tray holding two pieces of a beautiful sword next to its sheath. The intricate golden grip and guard connected to the broken blade glimmered in the light. "This is what you went to save."

"Don't touch that. It is mine," Mary stated. "You might get fingerprints on it, which would be quite a shame after somebody broke it." Her poisonous glare swung to Johnston.

"Do you know what you have done?" Johnston sighed.

"No, but I am sure you are about to tell me." She rolled her eyes. "Like you always do."

"You have changed history," Johnston stated with profoundness.

"History is written by the victors. Legendary events have been written and rewritten hundreds of times, each by whoever was in charge or needed to make a point, each time opinion tainting the fact just a little bit more." She smiled sweetly. "I just want to see what really happened, and maybe take a souvenir."

"I doubt that is what Churchill meant with that statement," Hajjar stated, shaking his head in disbelief.

"Well, maybe he did. To the victors go the spoils and history is written in their favor. I have heard that all my career." Johnston sighed. "But that is not what I'm talking about. You have *changed* history! There is a difference. You remember the bedtime story Dad told us—the harrowing escape of the Scottish Honours through the blockade to safety. History changed, so Dad's story changed. You corrupted our childhood."

"Spoken like the victor holding the control behind that shiny shield. I just made the story better," Mary boasted. "Now we are the heroines rescuing the Honors from the inevitable destruction."

"Mary, I have to take you in to the agency. You need to learn how to travel without changing our past."

"Why should I? If we don't protect the items, their stories and significance, they will be lost." She walked around the Ming vase, running her finger around the base. "Don't you see?" Pinkish red blotches started welling up as her eyes brightened with excitement. "I think it was said best whoever controls the past controls the future, but it isn't 1984. No, we can do more than rewrite the past. We can change it to our will for the betterment of everybody. The future will no longer be a place where we live in fear of the agency like you did for those eleven years, looking over your shoulder for that agent to show up again and take you away and brainwash you. There will be a change, sis." The red blotches combined forming lines, like curls of red smoke slithering over her skin, turning into tribal tattoos. They continued up her arms, weaving under her shirt to her neck and onto her face.

Hajjar watched the exchange, hovering next to the sword, slowly sliding on his glove. He knew that this was the reason for their trip. It was the only item so far that was altering history in the retrieval attempt. He watched for a sign from Johnston.

Johnston's head started shaking in disbelief. "It is nothing like that. I wish you could see what you could learn through the agency." She paused a moment, stunned, realizing her sister was convinced of her path in destiny. "I am sorry." Johnston lowered her head, continuing to shake slowly. "Go."

Hajjar grabbed the two pieces of sword and sheath then closed his eyes, hearing Mary scream as he jaunted, changing the cool damp air into temperature humidity-controlled air with solid gray walls. He stood a moment, holding the sword, the hilt in one hand and the broken tip in the gloved hand.

The moments drew on as he waited. Johnston should be right behind him. He hoped that he read the sign to bugger out, but he couldn't remember if she had given him the usual nodding gesture. On closer scrutiny, he could almost remember her saying go but not seeing her lips move. He shook his head slowly, deciding to write his own version of those last moments.

Bewildered, he slowly walked from the center of the room. Suddenly, he heard Johnston's voice behind him. "Wow." She paused. "I think I'm seriously going to need that drink after I take care of the sword."

Hajjar looked down at the two pieces. "How are we going to fix this?"

"We are not." Johnston passed near him, grabbing the two pieces from his hands. "According to all historic accounts, the sword was broken when it was smuggled out. Records can't explain when it was broken, but they suspect that it was in order to conceal the sword to smuggle it out of Dunnottar Castle. I guess we know now how it actually was broken." She smiled at Hajjar.

Johnston breathed deeply, her ears still ringing from Sarah's angry lecture on proper care of garments and "why should I issue you another dress when you're just going to bring it back bloody with a four-inch hole through it, on both sides?"

In through the nose, out through the mouth.

The focus on this trip needed to be precise, and her mind was hardly in a good bit of Zen after her last few moments with her sister after Hajjar had left with her prize possession.

In through her nose, out through her mouth.

People who did care about her were out there heading toward the ambush masterminded by…

In through her nose, out through her mouth.

The cool spring mist of the Ides of March caressed her face. The comprehension was not lost on her, stabbed by someone she trusted…

Focus…

In through her nose, out through her mouth.

She allowed her mind to clear of her distracting thoughts, focusing on March 15, 1652. She remembered the chapel, the side entrance, the meadow, the cool foggy air of the spring morning, the thick mist kissing her skin. Her eyes opened to the wooden door.

"Anne, here, take the crown and scepter." Father Granger's voice echoed from the other side of the church, high-pitched, tense with fear and worry. "We cannot leave her alone." A long pause, and then, "Where is Lady Ogilvy?"

Johnston closed her eyes, listening closely at the pounding of hooves riding closer along with the wailing. "They killed her!" Elizabeth Douglas frantically screamed. "She was defending the sword, and it broke. They ran her through! We have to go back to get her, to help her if we can."

A long moment of silence hung in the air before Father Granger forced calm into his unsteady voice. "Give the crown to Anne for safety. We will not have Lady Ogilvy's effort to protect us be in vain." His voice choked up a bit as he continued, "Take the scepter and crown into the chapel…now, Anne." He cleared his thoughts, and with stern resolve in his voice, he continued, "She gave her life to protect these. We will not ride back with them, giving the enemy the opportunity to make her death for naught." A long pause. Johnston imagined Elizabeth and Christian digging under their skirts, removing their concealed items as the father averted his eyes. "Lock all of the doors until we return."

Johnston opened her eyes at that.

"We must…" Johnston could hear Lady Douglas's voice continue.

Johnston twisted the doorknob, slowly unlatching the door and gently nudging her weight to coax the door through the creaky parts of the swing until the door opened mere inches, but enough to slip in. Her white cloak brushed over the ground as she glided over the stone floor to the main altar, standing in the center of the church in front of the rows of pews. She quickly pulled the two pieces of the broken sword along with the stealth from under her cloak, placing each piece on the altar before turning for the door. She quickly glided across the floor to the door, grabbing the handle and hearing the creaking of…

"Stop!" Johnston heard fear in Lady Douglas's voice, making it sound thin and scared.

Johnston froze halfway out the door, not looking over her shoulder, listening to the exchange behind her.

Footsteps ran across to the altar. "Lady Douglas, look," Anne's voice interrupted. "It's all here."

"I am looking at…" Lady Douglas's voice trailed off.

"No, the altar," Anne continued. "The Sword of State."

Lady Douglas gasped.

Johnston wished to leave as soon as possible before any more damage could be done. She took the opportunity to slip out the door before Lady Douglas's footsteps could catch up to her.

With a genital nudge of the door, the assignment was closed behind her.

The heavy green door opened with the welcoming sound. Johnston smiled, closing her eyes and breathing in the thick haze of nicotine and…marijuana…wafting in the air. "Follow me. The best seats in the house are right over here." Liz beckoned to Ryan. She walked around to the side of the bar that overlooked the stage. They stepped up onto the floor with the stools pulled up to the bar.

"Yeah, I know." He looked at her with pure amusement. "This is where I sat, remember?" Then his smile turned to pure enjoyment. "Oh wait, you *have* gotten old and senile since then."

"Watch it, you whipped snapper. I'm not even forty yet. And you, I doubt you are even old enough to drink. What, you've barely broken through puberty."

They pulled one of the seats up at the bar. Liz turned to glance at the stage as Hajjar flagged down the bartender. "Hey, Bridget?" he called, getting a disgusted look until she recognized him, and then her look made him want to hide under the edge of the bar. He sat crouched for a long moment, then consciously he peered up over the edge of the bar, looking for his impending doom to find her embracing Liz.

"Bethy, it is always good to see you." Their arms wrapped around each other tight, trying to catch up on lost time through osmosis.

Ryan quirked an eyebrow. "Always?"

"I may have snuck back every now and then. Helped pick up a few shifts before joining the agency."

"Two Maker's?" Bridget asked.

Ryan leaned in with his hand on his glass. "What did your sister mean by 'there will be changes?' She doesn't mean to end of the agency, does she?"

"Don't know." Liz looked at the ice cubes sitting in the amber liquid as she swirled them a bit.

"What will happen to the things in the cave?"

"My guess is they were long gone by the time any of the agents returned to clear it out." Liz sipped the bourbon, letting the warm oaky burn make its way to her stomach then out to her fingertips. "What about you? Looking to your solo career? This was your first assignment, and you *have* proven yourself."

"Oh hell, if you are asking for help after these many years, I just don't know." He smiled.

"You will be fine, and the one case that I couldn't give you advice on is behind us both, so you really can come to me for backup any time you need." She took another sip, swiveling her chair to face the bar. "If my sister is right, we all may need a good partner. I just hope it is later rather than sooner."

"What happens to your parents?" Ryan sipped his glass, setting it down and looking with concern. "How can you focus on your work while worrying about your parents, especially now that your sister is so…focused?"

Liz sat staring at the amber liquid swirling among the ice cubes.

"You should try to convince the academy to let your parents work for them on location. Keep a field notebook with them to keep them in the same reality that you are," Bridget stated.

"Do you know how many rules you have broken by telling her?" Hajjar gasped.

"I failed history. Ask me if I care." Bridget leveled a look, making Hajjar fidget uneasily. Bethy and I have only known each other for a year and a half. Within that time, I have seen her grow from a precocious six to"—she looked into Johnston's eyes—"what are you know, thirty, something?"

"Seven." Johnston smiled. "Thirty-seven."

"The altered timeline won't affect me." Bridget smiled, topping off Ryan's glass.

"It might, and that would most certainly destroy me." Liz knocked back the rest of her bourbon, setting down the glass as Bridget started to top it off. "Knowing that I have family actually preserving history makes me more motivated. This reminded me what I have to lose." She hoped that her actions correcting the bedtime stories to the same ones that she remembered would be the end of this, but a part of her just didn't want to find out the truth. She clung to the hope that the events would waive themselves into history, but reality soured her thoughts. She looked up into Bridget's eyes. "You are my family too, you know."

"Times like this, I wonder if I shouldn't have just shot him." She glanced over to Hajjar sitting inches away. "And kept you here, protected from all of those dangers."

Ryan set his glass down with a shocked look. "Me?"

Liz shook her head. "No, truth comes when we confront our demands, our doppelgangers, and realize that they are just as scary as our nightmares."

About the Author

D.Lewis was raised on a farm outside a rural town in Central Illinois with a passion for history and tradition. In her early teenage years, she moved to Dallas, where tales from her elders was replaced with schooling. As she pursued her degrees in chemistry and biology, the creative balance was kept, exploring distant realms armed with wit, paper, a D20, and a handful of D8s. It was there she started creating her own immersive worlds.

Through her childhood in the country, her teenage years in the city, and her adult career in science, one thing remained constant: imagination and inspiration found in the world of creativity found in books, TV, and movies. Now after years of writing technical procedures, balance comes again as she unleashes her creativity with a story that connects history and the future ahead, linking learned science and creative fiction.

CPSIA information can be obtained
at www.ICGtesting.com
Printed in the USA
BVHW072146200721
612420BV00015B/1389/J

9 781662 408977